Contents

Doug Clark

They Saw The Second Coming

An explosive novel about the end of the world!

Doug Clark

Harvest House Publishers
Irvine, California 92714

THEY SAW THE SECOND COMING

Copyright © 1979 Harvest House Publishers
Irvine, California 92714
Library of Congress Catalog Card Number: 78-71427
Cloth Edition ISBN 0-89081-196-2
Trade Paper ISBN 0-89081-190-3

Printed in the United States of America.

They Saw The Second Coming

Chapter
1

Night Attack

Night Attack

Near the ocean's edge, shadowy figures moved stealthily out of the protection of the tossing ocean waves and into the security of dense banana groves. They wore dark green and brown camouflage outfits and had long ski caps pulled down over their faces. Only their black, wicked looking eyes peered into the Israeli darkness.

Three hundred yards out in the blue murky waters of the turbulent Mediterranean Sea, their fishing boat, drifted without anchor, without lights, and without motors running. It was a moonless, dark night. The winds howled over the Sea and into the land of Israel.

The Israeli shore and sea patrols had just passed by thirty minutes earlier. The Arabs had waited quietly in their ship for the patrol boat to slip by them, not making a sound. They were undetected.

Radio communications from the shore told them all Israeli patrols had gone by now. This was the moment to come in, fast, in their swiftly moving motorized rubber boats filled with men armed to the teeth. Daggers were honed for the kill, and guns were hidden beneath their tunics. Automatic short barrelled guns were slung over their shoulders.

They had come as planned and met their contact man, who would lead them around the south end of Joppa to two Mercedes. These nine passenger taxicabs were parked in the darkness up an old abandoned road not far away from the seashore.

Ten heavily armed P.L.O. guerilla fighters had just landed and were fine tuned, completely ready for a vicious Israeli kill. The world must be kept aware of the terrible Palestinian problem of having no homeland, and these terrorist attacks would do it. The worse the ''situation'' was, the sooner world action would be taken to carve out a piece of this embattled land for them. The Palestinian Liberation Organization, long deposed of their land of Palestine in 1948 when the Jews came home, had tried negotiations and failed. They could not wage an all-out war, so this was their only apparent means of ensuring world awareness of both them and their plight. Guerilla action was their chief tool to prod Israeli leaders into political action.

They were Russian trained guerillas, and they knew their work well, having had previous experiences against unsuspecting Israeli citizens.

With their rubber dinghy boots secured in the banana groves, they made their way over the farming terrain to the awaiting cars. Their Arab drivers were dual citizens of Israel and Jordan, but were really Palestinians in their hearts.

The cars left, speeding up the back road forty miles to Jerusalem and the target for that early morning raid on the sleeping usurpers of that Holy City.

It had belonged to the Palestinians before the Jews had taken it in 1967. Now these terrorists were working feverishly to get it back and make it the capitol of the new country of Palestine again. It would take many raids like this, but in the end they firmly believed they would succeed.

Within an hour they arrived at a quiet tree covered street in the newer section of Jerusalem, known as West Jerusalem. Very few Jews chose to live in East Jerusalem—the Old City—just a few blocks away inside ancient walls. But in West Jerusalem three hundred thousand Jews lived with their families. No Arabs lived there.

The ten guerilla fighters glanced furtively in every direction and saw only empty streets. They quietly got out of the two cars, which had turned their motors and lights off. The drivers remained in the cars with the Arab guide. The ten men, trained to kill with knives as deftly as any fighter ever was, made their way up to two large apartment houses. There were no elevators, only outside fire escapes and inside stairs.

Five men went inside and five went up the outside fire escape darting like panthers as they surreptitiously crept up, prowling to the left and then to the right of the first floor up landing, looking for obvious open windows. They found two.

They gingerly, quietly, pushed up the windows and leaped like cougars into the adjoining bedrooms of two Israeli families. With their razor sharp knives in their teeth they approached the beds inside.

There were four people—two adults and two children in one room sleeping soundly. Within four seconds the two Arabs had knelt over the Israeli children and with a quick flash of their razor sharp blades, slit the throats of the unsuspecting ten and eleven year old boy and girl without a sound! Immediately, blood squirted everywhere.

Both guerillas in a flash were leaning over the parents. Suddenly, the father moved slightly, opening his eyes in instant horror and recognition. In that split second he screamed in utter terror as the blade flashed down over his stomach and pierced through the two blankets and sheet, penetrating his bowels and pinning him to the bed in indescribable agony and slow death.

His wife never knew what hit her. The second commando plunged his blade into her heart quickly and removed it before she knew life had vanished. She lay dead while her husband screamed wildly. The Arabs leaped out the window and jumped down the fire escape to the waiting cars, which now had their motors softly purring.

Three other P.L.O. guerillas had a similar experience in the right wing of the same apartment building. They had instantly murdered three people, two of the Jews had their throats cut from ear to ear and blood splattered all over the two Arabs. The third person in the room was a younger girl probably in her teens. She was stabbed right through the heart without a murmur from any of them.

The five Arabs leaping up the inside stairs had a tougher job on their hands. Inside apartment doors were locked tight. Knives were not the answer. They tried picking the locks, but to no avail. Two of them whipped out their handguns, blasting off two door locks at the same time with a thunderous roar of gunfire.

Three other P.L.O. guerillas raced into the two apartments and started shooting in every room, whether it was a bedroom or not. They had automatic machine guns and cut the bedroom doors in two as they went in firing first.

Hearing the sudden gunfire, two Israeli men leaped out of the bed in their separate bedrooms and reached for their hidden guns.

Both of them had military training and were in the standby reserve units, ready for action any time the Israeli government demanded it. They were combat alert most of these weeks, as things along the northern borders with Syria were going badly. Most of Israel was nervous these nights.

One Jew, without waiting, fired back before he knew who he was firing at. His wife screamed and fell under the bed as he yelled at the top of his voice . . .

"P.L.O., P.L.O., P.L.O." . . . And cursed them with a viscious oath while unloading his automatic gun on anyone intruding into his outer living room.

The first Arab was not as ready as he thought. He was immediately shot in the groin, and crumpled in agony to the floor, his gun shooting wildly as he fell crashing over two chairs and a nearby table.

His partner was shooting with everything he had, right at the Jew, who by now was nearly in the doorway returning the fire. Both of them instantly killed one another in bursts of gunfire that awakened the whole neighborhood.

It was five in the morning, but it sounded like all hell broke loose. Screams were coming out of every house. Windows were going up as men shoved the barrels of their Israeli issued guns out, ready to shoot anything that looked foreign or Arab. They had clearly heard the gunfire and knew it could only be the P.L.O. attacking as they cowardly had many times. Always at night, trying to kill women, children and unsuspecting men while they slept, unarmed.

One Jew picked up the phone and dialed an emergency military number. He screamed the message, in Israeli:

"The P.L.O. is attacking on Statton Street, number 48, hurry, there is shooting everywhere. They are killing us in our beds . . . Two cars outside, both Mercedes—waiting . . . Hurry!!! God, help us . . . Hurry!!!!"

He hung up and joined the shooting of the moving cars and men from everywhere trying to get into the cars. Three Arabs fell, mortally wounded in the street.

Two more Arabs were cut down, just as they entered the street from the apartment building. Three Israelis, one naked, two with their shorts on, were shooting with automatic, American made guns, and literally cut the Arabs in two, as they emerged from the doorway.

Their bodies leaped into the air as the three Jews hit them together.

The Israelis did not know how many there were. They were shooting the cars now. Gunfire was being returned from the lowered windows of the Mercedes as they sped away, tires screaming on the pavement.

Just as they heard other shots ringing out from the second floor of the same building, an Arab came smashing through the third floor window, flying wildly through the air screaming in terror. His body hit the pavement below with a sickening thud, laying in such a grotesque manner, no one wanted to look.

The two cars sped away, each in a separate direction.But there were only five men now, as only two P.L.O. members had gotten back to the cars, one in each, along with the drivers and the guide. They were being riddled with bullets from Israelis firing from their windows with their army issued guns.

One car suddenly burst into roaring flames as an Israeli bullet hit the oil tank and the car exploded. Flames raced everywhere, amidst the terrible screams of the men trapped inside.

As the second car sped down Statton Street, the Israeli military turned the corner. They had come in a jeep, armed to the teeth themselves with a machine gun mounted on the back.

Both racing vehicles sped right for one another, guns blazing out of the Mercedes windows by the three remaining Arabs, while the machine gun aimed at them, opened fire. There were four Israeli soldiers ready for hell that night.

The machine gun fire cut right through the windshield of the speeding car. It instantly cut the driver's head off. It fell out the window and rolled down the street with the momentum of the car, blood spurting on the road. The Mercedes went out of control, and the Israeli jeep had to veer up the sidewalk and into a driveway to escape the careening vehicle of death. The car crashed into the largest tree trunk on Statton Street and burst into instant flames scorching to death anyone left alive inside.

Pandemonium broke loose. There was screaming from every house, especially as the living investigated and found the dead with their throats cut or stabbed to death in their beds. Blood was everywhere. One Arab had his brains blown out and splattered over the wall and ceiling of the room where it happened.

Not one Arab escaped.

Children were screaming, parents were frantic and loved ones were waiting to see who was dead and who was alive.

Paramedics arrived, but very few needed them.

It took hours to calm the area down to normal. It would take many more weeks and months for that typically Jewish community to get over their intense grief for the deaths of ten Israelis.

The world wept for these Israelis and some wept for the Palestinians, too. Both sides had severe problems to deal with now.

How could this situation be corrected? How could this ticking time bomb be defused from producing World War III?

Chapter
2

Jerusalem

Jerusalem

Piercing the late afternoon bartering, arguing and haggling over prices of fly infested fruit, vegetables and some pathetic looking dry goods offered by the Bedouins, came the dismal wail of the muezzin calling the faithful of the Muhammadan sect to late afternoon prayers. It made little difference to the Arab bargaining to gain a days wages from their Jordan Valley fruit. Religion meant very little this hot summer afternoon to those whose life depended on selling their homegrown fruit and vegetables. Time enough for prayers on Friday, the one day they would sincerely devote to praying to Allah. "Muhammad must have been a wise man" they say, "but he had more food than us to pray so often." This was the common excuse for not praying five times a day, as the Holy Men advocated so sincerely throughout the Arab section of Old Jerusalem.

The day had been beastly humid, with the hot winds from Saudi Arabia scorching Israel like a giant fan blowing heat out of a blast furnace. It was unbearable. Tourists wiped the sandy heat from their sweaty faces while gazing at the ruins of Israel's past glory by the Western Wall. Aged Jews prayed at the Wall. The men, with heads covered in respect to the God of Israel; the women, mostly darkly attired, prayed fervently for the return of peace to their land. Several left their prayers written on small pieces of paper in the clefts of the giant stones.

It was a strange sight. No other city in the entire world could offer a photographer or student of comparative religions, or anyone interested in the varying social religious backgrounds of the peoples of the earth, more of an intriguing sight like this one. The Arabs answering the muezzin's wailing call through his electronic system to prayer on one side of the Wall; and Jews, separated male and female, praying on the other side of the Wall, with a smattering of Christian tourists praying in and amongst them quietly to their Lord, on the western side of this ancient wall,

But on this beastly hot day in June, no one cared much about Solomon or the Wall or Herod long gone, or of the bloody history of Jerusalem.

Away from the wailing at the Wall, and from the noisy muezzin calling the Arabs to pray, there is a shaded winding street. It's not too far from the orthodox quarter where only the orthodox Jews live with their peculiar rules and styles of dress. This oak treed street, heavy with leaves and overhanging branches, was cooler than the busy, bustling downtown area of West Jerusalem, where Sara Rosenberg had just come from. As she walked down the street, she was hoping to get home before her husband Moishe, or before her two sons, Ya'er and David, sped in for late afternoon sandwiches. She knew her only daughter, Ruth, would not be home for another hour. It was also the same street where last month's horrifying P.L.O. night attack took place.

Normally it was such a pleasant street and it was always so good to get home from the noisy bustling of shopping in Jewish Jerusalem. The only thing worse would be shopping in East Jerusalem where the Arabs were always far more willing to bargain than their Jewish counterparts in the other section of the great city. But the excrutiating heat and stench of animal dung and unrefrigerated meats and vegetables was far too much for Sarah. Only occasionally did they make that trip—when visiting relatives came from afar and begged to be taken inside the wall.

Today, she had bought some long needed colorful towels for the one small bathroom they had in their Israeli apartment. How long they had waited for this top story three bedroom apartment with a full bath! It was marvelous to have such privacy again after living two years with her husband's orthodox brother, his wife and family of four children in Tel Aviv. After last month's P.L.O. murders Sarah thought about moving back to Tel Aviv, but not for long.

The very memory of Dissendorf Square in Tel Aviv and that crowded flat with Moishe's brother, Sam, and his family nearly drove Sarah dizzy. Not only the difference in food preparation—Sam being so orthodox, and consequently Kosher in everything and Moishe being reformed Jewish in his belief—but the arguing of the children over religion, food, different schools they went too . . . it was too much!

Sarah had endured it for eight long years after they came off the Kibbutzim. The work had been so hard there, but many a time she had decided to go back to the Galilee Kibbutzim with the family to get out of the hassle of the older brother constantly trying to argue her husband into being orthodox or suffer hell fire!

There were times when hell fire, whatever it was, looked better than the painful living they had in Tel Aviv. But finally it ended with Moishe's graduation from night school and the diploma stating he had the equivalent of a normal secondary school education.

The children were proud of their Jewish father. He had worked hard and had come so far from those days in Berlin, Germany, where he was born in December of 1930. Moishe had already been through hell. He had lived through the Holocaust, as had their beautiful blond haired mother, Sarah. The stories father and mother would frequently tell about the Jewish persecution under Hitler would chill you through like a freezing winter's night in a Siberian forest. But now it was almost 40 years later, with three children virtually grown up, two of them in the reserve Israeli Armed Forces—as were all 17 and 18 year old sons of Israel—and one gorgeous raven haired blue-eyed German-descent Jewish daughter of 16 out of school and working at her first full-time position.

It was with a great sigh of relief that Sarah could push out of her mind all the tough, hard, bitter memories of the past; from Poland's Treblinka and horrible Auschwitz down through the journey to Israel, their miraculous escape from the Germans in 1944 through the extreme years on an Israeli Kibbutzim farm . . . Tel Aviv . . . and now she enjoyed a cool street and longed for apartment in Jerusalem so her husband could be a guide to the many Christian tour groups coming daily to Israel.

The past was past. She was not a bitter woman in her late forties, but a warm, happy, appreciative Jew, as she would always say, ". . . with so much to be thankful to God for, why shouldn't I be happy."

As she walked up the front steps and looked at the long branches of an old oak tree hanging over the verandah roof and down into the shaded area of the porch, she smiled, as she thought. "Never will we have to go through torture again. Israel is ours. And this is my home . . . Wasn't it the Psalmist that said, I shall not be moved?''

Ya'er and David were home early. They had found the aging refrigerator full of good things to eat. She heard them exulting over having free domination of the scrumptious sandwich meat and cheese they had found. She sighed . . . ''Maybe that's good . . . supper is going to be late tonight anyway.''

Sarah smiled most pleasantly at the sight of her two sons scurrying around laughing at their own awkwardness and sloppiness. In the midst of it, they both hugged their petite mother amidst loud shouts of excitement. "We're headin' out this weekend Mother! Our outfit is going to the Golan Heights for some real live training on location . . . right on the front lines!" they exclaimedf happily. "We are going to view Arab military positions and relive the 1973 war right where it happened up there . . . kinda simulated," Ya'er added thoughtfully.

''You remember how we pushed them back over 20 miles, Mom?'' David chimed in, though somewhat enthusiastically. ''Actually I'm not all that thrilled. Dianna and I have our first date coming up Saturday night, you know.''

Sarah knew of David's interest in the 18 year old beauty downstairs in the lower apartment. David almost had to beg her father for the privilege of taking his daughter to the dance over at the university. He had tried many times to get permission, but Rabbi Perla was not an easy man to convince when it came to his daughter going out on her first date. He had held the reins tightly over the past two years since Dianna had turned 16 and felt she should have some personal freedom of choice.

''Not so,'' said the middle-aged, balding, but good-natured Rabbi. ''A Rabbi's daughter is different than the rest of these Israeli sabras. You will only get out with my permission as long as you live in this house. We will not have your father's name and the good holy reputation of this family dragged in the mud of an unholy generation of Jews.'' He would repeatedly tell his only child that her time would come. Her man would come. ''As sure as the Messiah will come someday, your man will come. And when he does, I'll know him.''

''But father, I am 18, and I have never had a proper date . . . You know what I mean . . . alone with a boy of my choice. I would never disgrace you,'' she cried.

"The daughter of one of the most respected Rabbis in Jerusalem will only date when she is permitted by that father to do so, and not before," He would bluntly reply and then walk away muttering.

Finally the day came when he gave David permission to date Dianna, having watched him over a period of 6 months. He felt that after observing the boy, he would treat her as the Rabbi's daughter should be treated.

Only once had David asked her to go with him on a Friday night. The Rabbi blew his cork. "Friday night and he wants you to go out dancing with him when proper Jews are at the Wall praying with thousands of others for the peace of Jerusalem. He will never date my daughter," he answered brusquely and paced off, leaving her crying.

The Rabbi had many occasions since then to converse with David's father pleasantly over a glass of borsch or a beer on a hot late afternoon when Moishe wasn't guiding tourists through the streets of Jerusalem or Bethlehem. He learned of David's academic achievements and that he was finishing secondary school with the highest of honors and would be immediately placed as an officer in the Israeli military. David has stood at the top of his graduating class and was of the finest boys as far as his manners were concerned. His only error, the Rabbi mused to himself, was asking for Dianna on a Friday night . . . Imagine! . . . just as the sun went down declaring the Sabbath . . . he wanted to go dancing! But that was 6 months ago. Graduation was coming next week and so the special dance. Dianne could go.

The first son of Moishe and Sarah Rosenberg was a good boy. Conservative in his bearing, tall, he stood over 6 foot 2 inches and looked down on his shorter brother by three inches. David's deep brown eyes and jet black hair along with his concaved forehead and firmly set jaw, made him a strikingly good-looking boy. His parents, though not overly religious and certainly not orthodox, were very proud of him on his 13th birthday, when they had his bar mitzvah at the Wailing Wall, now called the Western Wall.

If David in the ensuing almost six years seemed conservative, it was because he loved Israel, loved to study about its illustrious past and felt that his father was such a great man for what he had endured in Poland at the wicked hands of the Nazis. He wanted to make his father proud of him, both academically and as a good soldier. He was an astute student.

His teachers had said this a hundred times when speaking privately to his parents.

Because of his depths of concentration, it was very difficult for Moishe to beat his son at his favorite pastime—chess. David would outmaneuver him virtually every time. Moishe could usually whip his younger son anytime, for Ya'er was not the student David was. He was the physically aggressive one in the family. Push-ups every morning, running every night he could, and then almost as intensely interested in the military as David, it was from a different point of view. He was a lover of sports, guns and girls, especially the latter of the three! He was broad shouldered, five foot eleven inches with a big broad smile and beautiful teeth that you thought might have been capped; they were so white and so perfectly arranged and set. His skin was slightly deeper in texture of permanent tan than was David's. He was more muscular and could usually topple David in arm wrestling and would outmaneuver him on the football field. He was nimble and had a skillful agility David never ventured to imitate. His younger brother was quick and good with a gun . . . good in maneuvers . . . good with girls . . . not as good by far at chess, deep studying or military planning as his brother, but both of them loved one another and probably if it came to it, each would give his life for any member of the family.

Ruth was something else entirely from the rest of this Jewish family. If her mother was a size 6, Ruth was a size 9 and was filled out where mother was somewhat lacking. But then mother was 48 and had seen the hell of the Holocaust, and Ruth was 16 and was a raven haired Israeli girl that every boy wanted to take to bed. So far, without any difficulty apparently, she had alluded all approaches—no one had succeeded. Her two brothers would have reason for murder had they caught anyone trying to seduce their beautiful sister. She was a virgin, and there weren't many left in Israel these days. She had many times been out on a date, but it was always double and triple dating with her brothers along as chaperones with their own dates. It had usually been good fun with only a half dozen times the guys trying to get fresh when David and Ya'er weren't looking. Sarah had taught her daughter well, however, and she knew the right moves to restrain them nicely. Her problem was her radiant beauty. Her skin was as soft as kid leather and had a look of soft Indian brown to it. She was not swarthy as were many Jews in Israel, but she had her father's tanned skin and brilliant smile that made you catch your breath when you saw her full head of long black hair gently swinging in the breeze of an Israeli summer afternoon. When she smiled, it was an experience for you to behold her.

Our fresh beauty of 16 had a personality to match her loveliness. Her manner of speech was delicate, ladylike and yet most dynamic at times. If she liked you and turned on the charm, you were conquered before your guard was up. She would ply her charms with grace and connivance so majestically and subtly, you hardly knew you were taken in and swept off your feet. And when you did realize it, you loved the feeling her attention brought to you and you couldn't help but love this creature created in the image of Diana of the Greek Temple . . . At times she looked like a Greek goddess—and she could act like one as well!

Sarah would often gaze adoringly at her daughter with great pride and say, ''How will you ever fit into the army darling? I just cannot see you in uniform. That trim waist and full figure will look so ugly in that horrible army get-up!'' Sarah dreaded the day her children would have to go off in the defense of Israel, but she knew the inevitable would come.

Moishe Rosenberg read the Jerusalem Post every morning. Today the news was more uncertain than ever. It appeared from editorial after editorial that Israel would soon be at war for the fifth time, and this time most seriously. Russia was coming; it was certain.

''God in Heaven,'' he exclaimed under his breath, ''where is justice anyhow?'' And with a grunt of disgust he looked up from the paper to Ruth and said, ''We went through hell when the Nazi's came in Germany, and it looks like we are going to go through hell when the Russians get here. The communists might be worse than the fascists.''

Ruth picked it up immediately that morning while frying eggs for herself. Being the Sabbath day, no one was going anywhere that early.

''Father do you really feel we are going to have war soon?'' She inquired anxiously.

''There is no doubt in my mind that Ben Gurion was right when he told our Nation the Russians would come and help the Arabs. None of the Arab nations can do it on their own. They've tried too many times and failed. This time ''. . . his voice dropped to a whisper and he spoke ever so slowly . . . ''the war the Prophet predicted may be on us.''

"What prophet, and what war did he predict?" Ruth was surprised at what her father had said about a prophet.

Her father frowned momentarily, and his lips tightened to a hard line. His gaze did not waver. "Fetch me the Bible, dear."

Quickly, with unusual anticipation, Ruth produced the only Bible they had. It was quite worn, not because the family had used it, but because of its former owner's use. It had been given to Moishe and Sarah by the Christian family who had so wonderfully befriended them and aided their miraculous escape from the Nazis. They cherished it as the only momento of Germany and Poland where they lived, and it reminded them frequently of how much they had to be thankful for in this great new land with their new life. If there truly was a God, He showed Himself through those people in the northern part of Poland.

David had read this Bible several times in his studies because of his desire to familiarize himself with the German language. Apart from that, Moishe and Sarah had studied it with the Christian Germans years ago. It was from them Moishe learned of the prophecies of Israel, the Russians and several other shocking subjects dealing with oil, war, the Temple and several other things he couldn't remember now. But his friend, the original owner of this book, Ludwig Kolenda, and his warm affectionate wife, Erica, had written at least two dozen prophetical subjects on the back page of the Bible and gave their references for further study. But they had never had time for the further study.

It took some time to find the prophecy while they all ate breakfast that Sabbath morning. The boys were gone to the Golan Heights on the planned military maneuvers the day before. David had arranged with Dianna to take her out the following Saturday night dining and dancing in an Arab cafe in the East Jerusalem area just ouside the wall for a real unusual treat for a Jew. He had made his explanation to her and her father regarding the cancellation of tonight's greatly planned date. All had agreed—duty before pleasure. Dianna was both disappointed and proud of him at the same time. "He does make some wise decisions, that boy friend of yours." said her Rabbi father . . .

Moishe suppressed a shiver as he read quietly to himself the passage of prophecy he inquired after.

He acknowledged at last that he had found it with a wave of his right hand while slowly running the fingers of his left hand over the lines. His eggs were cold now, so was the muffin Sarah had heated for him. He loved English style muffins with butter and jam the way the English eat their continental breakfast in the morning. He never did eat herring or cheese like the average Jew in Israel.

"I got it," he exclaimed excitedly. "Wow! Listen to this prophecy for Israel about the Russians . . ."

He read to them the following verses:

"Son of man, set your face against Gog, of the land of Magog, the prince of Rosh, of Meshech, and Tubal, and prophesy against him, and say, Thus says the Lord God: Behold, I am against you, O Gog, chief prince of Rosh, of Meshech and Tubal. And I will turn you back, and put hooks into your jaws, and I will bring you forth and all your army, horses and horsemen, all of them clothed in full armor, a great company with buckler and shield, all of them handling swords; Persia, Cush, and Put with them; all of them with shield and helmet; Gomer and all his hordes; the house of Togarmah in the uttermost parts of the north, and all his hordes; many people are with you . . . After many days you shall be visited and mustered for service; in the latter years you shall go against the land that is restored from the ravages of the sword, where people are gathered out of many nations upon the mountains of Israel, which had been a continual waste; but its people are brought forth out of the nations, and they shall dwell securely, all of them. You shall ascend and come like a storm, you shall be like a cloud to cover the land, you and all your hosts, and many people with you. Thus saith the Lord God: At the same time thoughts shall come into your mind, and you will devise an evil plan. And you will say, I will go up against an open country—the land of unwalled villages; I will fall upon those who are at rest, who dwell securely, all of them dwelling without walls and having neither bars nor gates. To take spoil and prey; to turn your hand upon the desolate places now inhabited, and assail the people gathered out of the nations, who have obtained livestock and goods, who dwell at the center of the earth, Palestine . . . You will come from your place out of the uttermost parts of the north, you and many peoples with you, all of them riding on horses, a great host, a mighty army." [1]

"Whew, that's incredible!" Moishe exclaimed as he looked weak and stared into space, considering the impact of the prediction.

Ruth was paranoid for a moment and while gazing over her father's shoulder read some of the predictions to herself as best she could in German. Her parents had spent sometime with each of the children teaching them their native German language. They had picked up enough to occasionally converse in it, brokenly.

"But Father, I don't understand this about Rosh and Magog. Who are they and what does this mean?" She really wanted to know.

"Darling, Rosh is the ancient word for today's Russian people. They were the ones living in the uttermost parts of the north. They went there after the great flood and one of Noah's sons whose name was Japheth had many sons, one of which was Magog who went to today's Russia and populated it. His brother was Meshech and he and his descendants became Moscow and another brother was Tubal, he became Tubolsk, the eastern capitol of Russia," he quickly answered her while peering into the text itself . . . "See here," he explained, "this part here says they will come into the land brought back by the sword . . . That is Israel, and it says so right here on this page. If we believe our Prophet Ezekiel to be a great man then he was inspired of God to write this prophecy. And remember, Rosh . . . or Russia has never attacked Israel in the past so it must be in the future." He ended his explanation and sat back, pensively staring into space considering the weight of it all.

Ruth picked it up and read slowly in German . . . "They . . . will . . . come . . . like . . . a . . . cloud . . . to . . . cover . . . the . . . land. Good God, Father, does that mean what I think it means?" She stared at her father with a frown on her brow.

"If the prophet is right at all, then he is right on all parts." He solemnly answered. "There is no doubt in my mind that the Russians will ally themselves even further in the Arab cause and attack Israel. That is exactly what it says," he grimaced.

"Then we can expect annihilation by the Russians in the next war." Ruth replied coldly and factually.

"Well, not exactly, if you read on." Moishe said a little more hopefully. "You know, I'm not the one to interpret these great prophecies . . . I should take it to the Rabbi downstairs, but here it says in the next chapter that they will be destroyed in the hills of Israel, and Israel will be seven months in burying the dead. I learned from our friends the Kolendas years ago that Israel would be a permanent state forever, and that the Arabs would be defeated and so would the Russians in that great bloody war.'' He added grimly.

"But how could we win such a war against millions of Russians and Arabs coming at us from all sides together, Father?'' She respectfully asked.

"By an act of God. That is all they taught us. I don't know the answer . . . Just by Divine intervention somehow, we will be saved . . . Maybe something like Moses and the Red Sea story. That was an act of God if there ever was one. And let me tell you, we would have to have an act of God if we're to be saved.'' His reply had been firm and solemn. Moishe got up and left the room and smiled lightly at his daughter's interrogation. The phone had rung.

"Mother,'' Ruth gazed at Sarah while asking, "Do you have any confidence in the beliefs of the Kolendas? After all, they were not Jews; they were German Christians . . . the kind who did all those horrible things to you!''

Sarah, catching herself quickly lest she come on too strong with her unknowing but honest daughter, lowered her voice and simply stated, "Ruth, those people were so honest and so kind, and,'' she raised her voice with a quiver indicating her intensity and profound sincerity, "*they* did not do those things to us! The Nazis were not Christians at all, they did not believe in God or any religion except the State of Germany under Hitler. The Kolendas were the most decent, respectable and kindest persons I have ever known . . . Never speak of them with disrespect again Ruth!'' She was obviously angered at her daughter's inferences even though she knew that Ruth could not know how it was.

"I'm sorry, Mother.'' Ruth rose, came to her mother's side and with a sweep of her arm caught her mother in a tight embrace. "I did not mean to hurt you at all. You know I love you too much for that.'' Ruth gently whispered in her mother's ear. "I only wanted to know what the prophecy said!''

"I understand, dear,'' Sarah caressed her daughter's hair and sat down. "If you knew what we had been through in those months and how the Kolendas were the ones getting us out . . . only then could you understand how deeply we feel about them. Everything they did was for our good. They put their lives on the line getting us out of Poland. They could have been shot immediately and very nearly did the nights we were in their fruit cellar that spring.'' Sarah lifted her eyes with tears swelling up and threw her head back as though to clear her mind of it once and for all and go on with the day's tasks.

"Wait, mother," Ruth asked. "Tell me about that episode . . . I've never heard it.'' She knew it would pain her mother to recount it, but her curiosity was too great. An insatiable hunger to know about her parent's exciting and dramatic escape always intrigued her. How could they have lived through all of that?

"Darling, that would take a long time, and I really hate to get back into it . . . but . . .''

"Please Mother, I want to know about it so much.'' Her sixteen years of age was showing and the childlike innocent sweetness was coming through and reaching her mother. She won.

"Well, it was not long after your father's family and our family, plus many other Jewish families in Berlin, were shipped out to the Warsaw Ghetto. Toward the end of the war thousands upon thousands of us were shipped out of the country to Poland. Just outside Warsaw they had barracaded off a large section and poured all of us in there with nowhere to sleep and hardly anything to eat. They herded us in like cattle, Darling.'' She paused, sighed and remembered with inner agony, "It was terrible. Thousands died every week. I saw them. I was only 13 and your father was barely 15, and I didn't know him at all. People were starving everywhere.

"We slept like flies next to one another in old houses, basements, garages. When winter set in in 1944, I sincerely thought we were all going to freeze to death. Our Jewish leaders encouraged us and bargained with the Poles and Germans for blankets, but not many of us got one. We always slept with our clothes on, and anybody else's clothes we could find. We stripped corpses each morning of their clothes, no matter how tattered they were. We had to survive. I had two brothers and another sister. I woke up one morning to find my little sister had frozen to death that night right beside me.'' Sarah stopped, reached for a handkerchief in her blouse and after wiping her eyes continued with the dreadful recounting of the disaster of her childhood.

"We took her clothes off . . .'' There were more tears momentarily, "there were other little girls who needed her clothes. The Nazis came, and that was the last I saw of her. She was buried in a mass grave. Some of our men did the burying and one of them told me about it" . . . she continued slowly. "The word had gotten out that they were taking all of us to Treblinka or Auschwitz-Birkenau. We knew these were not farms! The railroad engineer told some of our Jewish leaders who could mill about as we got on the trains: They were experimental camps and maybe even extermination camps! We were all frightened we were going to die some horrible death. Many didn't care; they felt they were living a life of death every day anyway. One engineer said he took in the weekly allotments of food and he knew there was not enough food to feed one quarter of the people he'd taken in over the past 3 months. 'Where were the people?' He said he asked and was told they were sacrificed for the cause of Arian Germany and most of them died under the euthanasia program set up by Hitler.''

"What is euthanasia?" Ruth interrupted abruptly.

"Euthanasia was a program of death for the infirm, elderly, incurably sick and unwantables, when Hitler wanted to rid society of undesirable diseases and costly welfare programs in homes and hospitals. He said the money should be used for the well and healthy. It was a quick death supposedly, mercifully for those sentenced that way." Sarah went on, with Ruth's nod that she understood the horrible meaning. You could read the pain in Ruth's eyes.

"We were told by the Elders that we might be going to our death. There was no proof, but they feared for everyone. Many ablebodied Jews tried to escape from the Warsaw Ghetto and some of them made it with the help of outside friends or Christians. There was a Christian underground movement for the saving of Jews and secreting them out of the country. We knew of it, and the word was out everywhere if you got out, where to go and who to contact. Many were shot trying to escape and others were beaten to death in plain sight of all of us by the guards as an example to the rest. My family never tried it. But our day came to be herded on the cattle cars . . ." Sarah's mouth was dry and her lips looked drained of all blood. "They put us on the trains in families, and we could stay together. We were told that upon arrival we would go through delousing showers, get new clothes and be assigned as families to our barracks, and our work would be assigned in a matter of days. We would be fed and clothed properly as we worked for the State of Germany on the farms raising crops, tending to cattle, milking, etc. for the soldiers.''

''What do you mean cattle cars, mother?'' Ruth was so full of questions.

''Cattle cars . . . where they had transported cattle and never washed them out, and we were herded in like cattle. We were so tight together you could not fall down if you wanted to. I found your father right next to me, a fifteen year old scared, skinny, Jewish lad, I remember how he smiled at me, a smile of reassurance that all would be fine. It was the longest trip of my life. It took two days to go where we were headed. On our car alone several died of the freezing cold and just eventually collapsed on the floor. We couldn't move them. Their bodies froze stiff and I remember how everyone urinated and defecated right there in their clothes on the car, and the stench was as terrible as anything you have ever known! You think Old Jerusalem smells bad on a hot summer day . . . Whew . . . and I was so embarrassed to have to go in front of your father. He felt the same, but we were right beside one another and could not move anywhere. Only after the first day and night when several had died . . . about 15 or so, could we then move a little. We walked around as best we could, sloshing in human waste and excrement from the dead bodies. Your father told me his name and we discovered then that both of us had been born and raised in Berlin, not really far from one another. His father was a gemologist who had been taken early in the war and never heard of again. His mother was on the train, and so was his older sister. He learned of my family, and my father being a machinist in a tool and die factory. He said maybe Dad would live because they needed skilled workers for the factories. I remember how good that made me feel. How wrong he was!

He asked me if I would try to escape with him if it were possible. I told him no, that I would go with my family always. Just as he asked me, the train stopped in the middle of the snowy, terrible wilderness of Poland. We watched through the boards of the car, which were slats bolted with two inch spaces between, as they unloaded two cars behind us . . .

The Nazis took them into the woods about one hundred feet away and lined them up. We could see the machine guns already set up and before anyone knew what was happening for sure in our car, they riddled them with bullets and murdered every Jew right in front of our eyes . . . I'll never forget the screams of those not dead . . . nor the extra shots from

Nazi rifles as they finished them . . . children . . . mothers holding babies who were probably dead anyway . . . It was so shocking. I was trembling from head to foot as though I had the palsy . . . Those monsters perpetrated the worst and most inhuman actions on fellow human beings I have ever seen. Some of the crawling ones were bayonetted while they squirmed . . . it was so awful . . . so awful . . . Everyone in our car was crying, shrieking and screaming . . .''

There was quietness for a moment as Sarah collected herself to proceed.

Quietly, with her heart pounding, she went on. ''Your father took my hand at that moment and whispered, ''We are going to escape. I know how. Stay close to me when they come for our car.'' And they came. I never in my whole life felt like I wanted to die immediately, but I did then. Moishe had looked out the other side of our car and had seen a deep ravine going down at least thirty to forty feet. He said, he surmised that when the door of our cattle car was opened, we would all rush out and topple on top of one another just as the others did. In the scramble, he thought we could get under our car and down the steep ravine in the snow covered by trees and thick underbrush, tall enough to hide two fleeing people while the Nazis were organizing the next group for the kill. It would be bedlam. Women were shrieking, kids were crying and men were weeping but ready to fight. Your father had turned around to the men in our car and said, ''Let's fight them and attack them as soon as we hit the snow before they know what is happening. Some of us might escape.'' The men stood frozen in their spirits, and only one man said he would. The other said they were no match for the soldier's guns and bayonets! ''But it is better to die fighting!'' . . . Your father was brave even at fifteen . . . What a man he was in my eyes at that moment . . .I remember,'' she smiled now lightly, ''he put us in the middle of the group . . . my family was up front. My father would fight, he said, with several other men.

''When the door was opened, the men suddenly jumped out throwing themselves at the guards, and the women followed fast. It was pandemonium. The guards were caught off-guard! They fell, some of them, with the men beating them furiously. Two Jews grabbed guns and began to shoot every German they could find. Other Germans started to run towards our car . . . Your father grabbed my hand so tightly I can feel it now . . . and pushed me out into that pile of bodies, screaming, fighting and clawing. We rolled under the cattle car while others fought and the soldiers attention was on the fighting Jews. We crawled like lightning to the other side of the car and leaped down the hill into the ravine, tearing our faces and hands on the thorns and branches. My eyes were closed, and I ran and leaped into the trees with all my strength. We rolled for ages, I tell you, and when we got up on our feet, we were at the bottom of the ravine. We ran through the deep snow leaving tracks just as plain as if we had planned for them to follow us!'' Sarah laughed nervously. ''We ran in the stillness of the forest and listened for the shots and the screaming in the distance, but it was somewhat muffled by the snow and sounds of the engine letting off steam. But no one came after us. Can you believe that? No one!

We ran until my legs would not move another inch. They felt like iron dragging on my hips. We dropped into the snow by a little stream, mostly frozen over, but with cracks through the ice in the center, and we drank like we had never seen water before. I had not had a drink in over 24 hours! My face was a mess of cuts, bruises and my nose was bleeding. Moishe was cut just as badly, and we were both drenched to the skin, but we were free!'' Sarah stopped talking, got up, walked across the room and put Ruth's face in her hands and bent over to kiss her and said, ''Darling, we were free! It had been nearly two years since we had been free of Germans everyday, everywhere.'' She looked so relieved.

''What did you do that night, mother?'' Ruth pursued the subject while Sarah paced up and down the length of the kitchen.

''That, my dear, was one of the best and one of the worst nights of your mother's life. It was the best because I felt safe with Moishe, and we felt free with no one in pursuit. But we knew it could mean our death in the freezing cold. However, we had survived the preceding night on the freezing cattle train, and Moishe said if we could last another night, we might find some help. Help for Jews was not easy to find in the country. In the cities, there were the underground contacts most of us knew of. And, if you didn't know where they were, there were ways and means of finding out. But this was the country, and it was very cold and very dark.''

Sarah remembered something special and smiled at her daughter. ''That was the first night I had a boy's arms around me all night long.

We were wet, lost, dismayed, because we knew my parents and brothers and sister were unquestionably dead, along with all the others who were on our car. If the Germans had not seen us fall down the hill or saw the tracks later after the miniature battle, then there would be no hounds and no pursuers. We knew they did not have a count of how many were on the car to begin with.'' She added. ''They had been too interested in getting us on the car to count us. So we felt we had a chance to escape, but where to? This was Poland and believe me there was no more love for a Jew in Poland than there was in Germany.

We finally sat down under a large tree, as it was really snowing, and made our plan . . . or should I say Moishe made the plan—all I did was agree . . . agree to anything! We would spend that snowy night by the tree. The snow would cover our tracks some. Next morning we would follow the stream wherever it led. At least we would have water, and it might lead us to a farmhouse. We figured every farm had its stream. We weren't wrong. The next morning, after about four hours of walking, we came to a fence . . . an old broken-down wood fence. It had to lead somewhere. We left the stream and followed it, and found our farmhouse. We couldn't run any longer. Just then, we saw an old Polish farmer going to the barn to milk his cows. He was carrying a couple of pails and had a stool tucked under his arm. We yelled and waved as we were quite a distance. He stopped and never said a word or waved back at us until we got to him. He knew we were in trouble and knew we were Jews. I could have passed for just a German fraulein, but Moishe was distinctly Jewish. The farmer understood our German. Probably not all of it but enough to know we had escaped a Nazi extermination train, and when we told him my father and mother were murdered along with my sister and brothers, he dropped his pails and stool and motioned for us to enter his old house.''

''Good Lord, Mother, how could you do all that at 13 years of age?''

''You do exactly what you have to do when you are starving, cold, wet and dead tired. I remember his elderly wife fixing us some good tastin' food of some nature . . . hot and fast . . . And that fire felt so good I nearly fell asleep eating . . . but it was so good . . . food never tasted better. That old farmer's wife listened to our story, and though she could not speak much German, she motioned for us to eat the bread and porridge she had prepared and then lead us upstairs to a bedroom and motioned for us to take off our clothes and give them to her and get into bed. That bed looked like heaven to me. And you know . . . I tore my clothes off with my back to your father, and he did the same . . . neither of us thinking about what we were doing until I turned around. At 13 years of age I had never been naked with any boy, including my brothers, and saw him standing there stark naked.'' Sarah smiled. ''We both burst into uncontrollable laughter looking at one another's nakedness. It was so funny to me and so hilarious to him. We quickly jumped into bed. The sheets were made of some wooly substance and felt so good, and the warmth of my body warmed up my side of the bed immediately. He jumped into bed with me . . . away over on his side,'' Sarah pointed out with her hand. ''We were both laughing at it all, and we both went out like lights and slept around the clock . . . twelve hours.'' Ruth smiled at her mom's first episode in bed.

''That next morning, that dear old farmer's wife had not only washed, but ironed our old tattered rags. Can you imagine—ironed them! And when she came up, she had some hot biscuits and bread with jelly on several pieces and smiled and talked so cheery in Polish. She gave me some old garment that she had had years before, no doubt. It looked so old. But I put it on and some underclothes she gave me too. They were the funniest old bloomers I'd ever seen. Never had I seen anything like them in stores anywhere. But, that's what you get free on a Polish farm, and I took them and put them on gladly . . . By the way I dressed privately the next morning. Moishe had gotten up and put on a pair of the old farmer's pants . . . Well, anyway to make a long story short . . . They took us on their horse-drawn sleigh to a neighboring farmhouse several miles away. It had been my first sleigh ride with horses. It was fun, and I was full of good food and was warm and happy snuggled next to the man who was going to be my husband and the father of my children some day . . . I just didn't know it at the time. But I had already slept with him! How do you like that?'' Sarah chided her pleasantly. ''But I was innocent; I hardly knew what sex was . . . I guess just enough to be scared silly of it all.''

''Hadn't your mother told you anything about making love or having children like you and father have taught the boys and me?'' Ruth inquired.

''Not in those days, dear. Sex in an old-fashioned Jewish home, even though we were not orthodox, was just not spoken of. Mother told me nothing. And I knew better than to ask.''

"That's funny, you sleeping naked with father at 13 years of age . . . and never thinking anything about it." Ruth exclaimed with humor.

"We had far more important things on both of our minds than love-making or sex exploration, my child! And I knew it was a new experience for your father too . . . just in case you are thinking anything, darling daughter!'' . . . Mother looked seriously at her when she made that last remark.

"Oh, Mother, I hadn't even dreamt anything different about my father. Goodness, he is so great in every way . . . I have to tell you it's really hard for me to think of the two of you like that even now . . .'' she quietly smiled hardly believing it yet.

"But what about the Kolendas, mother? Where did they ever come in? I remember the story of the boat trip from Poland to Israel that father so often tells, but I have forgotten the part before that."

"The farmer and his wife took us to a farm house several miles away. We passed many other farmhouses, but did not stop. They took us to a farm where, as soon as we alighted from the sled we heard German voices speaking, and they came running out to meet the farmer. They spoke in Polish, and the farmer and his wife waved to us and drove their sleigh back home leaving us standing there in the snow with the Kolendas. They immediately took us inside their farmhouse and were chattering like birds at us in German, and we back to them as fast as we could. They heard our whole life story in ten minutes! They seemed to understand all about us. We hadn't been with them for 20 minutes when they told us they were part of a large group of Christian Germans and Poles who were smuggling Jews out of the region onto boats at night bound for Israel. We had never dreamt of going to Israel! It was the farthest thing from our minds! All we knew about Israel was history from the Old Testament books and Rabbinical books we had studied in school. We knew a few Jews still lived there but that it was under British control, and they didn't want any more Jews in."

Sarah stopped to reminisce. "Those precious Christian farmers, the Kolendas, hid us in their fruit cellar downstairs where the only approach to it was in the kitchen when they lifted up a hinged part of the floor. Over that doorway on the floor, was placed a large mat and the kitchen table at all times whether we were up or down. Your father and I stayed with them over two weeks, and they fed us daily so much we were stuffed and put on weight for the first time in two years. Frau Kolenda gave me clothes to wear that had been her daughters, and Moishe received clothes from Ludwig Kolenda. We laughed and had great fellowship with them even though they were Christians and we were died-in-the-wool-Jews and had little or nothing to do with Christians while growing up in Berlin. My eyes were opened to what a real Christian is.'' Sarah stopped for the realization of what she had said to sink in. It did.

Ruth paused before saying anything to her mother, before the story continued, and thought about what her honest mother had just said. Ruth had never given any thought to Christians as to what they were or much of anything about them. Israel had very few Christian Jews, and the only ones she could think of at that moment were Christian Arabs in Bethlehem, less than 10 kilometers away. Her vision and understanding of Christians was limited to that, apart from some Christian Catholics down in the center of the Old City inside the walls. She had seen American and European tourists who were no doubt Christians too.

"But wasn't Hitler a Christian and isn't Yasser Arafat, head of the PLO as well, Mother?" It was a good question. Sarah thought for a second and then answered, "Christians in word only. Neither of those maniacs follow the teachings of the Old or New Testaments. Christians follow the Bible well. Many of them have great respect for the teachings of the Talmud and the Rabbis along with the Pentateuch. They don't keep our feasts or holy days, but they respect the Old Testament just as they do their own Testament. Would you believe it if I told you that the Kolendas were waiting for the Messiah to come just as we are told and taught that He will. The only difference between us and them is that they believe Jesus Christ will be the Messiah, and we certainly know that He won't be, no matter how good a Rabbi He was. But, they did help us inestimably with their love, their food and their house. The best apples I have ever eaten I ate at night in that fruit cellar . . . They were so delicious . . . Mmmmmmm . . . . I can smell them now. But such gracious people they were!" Sarah thought out loud . . . "You could find no finer people anywhere."

"Weren't they the ones who got you to the coast and put you on the boat for Israel, Mother?" Ruth was remembering part of the ancient story now . . . it seems so long ago that she had heard it for the first time.

"They were the ones. The Germans searched their house many times with your father and I buried beneath old blankets in the cellar with our hearts pounding like machine guns. The Germans never dreamed of where to look for escaping Jews. They had a hunch the Kolendas and others in the community were tied into the underground for we heard them yell it at them one night and threaten them with immediate death if anyone was ever caught in their house. It wasn't long after that they took us to the coast, placed us safely in the hands of Jewish sailors and with other Jewish escapees, we were soon bound for Israel. It took three weeks to cruise out of the Baltic Sea through the North Sea and into the Atlantic Ocean and then into the Mediterranean and home. We even had to land at night up the coast so as not to be seen by the British when we got here. They were going to send us back to Germany!" Sarah exclaimed, looking mortified at the horrible thought of it. "Your father and I never split up. We were sent to a Galilee Kibbutzim, in those early days, where we lived separately, of course, and we plowed, harvested and ate good and lived primitively for several years. Later we finally got married, had you and your brothers and moved to Tel Aviv to live with Sam until your father graduated, and then we moved here as you know three years ago when he became a guide. You think I should write a book on that story, eh?"

She knew there were stories far more horrible and spine tingling than hers . . . It seemed that every third middle-aged Israeli had a story. Thousands had escaped to Israel but had lost all their loved ones in the gas chambers of Nazi occupied Poland in those terrible years. They used to tell stories of Jews melted down in giant frying pans for soap and how they tore the skin from their bodies to make lamp shades . . . She shuddered to think of the stories she had heard in her 35 years now in Israel. The stories were always the same—horrible to the superlative degree! But the younger generation must know what their fathers and mothers went through to get this land back. So they tell the stories occasionally, seriously, soberly and the stories sink in.

---

1. Ezekiel 38:1-16.

Chapter

3

London, England

London, England

"Doctor Steven Scott's residence, this is the maid speaking."

"No, the doctor and his wife are not in right now, and they can't be reached. Can I give them a message from you, sir? Thank you, I'll tell your brother-in-law you called, Dr. Morgan. He'll be glad to know you arrived safely. They had been waiting to hear from you. Thank you, good-bye."

The young black maid jotted down the address of Dr. Scott's brother who had just arrived in London from Vienna.

The family had talked at length about Dr. Morgan and his family coming from Vienna to set up practice in the doctor's field of Psychiatry for some time now. They had at last arrived. Emily thought to herself . . . "Wish I could travel around this world like the rich do. But I really have no room to complain, look at me, she thought . . . my brothers and sisters would give their right arm to be here in London— doing exactly what I'm doing—off that British West Indies Island . . ." she muttered to herself while getting the dining room table ready for the family dinner.

Emily had been with the Scotts twelve years and had seen the children born there in London and grow to the ages of twelve for Steven Jeffrey and eleven for his sister, Marsha Ann. Emily loved those children. She had virtually raised them as their beautiful mother had worked hard with her husband, after his graduation from the Royal Academy of Chiropractic Doctors, in those early years at the doctor's office in Kensington. She remembered when they had first hired her as a maid for their fashionable Victorian styled house in a better end of London than Emily had ever worked. She had come over from the Islands only five years earlier anyway, having been born a British subject, and even though she was black, England let her in to do maid's work. Now it would be tough to get in, for the immigration quotas did not allow any more blacks into England. Working for Dr. Steven Scott and his beautiful blond wife, Pamella, was the greatest job she had ever landed.

It was one lucky day when Princess Margaret inquired about Dr. Steven Scott's chiropractic ability and had him come to Buckingham Palace itself to treat her when she had fallen off that Arabian steed Prince Phillip had gotten her for her last birthday. From that day till now, the Scott's chiropractic center had grown by leaps and bounds. With three new young doctors joining Dr. Scott on the staff, the load is easier for him now, and he only works three days a week without his lovely blond wife by his side. Four able secretarial assistants have been hired to do the insurance papers, medical examinations and preliminary investigations for the doctors. The doctor practices Monday, Wednesday and Friday and loves it. He is so devoted to his work, she mused . . . And that wife of his loves him so and those kids . . . my goodness . . . they live a busy life now.

Just then, Dr. Steven Scott and his blond wife came running up the front steps of their home, burst through the door and impatiently ran and turned the television on.

"There just has to be a program preemption for this news." he hastily said, while eagerly pacing in front of the set.

"I just can't believe it; I cannot bring myself to believe this is happening. Those crazy Russians . . .Blast them anyway for their greed; they're a murderous group of warmongers, those communists!" Steve was angry.

"Sir, whatever happened to make you take on so?" Emily had come rushing into the television room as fast as her feet would go from the kitchen. She was preparing the doctor's favorite recipe tonight. It was New Zealand lamb with special mint sauce and roast potatoes, onions and carrots all roasted together as they did, "down under," where he was from.

"The Russians have attacked Israel with the Arabs just this morning, Emily, and I can't get any reports on what is happening, AND I AM DARNED PERPLEXED . . . that's what's wrong!"

"Oh my God, what are they going to do, sir? That is terrible. How can that little nation survive all the Russians and Arabs coming at them?''

"They can't survive on their own, Emily,'' . . . the doctor paused as he flipped the channels . . . "Only if God helps them will they make it. Here it is.'' The news had been running for several moments before the doctor got it tuned in . . . an announcer was reporting on the Middle East.

"Word from Beirut states that the Soviets attacked from Syria, Egypt and Jordan for the land portions and swept in from the Mediterranean Sea hitting Haifa and Tel Aviv hard and fast at 4 a.m. Israeli time today. Residents were sleeping, but some of the military were on alert. Reports had been coming into Israeli Intelligence headquarters from various areas reporting a sudden Soviet build-up in many areas of the Arab world recently. Arms had been shipped in during the last thirty days to Amman, Cairo, Alexandria and Damascus. Overnight, from ports near Odessa on the Black Sea, large transport planes brought fully equipped Soviet soldiers with several brigades of tank corp and heavy artillery troops.'' The announcer continued with a map of Israel behind him. "It was an overnight mass movement of combat ready troops. So far'' . . . the announcer hastily went on to say, "the Soviets have used conventional and non-nuclear weapons. With Arabs at the forefront, the Soviets moved in before dawn and attacked savagely. Russian MIGS were in the air straffing and bombing Tel Aviv, Haifa, the main Israeli seaport. They were also flying low over Jerusalem in reconnaisance, but not shooting there as yet. It was a fearful sight to those of us here for the BBC in Tel Aviv. Untouched bodies lie in the streets outside our broadcast windows. The only Israeli television channel was destroyed shortly after dawn. Radio is still functioning as this tiny State of Israel battles desperately for its very life. Naval artillery fire is wrecking havoc in Joppa, Tel Aviv and the seaport of Haifa.''

"My God help them . . . Steve prayed openly as he gently clutched his wife's hand watching the set as the announcer hastily went on. Israeli resistance is the stiffest I have ever seen. These Jews are girding themselves and fighting like mad. I have never seen such a coordinated effort in my life. No one knows how many Arabs there are fully armed with Soviet weapons. We cannot tell how many Soviets there are, either. Casualties are evidently high both with civilians and the military. The Arabs are apparently suffering the worst. They are no match for the

Israeli fighters. It is the bloodiest battle this reporter has ever witnessed!'' He exclaimed excitedly.

''The Russians have not been able to penetrate too deeply thus far into the coasts of Israel. Naval bombardment is taking a heavier toll inland than the infantry or advanced ground troops. Eilat has fallen as they came across the Red Sea from Egypt and Saudia Arabia early this morning. The Gulf of Aquaba has fallen into Soviet-Arab hands. Israeli troops have withdrawn under the heaviest bombardment of any location. The civilian population is under the control of the Soviets now in that southern Israel beach and resort area. They swept in there early this morning from Jordan as well. Haifa has not fallen, but is under terrible seige. Most of our communication from that area is cut off. The news we have this late afternoon is from the military standby radio transmitters.

''The Israeli Knesset is jammed with ministers in an emergency legislative meeting.'' . . . ''Word has just come that Jordan . . . the Jordan Valley . . . with the Arab city of Jericho has completely fallen to the Soviets. Israeli forces perched on top of the Judean mountains have the vantage point, however, keeping them from coming up the Jericho Road to Jerusalem. Jerusalem is not the center of the attack as yet. The great pressure in the Golan Heights from the Syrian troops and Soviet tanks is being met with fierce resistance by the Israeli tanks and those valiant fighting men. They are led by General Zev Gordon. Major General Tzur is the commanding officer in Tel Aviv with Major General Shoshani in Haifa. Gordon, Tzur and Shoshani's latest reports indicate the Israeli's are holding ground. But more troops are being moved in from Saudia Arabia and Egypt. Libya is on its way via the Mediterranean Sea with large Soviet forces and military equipment that have been there for months. We return you to London awaiting further communiques from Jerusalem and Tel Aviv . . .''

''This is London . . . from the BBC we further report—The Prime Minister and Joint Chiefs of the Military Staff on the United Kingdom have just entered into an emergency session called in London's Parliament Buildings one hour ago. While they are meeting here, the United Nations Security Council in New York has been in session for two exhausting hours attempting to determine other nations' policies toward this invasion of Israel by hostile forces of an insurmountable nature. It hardly seems likely that Israel can hold out without immediate aid from Europe's NATO forces and from the United States of America. Jewish lobbyists in Washington and New York are screaming angrily for immediate intervention by the foreign powers and America. The Pentagon is the scene of a series of meetings with the American military Joint Chiefs of Staff. No news has come to us of any decisions from either New York or Washington where the President and His Cabinet are also meeting with military leaders reviewing the world position today . . .''

"Oh, here is annother communique from Haifa . . . General Shoshani has reported a fresh naval task force replenishing Soviet losses in the Mediterranean Sea at Haifa, scene of ferocious naval battling. It consists of transport ships with heavy-duty tanks, trucks and gun replacement parts on board. Already they are taking over almost all of the sea basin of Haifa. Major General Shoshani has had to pull back to the tip of Mount Carmel where Israeli shelling of Soviet landing forces is severely heavy. It appears that several of the Soviet Naval vessels may have nuclear tipped missles on board. If they have nuclear tipped naval guns, Israel may not last more than two days. Israel does possess nuclear power, but if these weapons are introduced into the war only God knows what will be the outcome. Common market leaders are meeting in Brussels with NATO leaders concerned with the serious implications this has for the world. If the Russians win, vast oil reserves will be under her power in the Middle East . . .'' The BBC Commentator ended his news report by stating; "our regular program schedule will be interrupted as news reports on the current Middle East situation come in.''

There was silence for a moment in the Scott's home, and the maid dared not speak though a million questions pounded in her head.

"My Lord," she thought . . . how would this affect London . . . her . . . the job . . . could it?''

Steve read her mind . . . "This is not the end of life, Emily, for Israel or for us. Don't worry about it, just get on with dinner, if you don't mind; I smell that lamb cooking . . . and I am dying for some. It's been weeks since you prepared my favorite . . .'' With a sweep of his arm he pleasantly motioned for her to be gone while he discussed this serious blow to the world with his wife alone.

"I can't believe what is happening.'' Pamella Jean Scott whispered softly in her husband's presence as they sat side by side on the couch.

"It hasn't been a year since we visited Israel with mother and dad on that Lands of Prophecy Tour . . . Why, I can just see Tel Aviv and Haifa now when we stood there that day on Mount Carmel and looked down over the Baha'i Gardens Temple at the blue Mediterranean. It is so hard to believe that all is being destroyed by the Russians . . . so hard to imagine it . . . '' Pam sighed.

Her husband sat in deep contemplation and said nothing for several moments. She knew better than to disturb him at that serious moment. He would speak when he was ready, but she was bursting with inquisitiveness to know what he was thinking. Her husband understood the prophecies of the Bible as well as anyone she knew personally. He had followed the teachings from his childhood on up till now. He had taught her so much about Israel and the Russians and the position of the Chinese along with the Ten Nations of European Common Market including the United Kingdom. Sometimes these Biblical predictions scared her. She would think, "Will we have time to raise our family before all these things begin to happen." It was a real concern to her especially when they would read the books her husband ordered on the coming world events as predicted in the Bible. Some of the writers predicted the worst things she had ever heard of. But this was one of the major prophecies. She remembered studying it with her family. Russia, from out of the uttermost part of the north, would attack Israel. But she couldn't remember what happens to Israel in the teaching and to what extent the rest of the world was tied in.

Pam and Steve attended church regularly with their two children, Steven Jeffrey and Marsha Ann and full-time maid and baby-sitter, Emily Barnes. The rector of their large interdenominational Center in the Kensington area of London was a dynamic minister majoring in the prophecies of the Scriptures both Old Testament and New. He had taught them for nearly ten years now, in special Sunday evening courses, nearly all the prophecies of the Bible. The minister had announced through the pulpit for two months in advance and circulated announcements everywhere of the PROPHECY SERIES to begin June 1st, 1973. That was almost ten years ago, and now the sanctuary has more in it Sunday night than Sunday morning! People from all over come regularly for this special series on prophecy. What was really interesting was when their minister did his two month series on the Position of the Jew in New

Testament Prophecy. He had invited every Rabbi in London to come. Many did, simply out of curiosity, and he had several of them pray publicly from the platform for Israel and for peace. Many leading members of nearby synagogues had attended the lectures and said they did not offend, but were extremely intriguing and most informative. Dr. Robinson, did not try to push Christianity down the Jewish throats those nights, but merely presented the texts as they were and told everyone to analyze their own conscience as to what to do with Jesus Christ—to which all prophecy actually pointed. [1] Afterwards, coffee was always served for those wishing to stay and chat and only one night was there a heated reaction from a Rabbi to Dr. Robinson. It was controlled anger on the part of the Rabbi who did not believe that Daniel was referring to Christ when he predicted the Messiah was going to die in Daniel 9:25-26. Dr. Robinson asked the Rabbi to interpret the passage for him in Hebrew then and there. The Rabbi pulled out his Bible and read the very teaching Dr. Robinson had presented! The aged Rabbi stormed out of the Center never to return again. He could not deny factually what the rector had stated.

Steve sat up so quickly that it startled Pam who was deep in thought at the moment. He turned and stared deeply into her blue eyes and said seriously, "There is no doubt in my mind that it is now beginning to happen exactly as we have studied. This is part one."

"What's part two, for heaven's sake." Pam exclaimed somewhat dejectedly.

"Part two is really not clear to me, and I don't know who understands it to tell you the truth. Part one: The Soviets and Arabs attack Israel. [2] Part two is how Israel survives if this is the war predicted in Ezekiel. We know Israel survives in part, [3] but it does not state how much death and bloodshed Israel will go through although the implication is that a heavy toll will be taken in life and limb for that tiny state . . ." Steve went on to say, "Only God knew how Israel was going to be protected in all of this and the Bible is not that clear. It just implies that Divine intervention will take place and Israel will be preserved." [4]

"Honey, how can Israel survive two or three days with this onslaught?" She has at least six countries and Russia against her and all those arms . . . and men . . . and ships . . . I can't believe it . . . I can't believe it!" Pam uttered in despair thinking of the friends they had made in Jerusalem. Her mind drifted off momentarily to the shops she had stopped in down in Jericho when they got off the tour bus and ate those Jordon Valley oranges together with friends on the trip. She recalled the dilapidated shops in the Old City where friendly Arab shopkeepers offered to give big discounts on everything. One had sold her some 18 karat gold rings set with beautiful diamonds and emeralds. Steve had bought her three beautiful rings and a matching bracelet of diamonds, emeralds and rubies. When they had arrived back in London, she found them to be valued at least four times higher than what they had paid! How she longed to go back . . . sometimes she wasn't sure it was for the sights of Israel or just to go back to those Arab jewelry stores . . . Mmmmmm they were the greatest! She exclaimed inwardly.

"Didn't our guide . . . ah . . . Jacob . . . live near Tel Aviv, Steve?" Pam asked.

Their minds drifted off to the land of prophecy and the trip . . . and friends they had made . . . like the terrific guide, Moishe Rosenberg along with his assistant, Jacob Davids from Tel Aviv . . . Moishe had lived in Jerusalem with his family . . . He remembered meeting them all at the Intercontinental Hotel one night when the guides and drivers brought over their wives and families to meet the illustricus group of doctors and their wives. That arrangement turned out to be a most memorable occasion for it was that night Pam learned that Moishe's wife, Sarah, had been raised in Germany and had escaped so miraculously from the Nazis through Christian friends. Sarah had told Pam the story in the three hours they were together that evening. Pam found it so intriguing; she continued a letter writing friendship with Sarah really on behalf of helping her understand Christianity a little more. And besides, it was thrilling to have a friend living in the Holy City to write to every month or two. And write they did.

"I guess Moishe and his boys are fighting at the front today . . ." his voice drifted off . . . thinking of that friendly family so interested in the prophecies.

"Yes, and probably his daughter, Ruth, too. She is nineteen now and soon going to be twenty. When we were there her brothers had been in the army for three years full time. I think they were in their early twenties." Pam replied quickly.

"Well, we have known for several years now that things were heading up fast for the fulfillment of these predictions. Frankly, everything is right on time. It was just over three or so years ago that the treaty to protect Israel was signed by the President of the Market headquarters in Brussels and all the United Kingdom agreed and so did the Common Market leaders. You remember Stanos Papilos, head of the Common Market since 1979, came up with the arrangement. All the participating nations agreed to protect Israel's borders for at least seven years in that treaty."[5] Steve recounted as they now prepared for dinner, washing and refreshing themselves from their day at business.

"But didn't the Arabs hate that treaty, honey?" Pam asked while changing from her exquisitely fitting blue velvet dress. It had a slightly plunging neckline that Steve liked so well and had bought for her at the last chiropractic convention in Paris two months ago.

"Yeah, they hated it . . ." he muttered through the soap and water as he got through splashing his face and neck and arms, having taken off his shirt and tie and was readying for some casual wear for the dinner hour. Steve didn't know which he wanted first, the roast leg of New Zealand lamb or to pick up the books and follow the news as he found it relevant to Bible prophecies.

With Emily serving as she always did, the lamb was a hit that night with the whole Scott family. Emily joined in the sumptuous dish later before cleaning up the kitchen when the family retired to the library to finish their coffee and discuss the earthshaking news of the day.

The children had heard part of the discussion at the table. They were vaguely aware of the fact that a war was going on, in the country they had visited last year where Jesus lived and died. They would never forget riding the camels on the Mount of Olives outside their hotel or the boat ride on the Sea of Galilee.

"You mean, Dad," Jeff absorbed, "that the Jews are fighting the Russians and Arabs up there near Tiberias where the Sea of Galilee is?"

"Right where you were on that boat, son." Steve answered his son with a serious frown on his brow. "Right where you were swimming . . . just a short distance from that beach, heavy fighting is going on right now. Many are being killed . . ." His voice drifted off quietly, making a profound impression on both children as they thought of their recent trip there and the events that brightened their life by going to Israel.

"The truth of the matter is," Steve continued the dinner subject, "that if Stanos Papilos is the predicted head of the revived Roman Empire and the Common Market Ten Nations happen to be the fulfillment of that partial revival of the Old Roman Empire, as Daniel predicted,[6] then, we have to be hideously close to the middle of the predicted seven years of hell on earth."[7]

"What seven years, Dad?" Jeff chimes in cautiously, not wishing to upset his father's trend of thought.

"You remember Dr. Robinson telling us that night he was over here for dinner Jeff, about Daniel . . . you remember the story about Daniel and the den of lions and all of that?" Steve queried.

"Yes sir, I remember that and about the three Hebrew men who wouldn't bend, budge or burn . . . I remember those stories. Mr. Williams told them to us just recently again by the fireside." Jeff quickly answered, wanting to get on with his original question that was really important to him.

"Well, Daniel predicted, as Dr. Robinson told you that night, and I remember he took you and Marsha into this very library and read it to you from that very Bible there" . . . pointing to the one the good doctor of theology had used, "that a man was going to rise and take over ten nations probably rising in Europe or Asia, and that he would be a world dictator."[8]

He is called the Antichrist,[9] or beast,[10] or little horn[11] in the Bible. He said that this man would take over ten nations as they asked him to,[12] in their plight to run the world, and that he would use them to become a world dictator[13] . . . Do you remember that?" Father asked.

"A little," Marsha answered timidly, not wanting to appear absolutely dumb about these grown up matters. Jeff just nodded affirmatively.

"We believe that Mr. Stanos Papilos, who took over the Common Market Ten Nations about four years ago now, is that man. If he is, then this war will result in him moving from Brussels, Belgium where his headquarters is now, to Jerusalem after this war with Russia.[14] If that happens—and we don't know how long this war will last in Israel—then we are going to have a new kind of money issued, in the form of a stamp on the back of your hand or forehead.[15] You'll use it when you go to the store or for petrol in the car or for groceries or when we go to pay the accounts where your mother carries charge cards, or for anything we would ever have to buy,'' Dad answered gravely.

"Daddy, would I have to take that stamp on my hand?" Marsha asked, with a look of bewilderment on her countenance.

"We will never take that mark at all, Marsha,''[16] Steve firmly replied. "We will not stay in this country if that system is used in England.''

"Where would we go, Dad?'' Jeff immediately inquired, thinking of all the friends he had and would have to leave behind. That was the saddest thing he had heard through the whole meal. Not too much of the war goings on had bothered him but this shook him up visibly, a lot.

"Your mother and I have known for about four or five years, after studying with Dr. Robinson at length, that these things might come in our lifetime.[17] If we see any of them start happening and other prophetical points follow close at hand, then we will know that this is it. We had always planned to leave England and go to the United States, as quickly as we could sell the practice and pack and leave. I'm not saying we are leaving now son, but it could happen in a little while—a year or two maybe, depending on events in the world. It has been in the back of my mind for over five years. I know exactly where we are going.'' Steve answered rather methodically, as though explaining an internal muscle problem to a patient lying on his manipulation table.

"Perhaps this would be as good a time as any, honey, to explain to Marsha and Jeff where we could go and what might happen?'' Pam requested of him softly and yet with grim determination written all over her face.

"I'd rather not go into all the details tonight, children, but I will tell you this. Your father has a plan should England and all of Europe become embroiled in this thing.[18] We will live in the state of California, as far as we can from Europe, and stay away from the Mark of the Beast,[19] as it is called in the Bible. I'm not sure it will ever reach the United States for various reasons.

"Why are we so afraid of the mark, Father?''[20] Jeff piped up once more.

"The Bible says if anyone takes that mark they are doomed in Hell, that's why.'' Dad said emphatically. "You cannot take that mark and be a Christian. It says that in Revelation 14:9 . . . it's just that simple. It also means we would be pledging our allegiance to this Stanos Papilos, as our political and religious leader forever. If he is the man, we will see our church closed down, our minister banned from public speaking and all Christianity ended, as we know and understand it. This will be a terrible place to live with murderers and thieves in control of our world and country. I do not want to raise you and Marsha Ann or keep your mother in this environment.'' . . . his voice trailed off . . . ''But listen you two'' . . . he came on strong now . . . ''You let me and mother do the worrying . . . you leave us alone for a few minutes and then we'll join you in the television room for some dessert. Why don't you go and do your weight lifting, Jeff?''

With that, the children slowly left the room. Marsha Ann went to the television room to watch a favorite BBC humorous program after that heavy conversation and overwhelmingly good dinner . . . ''After all'' she thought, ''that's what mothers and fathers are for . . . to think all the big thoughts!''

For Jeff, life was entirely too busy to think of Jews, Russians and a war a million miles away. He had good memories of Israel and liked the mules and camels in Jerusalem. But it was hard to imagine war there now. On to the weights. Dad had taught him some weight lifting techniques for a young boy to produce stronger muscles for soccer and basketball. After, all, didn't his dad know more about weight lifting than anyone else he knew in England? He had won two awards in weight lifting back in Sydney, Australia before he met and married Mom . . .

Emily came rushing into the library without knocking. She hurriedly apologized and breathlessly panted out the message, having run from the kitchen down the long hallway decorated with beautiful paintings and busts from Greece, Rome and Paris. ''I clean forgot, Missie Pamella,'' an affectionate term she had applied to her employer. ''Your brother called, Dr. Raymond Morgan,'' . . . she was reading her own writing. ''He and his family arrived in London today . . . this afternoon before you got home. He called and told me they would be staying tonight at the Hilton Hotel in room 323 and for you to call when you came. I am sorry, ma'am, I forgot to tell you in all that wild excitement about Israel and Russia. I just found my note.'' Emily handed the note to Pam, who hastened to pick up the nearby phone and call her brother and his family at the Hilton.

Pamella's older brother, like herself, was born in Brighton, England, on the south coast of England, opposite France on the English Channel.

Dr. Raymond Morgan was 48 years of age and had accomplished a great deal in the medical world of Europe, first as a general practitioner in Brighton, then, after four years of practice, at the Freudian Center for Psychiatric Studies in Vienna, Austria. He had been there for 11 years now and had just resigned his post at the University of Vienna, Psychiatric Center. He had been asked to stay on at the Freudian Center, inasmuch as he was such a brilliant psychiatrist and was loved by his teachers and peers.

Dr. Morgan was anything but religious. After a similar Christian background of teaching such as Pam had by nominally Christian parents in Brighton, he had virtually given up on all religions and decided the study of the brain and all its microscopic wonders would be far more satisfying than life in the monestary, as his father had once suggested.

Pam put down the phone and announced that they were all having dinner at the hotel tomorrow night at seven with her brother and family.

Steve inquired why they would not come to the house and stay. Pam merely said, "My brother is too independent for that. He'll come, but in his own good time. He's not snobbish or anything like that; just totally unpredictable. Sometimes I think he needs a psychiatrist himself."

"What's their daughter's name?"

"Tonya Rae, honey" . . . Pam's voiced trailed off as she had already left the room for the news on the television.

It was nearly 9:30 p.m. London time and that meant it was past midnight in Tel Aviv. The news was worsening as had been expected. Steve came in shortly hearing the BBC in the other room.

"What we feared is happening in Israel tonight," the announcement came. "Tel Aviv has fallen along with Ben Gurion airport to the Soviets and the Arab legions with them. Walking through the streets one can see blasted-out houses everywhere from the naval bombardment. Most ministry buildings, the art building along with the downtown shopping areas are thoroughly in ruins. People have succumbed completely, though there is the occasional sporadic gunfire in the suburbs this early morning hour in Israel. All Tel Aviv communication has been taken over by the Arabs who are broadcasting their victory constantly and singing Arab military victory songs to listening Arabs and Jews alike. All armed resistance from the beaches to the airport ended at 6 o'clock tonight, Israeli time. The Israeli Defense Forces conceded the loss of Tel Aviv shortly thereafter and retreated to the hills between Tel Aviv and Jerusalem for good protection. They are thoroughly dug in militarily.

"Aerial forces are hammering the Israeli strong points on the road to Jerusalem at this hour as Israeli fighters based out of Jerusalem are fighting fiercely in retaliation. Several Israeli jets have been downed in fiery dog-fighting between Israeli and Soviet fighter planes.

"Israeli forces are still holding the Jericho road—closed to Soviet forces coming in from Jordan along with fierce fighting in the Sinai where many Israeli soldiers are fighting almost suicide-like missions to blast out the Egyptians and Russians in their several thousand tanks coming across the desert from the Suez. Egyptian losses are heavy. Soviet losses are just as heavy in the Golan Heights where Soviets are leading the pincer movement against the Israelis firmly entrenched in and around Mount Hermon. The Israelis still hold the high spots making it a terrible loss in lives for the Syrians as they fight fiercely to take the Golan Heights again and Mount Hermon. It is less than twenty miles to Damascus, and the Israelis can see the lights of the city in the sky at night. They are counterattacking and missiles of a non-nuclear nature are falling on Damascus killing thousands of civilians in this retaliatory raid by Israeli air and ground forces." The announcer droned on . . .

"The United Nations has gone into an emergency session in New York tonight. They did not come out for dinner, but delegates speaking on resolutions for hours have as yet come to no united end."

"A report just in to the BBC states that the United States of America will declare war on the Soviet Union in 12 hours if the Russians do not pull back within that time! Good Lord, ladies and gentlemen, this is the beginning of what looks like World War III!" The announcer took out his handkerchief, blew his nose and wiped his brow and said publicly, "Blimey, we are into it now, folks. This is a major war all over again." He announced that all regular programming on the BBC would be preempted that night and with that, a station break came.

"This is it, then," Steve said emphatically and soberly with his lips pursed tight and bloodless. "We are all going to be at war by noon tomorrow. The United Kingdom will go the way of the States; we need that oil just like they do. The Common Market is already committed to

Israel's defense and has to send NATO's troops in order to keep Papilo's seven year protection treaty with Israel. By this time tomorrow night you can bet that the entire European forces will be thrown into the fray in the Middle and the US 6th fleet will be steaming into the eastern Mediterranean for Israel.'' Steve explained ''I'll bet the 7th fleet will come up from the South Atlantic and go through the Indian Ocean to try to get to the Red Sea and the Gulf of Aquaba and Elat at the southern tip of Israel. They'll work a two-way movement from the northwest and from the south. Then the Europeans will hit them from the direct north and west as they can.'' Steve was staring at his world map while talking. His fingers ran over the areas he was speaking of for Pam to understand.

The rest of the evening was filled with watching and talking over the news from around the world. Shocked amazement filled the world at America's decision to declare war on Russia. It was really unbelievable!

It was the talk of London and the world the next day. Newspapers blazed out the War threat from America to Russia. The deadline was 6 o'clock p.m. New York time—today! It was chilling to think of the ramifications internationally.

The American President stated flatly that an attack on Israel was as good as an attack on the western nations since their oil supply was threatened.

There was no word from Moscow by evening dinner time at the Hilton Hotel in London's most fashionable downtown district. The Morgans met the Scotts in the finest restaurant the Hilton afforded. Both families got along well. Raymond and Charlotte were more than ten years older than the Scotts, man to man and woman to woman, but that made little difference. Nor did the difference in the fields of academic achievement make any difference between the doctors. They both respected one another highly, Raymond commenting on Steve being the doctor of chiropractic for the Royal Family.

''Not of the whole Royal Family, Raymond.'' Steve replied somewhat regrettably, but the Princess is enough to keep me busy in Buckingham Palace, oh . . . at least once or twice a month as she calls.''

The Morgans only daughter Tonya had never married to date. Nor was there seemingly anyone who suited her specialized taste. She was extremely attractive, being so tall and so slender with long flowing blondish hair. She looked like an English or European model. Her facial features gave her a stunning Grecian beauty. She had done modeling in Vienna for some time, for some very exclusive fur houses and fashion centers. She was about 25 Pam thought, and certainly beautifully dressed, spoke impeccable English in spite of her nearly 20 years in Vienna where her father had practiced and taught and furthered his career in medicine. Her mother was petite and well bred. Charlotte had been born outside of Paris and being French through-and-through brought a culture to the dinner of Englishmen and Australians quite enriching and flavourful. Pam adored her French accent and parisian ways.

While the three women spoke of skiing and fashions and life in London and a million questions about Buckingham Palace and what was the Queen like; the doctors spoke of their individual practices and ended the evening on the subject that had to come up—prophecy and the current war.

Raymond knew pretty well where Steve stood in Christian thinking and evangelical thought and theory. What Steve did not know about Raymond was that he was bordering on atheism. After having studied all religions and their various effects on the minds of recipients and mental patients, he could not bring himself to believe in God at all.

"Steve, if there is a God, then He is far away and is totally uninterested in what is going on here on earth." Raymond quietly admitted. "I have no desire for God or even to believe in Him or His existence. I just never had any reason to believe that one exists any more than Zeus existed." He paused and then continued, "I really admire your real religious conviction and most of all admire and respect your faith. You had it when I first met you, and you seem more adamant in it now than ever. Where did you ever acquire such faith in such an unknown entity as God?" His voice faultered somewhat indicating a longing to believe in something more than just what was around him. "Frankly, I see things in my psychiatric world that, if I could believe in an all-powerful God, like you do, it would help me tremendously. Believe me, psychiatry is not the end-all to the world's needs, emotionally and spiritually. I see people every day that I wish I could impart some faith to. But I have none and so" . . . He looked at Steve, shrugged his shoulders and lifted his hands, palms up as though wishing he could do something really tangible about his tragic lack of understanding faith.

Steve came back with a clever piece he had picked up out of one of Dr. Robinson's sermons one Sunday morning that had really made an indelible impression on him. He recounted the message this way.

"Raymond, a very learned man once told me that the human being psychologically, intellectually, physically and emotionally is made up of four basic hungers of his personality or character. Perhaps you will concur with him to an extent." Steve cautiously pondered a moment thinking of them all, then continued, "First, this doctor taught that when an infant comes into the world he possesses four hungers or appetites that make him click all through life. Everything he does is wrapped around these appetites. The first one manifested at birth is the physical appetite for milk and then more solid nourishment. The second one is the emotional appetite for love and affection—to give it as well as receive it. Thirdly, comes the intellectual hunger or appetite for learning and acquainting himself with everything round about him . . . So far do you agree with his analysis?" Steve asked Raymond looking him square in the eyes.

"No doubt about his analysis at all. Your friend surely described the human character and personality." Raymond pleasantly observed.

"Well, the good doctor added one more appetite and said without it we are incomplete and that many times we treat another appetite for a malfunction when it is this last predominent one that is out of whack and not being fed. He called it the 'spiritual appetite of man's soul.' " Steve paused and then went on . . . "He said if we fail to feed this appetite with things greater than food, rest, recreation, fun, love and intellectual satisfaction then we are like an automobile going through life with a flat tire. You may feed the physical with food, rest, beverages, etc; and feed the emotional with love and affection both giving and receiving; and you can even feed the intellectual with profound material; but if you fail to do anything about your inner spiritual hunger, you cannot be complete or genuinely, internally at peace with yourself. There's a missing link in your make up . . . What do you think of all this, personally, Raymond?"

That thought hit Dr. Raymond Morgan, Psychiatrist, right between the eyes head on . . . He dropped his head and said quietly, "That is . . .

without a doubt the story of many of my patients . . . but better still, Steve, it sounds like my story,'' he swallowed hard. Steve thought for a fleeting second Raymond was going to brush a tear from his eye, but sniffed a little instead as he pulled his handkerchief out quickly. He had been very obviously touched by what Steve said. He thought to himself . . . "Blast it, how could a guy not majoring in my field of study come up with such a unique explanation for something I have been searching for for years. He's just described me! I can't believe what I have just heard . . . Keep yourself in control, doctor . . . no need to make an evangelist out of your brother-in-law the first night together after many years. But darn, that was good thinking even for a man in psychiatry . . . Could that be my answer?'' He mused to himself, pausing to have another sip from his glass of dry red wine.

As a foreign-born waitress poured Raymond's third glass of wine, Steve looked over at her and said, "Say, have you heard any news tonight of the Middle East situation?'' . . . "Yes, she said smiling brightly, we are soon going to have our homeland back again. I am a Palestinian working here in London. I follow the news every minute on my little radio back there . . .'' she said, pointing to the kitchen area.

"What has happened then?'' Steve never winced or changed his expression at her obvious elation over Israel's pending defeat. How could he blame her; she had lost her home and she felt very naturally about it.

"The Russians'' . . . she paused speaking with a strong accent and having some difficulty with English . . . "have taken Tel Aviv with my people helping them. They are all over the area north of Jerusalem in a city called Ramallah and hope to have Jerusalem by tomorrow. Jericho and the Dead Sea area is in Palestinian hands and the Gulf of Aquaba too.'' She hurried on to further report that, "Ben Gurion airport is ours and the town of Caesarea has been taken north of Tel Aviv.'' She exclaimed very happily.

Most of that news was old. Nothing too astonishing yet. Steve thought to himself, while others chatted with the waitress about her background.

He interrupted them . . . "Was there any news about the Golan Heights?'' She thought for a moment and said . . . "I have not heard anything about it so there must not be any new development there, sir.''

No news is good news, Steve thought and the evening wound up on a most pleasant note with everyone toasting Dr. Raymond Morgan's new post in London as Assistant Chief Psychiatrist for the Royal Academy of Psychiatry. It was a cherished post and an extremely well paying one. Not that Raymond had lacked for anything financial in Vienna either.

The families made plans to get together again soon after the settling-in experience and would be talking on the phone concerning the date.

As Raymond went upstairs in the hotel to their lovely suite, he was in deep contemplation of what Steve so simply and candidly had come out with. Charlotte, sensing something troubling her husband, inquired what was bothering him.

He looked at her and Tonya Rae both as they sat momentarily in the lounge area of the suite and said to them, "I may have learned something so profound tonight from Steve that I am still stunned from the blow . . . and I cannot fathom something so wise coming from someone not, ahh, in psychiatry . . . Now, I don't mean to belittle Steve, dear, at all. That's not it. For years I have thought and thought about life's little missing link. He may have unearthed a new mine for me to dig in to-night . . ." He looked shaken, uneasy as he shared his thoughts on what Steve had said.

Tonya Rae spoke up and said, "It was impressive, indeed. Maybe it does account for the unhappiness of so many people."

"What you two are saying," intruded Charlotte, not to be left out of the intellectualism her daughter and husband were enjoying by themselves, "is that most of us spend our lives feeding the physical and the intellectual, like you two," quietly admitting that both of them had entered a world of intellectualism she had no desire to enter, "along with feeding the emotional, never realizing there was another little mouth down there looking like a baby bird wanting to be fed. Is that it?"

"Yes, that's it." Raymond answered, only it isn't just a yearning of just wanting to be fed. I think in most cases I have observed the rich and seemingly satisfied persons I have treated. Their spiritual hunger is screaming and clawing to be fed!" He eagerly exclaimed . . . No one said a word, but in deep contemplation Raymond reached over and picked a Gideon Bible from the table.

"Cripes, where do you start with one of these things?" No one answered as mother and daughter went into their separate bedrooms looking at one another as though to say fleetingly—"What do you think

of that?'' Everyone turned in . . . with Raymond coming much later—
his eyes blurred and tired from reading the Gospel of John omnivorously.

---

1. Revelation 19:10.
2. Ezekiel 38.
3. Ezekiel 38:8.
4. Ezekiel 38:21.
5. Daniel 9:26-27.
6. Daniel 7:1-26.
7. Matthew 24:21-22.
8. Daniel 8:20-27.
9. 1 John 2:18.
10. Revelation 13:1.
11. Daniel 7:8, 19-28.
12. Revelation 17:12-14.
13. 2 Thessalonians 2:1-8.
14. Daniel 11:45.
15. Revelation 13:16-18.
16. Revelation 14:9.
17. Luke 21:28.
18. Daniel 7:22-24.
19. Revelation 13:16-18.
20. Revelation 20:4.

Chapter
4

Jerusalem Under Seige

Jerusalem
Under Seige

Rabbi Perla came rushing into the apartment building almost pushing his heavy frame through the door panting and out of breath. It had been a long walk and was a dangerous one tonight anywhere in Jerusalem. But he had never had a car and would never spend money on a taxi. Both families met him at the door . . .

Dianna had married David, the young handsome boy upstairs, to the happiness of both families and she was great with child at this moment. She was so beautiful. He may have missed his first date with her four years ago, but he made up for it a year later by marrying her. It had been one gala occasion with the Rabbi's relatives on the orthodox side of Jewry, and the Rosenbergs side with conservative and reformed Jews in attendance together. They had sung far into the night, true Israeli style. Everyone was so happy then and within the last three years David and Dianna had learned to love one another with a deep, richer than usual kind of love. It shone on both of their faces when together. They adored one another and never wanted to be apart.

But these were terrible days to be bearing a child. David was presently at the Golan Heights fighting under General Gordon, holding back the Arabs and Soviets only because they held Mount Hebron and had the high vantage point. In addition, Israel had faster maneuvering tanks than the bulky Soviet tank. They could outmaneuver Arabs and Soviets alike, and the anti-tank brigade that David was in was a crack team of experts.

Ya'er was fighting in the Sinai Peninsula with other Israeli divisions, keeping the Egyptians at bay. Soviet armor crept over the Suez Canal via pontoon bridges and into the regions presently occupied by the Israelis in great strength. Thousands of Egyptians had already been killed while many fled in frenzy and fear of the Israelis.

Everyone was shocked at the suddenness and the swiftness by which the Soviets had taken Tel Aviv. Politicians in the Jerusalem Knesset were blaming every other man's party—especially the Minister of Defense and the Prime Minister who should have known this was going to happen!! Pandemonium was in the streets of Tel Aviv and Haifa and would certainly break out soon in Jerusalem.

The tired, weary with life, Rabbi hugged his wife, Miriam, telling her and the Rosenbergs of his praying at the wall with thousands of Jews and that nothing new had developed there. The news was terrible about Tel Aviv; armed resistance was being flattened and loudspeakers on Soviet tanks told the Jews to stay in their houses. They were not to come out for any reason or they would be shot.

The Rabbi had heard that the American 6th Naval fleet was on the way and that NATO troops were expected any time. They tuned in their radio and listened as they ate cold fish, cheese and tomatoes. With static and short wave sounds periodically piercing their ears, they heard another message. A shocking one!

"Warsaw Pact Forces have taken Berlin this afternoon and though there was much resistance by the American forces stationed there as a part of NATO, all resistance is silenced now. Berlin is no longer a divided city. It is totally under Soviet control." The announcer went on to say, "Soviet forces are pushing out of East Germany to take all of Germany tonight. Without any announcement, a Soviet invasion of Europe has started at nearby NATO bases. All-out war has begun in parts of Europe with the Warsaw Pact Forces against the North Atlantic Treaty Organization military powers." . . . there was a lot of static . . . a longer pause and the short wave set again blazed new information from some point in Europe. "The Common Market Nations with their President, Stanos Papilos, have announced their intentions of an all-out war against the Russians and the Warsaw Pact Nations tonight. I repeat, NATO, and the Common Market Ten with President Stanos Papilos, have announced a Declaration of War against the Soviet Union and Warsaw Pact Nations late tonight. Europe is going to war to defend itself against the Russians. Word has it from official sources that the Russians have been building up to this moment for 10 years in Europe and NATO leaders knew of it, but did little. It's too late to cry tonight; they said, and declared war.

"British, French, German and Netherland leaders have agreed to a summit meeting of all western powers in London tomorrow morning to convene at 9 o'clock, London time. Military strategists from all nations will be involved and leaders from the International Monetary Fund and the United States will be present. Our President of the Common Market Ten, Stanos Papilos, called the meeting just before dinner hour tonight after announcing Europe's declaration of war with the Soviet Union . . . NATO leaders indicated it will not be easy to fight a two front war both in Europe and in the Middle East but with strong American aid, they feel they can win the war—though at high cost. Several of our Big Ten military leaders said we could not hope to win the war no matter how hard we try. The Soviets were superior in training and vastly superior in military hardware. So far nuclear power has not been unleashed anywhere in the fighting areas. Only conventional fighting and armament is in use . . ."

Moishe Rosenberg, at home with his wife and daughter, looked up from the broadcast at the Rabbi and Miriam to say, "Daniel, Chapter 11, Verse 40 is now being experienced."

The Rabbi, having already heard Moishe's interpretation some time ago, lifted his eyebrows and inquired what is said in that passage. Most Rabbis kept themselves busy with the first five books of the Bible and the Torah and seldom looked beyond the Book of Moses commonly called the Pentateuch.

"It says," Moishe respectfully reminded the Rabbi, "the King of the North will attack and the King of the South will attack at that same time. That is what is happening now. You have Russia from the north and the Egyptian powers backed by Russia, and many nations in black Africa pushing at us from the south. It is happening exactly as the prophet said."[1]

The Rabbi nodded his seeming approval. He respected Moishe for his knowledge of parts of the Holy Writ that he had not delved into. They had long ago stopped talking about Who the Messiah might be, but this was interesting.

Just as he was about to ask Moishe about what was supposed to happen next in the prophetical record, the radio became clear again and the news announcer said, ''And now a message from the Prime Minister of Israel: Your attention please:

''Mt. Hermon has fallen and many of our Israeli soldiers are dead or are taken prisoner. The Golan Heights are being overrun with Soviet military strength. It appears that the entire area around the Sea of Galilee including Tiberias has or is now falling into Soviet and PLO hands. The latest word we have from Israeli commanders in that area is that they are pushing us back to the hills of Samaria, south of Tiberias and the Galilee area. Israeli losses are great, but our men are fighting as never before in the history of this country. If this nation can hold out till morning, American forces and NATO powers should be here to aid us and to route the Russians. Any delay in them arriving will mean that when they get there it will be too late! We are being pushed back at every area of the battle. In the Sinai, black forces have arrived to assist the Egyptians. Black armies from Uganda and Zaire and several other unrecognizable African countries have moved in in large numbers. It appears there may be more black soldiers fighting than Egyptians.

''We are up against forces from Africa and Egypt on the south. We are up against the Soviets and at least seven Arab nations in the west, east and north. Never in the history of our tiny nation—in our 35 years— have we experienced anything like this mighty armada of armies coming against Israel. If you have any belief in God as Israelis, then pray.'' The Prime Minister pleaded with his nation. ''It is our last hope as help from our allies is very slow in getting here and may be too late. This is Israel's most difficult hour yet. We are being battered in every city and area except Jerusalem. We need our aged men and mothers of Zion to pray to God for our salvation. You may accomplish more on your knees than we will accomplish here in the Knesset for our boys in the bloody fields of battle tonight. Pray Israel, pray! We beg you to.''

The Rabbi was weeping quietly and praying. You could see his lips moving. His wife wiped tears from her eyes and sat moving back and forth in psychological agony thinking of what was to come.

Moishe, Sarah and Ruth went upstairs to listen to their own short-wave radio. All normal radio stations were off the air, taken over or destroyed by the PLO or Russians. All communiques were coming in from field transmitters set up by the Israeli Defense League or in the Knesset.

Sarah and Moishe did their best to comfort their almost twenty-year-old daughter, Ruth. Her boss was on the battlefields of the Golan Heights, and had led in the battle against the Russian tanks. She was imagining the worst about him and the others who had worked in the defense plant, but who were now fighting all over Israel for their very lives.

There had been no word from David or Ya'er on either front. The news was the same from all over. There were many casualties. Many Israeli civilians in Tel Aviv along with the military were dead. The hospitals were jammed already. They were calling for volunteer nurses, or trainees, or just any wives who would donate time to help in any way. Ruth wanted to go badly but was so far forbidden by her father to do so.

"Two sons at the front is enough right now!" Moishe had said, and that ended the matter for then. "The irony of it all," he thought as he pulled on his pipe and prayed inwardly that he would see those precious boys again.

Dianna knocked on the door and came running in.

"I have news of David," she said breathlessly, "He is alive and hopes to see us soon."

"Where and how did you get that piece of information?"

"A telephone call from the hospital. One of his buddies called to tell me. He had been shot up badly with shrapnel, and they brought him and a load of others who may be amputees down to Jerusalem. He had seen David last night." She sat down, breathed heavily and smiled at their good fortune.

Washington had received no direct word from Moscow nor had any ambassador from any other nation conveyed a message to the President. All signals were go. The war was on. The US 6th Fleet had been steaming eastward in lieu of these predicted circumstances. NATO forces were on their way by sea and air to Athens, Greece and nearby air strips. Turkey had declared its position on the side of the Soviet forces on another news broadcast. That had been no shock to the western world at all. Twelve months ago Turkey had ordered all NATO radar observation sights to be dismantled and removed from her land.

The Russians had been bringing troops and machinery of war down through Istanbul into the Sea of Marmora, out of the Turkish Bosporus, and docking much shipping there before entering into the Aegean Sea and then into the Mediterranean Sea. Much of this had gone unnoticed, as NATO had been out of Turkey, and the usual reconnaisance flights of the Big Ten or NATO over the Bosporus and Aegean Sea were not allowed. It was not always easy for spies and undercover agents and Turkish sympathizers with the western powers to be sure whose ships were whose, and what was on board. They had been getting ready for this invasion ever since the NATO powers were kicked out of Turkey. Russia must have bought off the ailing Turkish nation with much financial aid.

The element of surprise was in spite of NATO observers and Israeli intelligence. They had been thoroughly caught off guard, because of the TREATY OF ROME. It guaranteed the borders of Israel to be safe from the P.L.O., or anyone. An attack on Israel meant an attack on Europe—so said President Stanos Papilos, the newly appointed leader of the Big Ten, commonly called the Common Market Ten Nations. He had been installed in early 1979 and by 1980 had guaranteed the State of Israel's security.

Because of Papilos' guarantee of security for Israel, backed by all the powers of the west, the Arab nations were completely silenced. There had been vital peace in the Middle East [2] and even Egypt had opened her borders to Israeli-Egyptian interchanges of commerce, along with what Jordan had been doing for over ten years through the Allenby Bridge, over the Jordan River.

Lebanon had done the same. Only Syria had remained adamantly opposed to any trade with Israel during this time, primarily because most of the P.L.O. were based in Damascus, and pitted their voice and strength against any open border policy. Thus, Israel had felt at ease [3] and military relaxation set in. Not near as much of her annual fiscal budget had to go to defense and her inflation rate had fallen. Her people enjoyed a new era of success and prosperity. Her valleys produced in abundance. Her people felt at peace with most of the world, and no longer daily wondered about P.L.O. intrusions. They had been unusually quiet and almost nothing had been done by the P.L.O. in nearly three years, until now. They feared the super powers would move in against them as Papilos had said. At least that was the current running opinion, and Papilos' tight rein in Europe almost stopped all terrorism of the airway and airports. It appeared to the world that the P.L.O. had been silenced and terrorism curtailed.

When Papilos came to power in 1979, three nations bucked him [4] — England, Ireland and Denmark. All three of them were in the northern most regions of the Common Market Ten. Greece was the last nation to join in 1979.

The immediate threat of complete economic boycott of those three nations, produced a war of words and politics, shaking Europe's unity. While the Ten Nations fought their wars of words and sanctions on the three northern nations, the Russians were moving in with the P.L.O. The attention of the world had been diverted from Russia to the great rift and diversion in Europe's unity.

After economic boycotts had been imposed nearly a year, and Britain's economy, along with Ireland and Denmark was going quickly down the drain, they aquiesced and Papilos had been accepted by them, but with grave concern that he might become a Napoleon of modern day Europe with all the power he presumed to take upon himself. English people still revolt at times against him and his policies. They call him the "beast of Brussels."

That Treaty of Rome, as produced by the "beast of Brussels" was Israel's downfall. Had she not confided in that piece of paper so completely, her defenses would not be down tonight as they were. These were the words spoken by the Prime Minister in midnight session.

"Hindsight is always so much easier than foresight. Our fate is in the hands of this European leader and where is he tonight?"

"He could not be reached Mr. Prime Minister, and we have been constantly trying to do so. The latest word is that help is on the way," one of the minister's replied.

"Help may be on the way, but they do not realize how small this country is and how vulnerable we have allowed ourselves to become because of their confounded treaties . . ." he paused for emphasis on the next statement. "And, if their help comes tomorrow night or the next morning, they will find our corpses strewn all over the hills of Zion. There will nothing left in 24 hours at the rate the Soviets are pushing!"

"Mr. Prime Minister sir . . ." What about using our atomic weapons now?" one of the ministers frantically inquired of his superior.

"We have already started. Three hours ago the word was given to save

Mount Hermon and we introduced nuclear tipped weapons in the war for the first time in human history since the Bomb was dropped on Hiroshima. The Soviets still came through and took us. We are fighting, Sir, with every weapon known in the Israeli arsenal. Nothing we use is holding them back. They could be at Jerusalem by morning if they push hard.''

The Prime Minister sat down and wiped his brow. The men were working in their sweaty shirt sleeves, without any food for hours. No one had stomach to eat. They suspected that they would be dead by morning.

The Rabbinical members of the Knesset had long disappeared and had called the people through the remaining broadcasting facility to pray at home or join them at the Wall. Over twenty thousand Israelis were at the Wall.

It appeared that before dawn the Holy City would be taken and the people would have nothing left. When Jerusalem was taken, that would be the last.

At 2:45 a.m. the Prime Minister called Washington, D.C. and told the President that it was all over. Israel could not last another hour, much less a day. The President was to signal Moscow that Israel had surrendered in full. They were urged to cease-fire immediately.

At 2:50 a.m. the President of the United States called Moscow on their hot line and announced that Israel had surrendered. Would they call off the fighting in Israel immediately? The Communist Party Chief said they would. When the American President asked him secondarily what his intentions were in Europe, he very sternly replied, ''That ought to be obvious to you and the Europeans'' and then promptly hung up on the President; but not before he elicited a yes answer from the President on keeping his American troops out of Israel.

At 2:57 Israeli time, the Commanders of the Soviet forces were told to cease-fire, as Moscow called Jerusalem to confirm it at 3 o'clock in the morning.

With the Prime Minister of Israel indicating clearly the will of the leaders to cease-fire and surrender completely, before everyone was destroyed, the word went out on Israeli radio and Soviet wireless to cease-fire. Israel had surrendered unconditionally, to the Russians and Arabs.

But the P.L.O. did not cease fire with the Soviets. They were angry that the Soviets had ordered a cease-fire. They ran into houses, murdering people in their beds, on the streets, herded them like cattle, and machine gunned Jews on sight. The Russian soldiers were aghast at the lack of protocol, and tried to command the P.L.O. to stop. Bedlam broke out in the streets of Haifa, Tiberias, Tel Aviv, Bethlehem and Jericho. The P.L.O., in their jubilation, didn't care what they did or who they killed. Suddenly they turned their guns on small bands of Russians attempting to bring order out of the pandemonium. Pockets of Soviets fired back at the P.L.O., easily identifiable in their white tunics and black turbans. Even when they were not fighting one another, the P.L.O. took the Russians by surprise and started opening fire on them. [5]

Every Israeli was awake, up, dressed and ready for death or whatever might come. No one knew what the consequences of surrender would be. Women screamed in terror, grown men wept and children held to the parents' legs, as if drifting out to sea in a storm.

Stanos Papilos had begged the Israeli Prime Minister not to surrender, but it was futile. He could not help Israel now. It was surrender, or be completely annihilated as a Jewish race. They had no choice.

Black leaders to the south, with Egyptians leading the way, heard the message. There was an immediate cease fire in the Sinai, with Israeli troops doing the same, prepared to hand over arms and come out in the open when the sun came up. No one wanted to move in the darkness, though all had the message.

Every civilian knew of the action of the Knesset. Whether they agreed or not, the Prime Minister had said to all listening, and to many nations listening on shortwave around the world:

"It is surrender for us now, or annihilation by morning for all Israelis. I cannot take the responsibility as your Prime Minister to sign your personal death warrant, even if it means losing our country. We will save lives this way. It is with the deepest of sorrow and humiliation that I tell you, our people, and our fighting men, we have just surrendered to the Soviets through Washington D.C. and in a few minutes the Soviet commander will be here in the Parliament building to receive the formal treaty of surrender, being drawn up now for our joint signatures. Never have I wanted to pen my name less. Death for me would be better. But that is not what you need now. There is enough death. Thousands of our men have perished, as have the enemy. We have inflicted the heaviest of tolls on the enemy. But they overwhelmed us in numbers," the Prime Minister admitted. "It is futile to fight on till we are all in the dust, dead . . ." His voice cracked terribly, under the strain . . . Softly he went on . . .

"The President of the United States, and Mr. Stanos Papilos, have assured me they will do everything they can to either get us a piece of this land to live in, or safely secure our people out of Israel to refugee camps in America and Europe. Our people in the United States and Europe, our Jewish brothers and sisters will take us in, if this is the end of the State of Israel." He ended his pathetic speech . . . The announcer came on . . . and reminded all to stay tuned for the final developments. They would know shortly what the plan was for the remaining living Israelis in all cities, towns and villages.

Steve Scott called his brother-in-law in London to listen on the BBC.

It was late afternoon in the U.S.A. when it was happening in the Middle East. It appeared that every ear was listening in America and Canada. African nations were now aware of the giant participation of the blacks with the Soviets and Arabs, and they too were listening to the south. South America was in the same time zones as the U.S.A. and anxious ears listened intently in the southern regions there.

As far away as Australia, New Zealand Singapore and the nations of the Oriental communist world—all were listening. China, with headquarters in Peking, had already stated her disappointment that the Russians won.

The ears of the world were listening as the Soviet commander stepped into the Knesset Building, and as a lone Israeli announcer gave the story, step by step. The world translated the message into each native tongue simultaneously, while hearing the native tongue of Israel in the background. The miracle of communications never had such a primitive hook-up as that morning by wireless to the radios of scores of nations and into millions of homes around the world.

"Rachel is weeping for her children." The Israeli leader said to the Soviet commander when he climbed out of his jeep and walked into the buildings housing the Lords of Israel.

"Israel weeps more than in Egypt, centuries ago, sir." It appeared that the Commander knew little about what the Prime Minister uttered.

They were about to sit at the table and sign the treaty of surrender when the Knesset building began to tremble as though taken up in some giant hand and shaken terrifyingly. The chandeliers suddenly fell, crashing on the treaties, and the papers were dashed to the floor along with the Soviet delegation.

Ministers in the Parliament building crawled to the windows which were instantly shattered. Everyone believed they had been hit by a missile or a bomb. The building stood still a moment, though all hell broke loose inside it, with Russians and Israelis trying to stand on their feet—those who had not been hurt or killed in the shuffle—while pieces of the ornate ceiling hit them from above.

They were suddenly drawn by one minister screaming, "Mr. Prime Minister, hurry over here and look." The man was obviously in the greatest state of panic. His voice indicated unbelief and incredulity.

He screamed, "I can't believe what my eyes are seeing. I can't believe it."

The others rushed as best they could over fallen ceilings, broken chairs, wooden beams half hanging, half in place.

To their combined horror and consternation, it appeared that the sky was lit up by a giant explosion that showered sparks all over the land. It was as though a thousand fourth of July's had suddenly erupted into the sky and the fallout from the smattering skyrockets had illuminated the entire area of Jerusalem. You could see to Mount Scopus, several miles away. People were running and screaming everywhere.

The very large brass Menorah that had been standing outside the Knesset, had toppled and smashed over the Prime Minister's nine seat black Mercedes. The top was as low as the hood, completely pushed in by the weight of the brass Jewish replica.

The land was filled with complete pandamonium. Israeli soldiers mixed with Soviet and P.L.O. officials were running, each screaming in his own language, attempting to find out why the sky was lit up like a million meteoric comets. The explosions were now descending to the earth slowly fully lit as they came. It was a shocking sight. Everyone was aghast at it and wondered who shot up what fire power? [6]

The soviet General staggered to the doorway and instantly caught the scene. He had been partially hit by the falling chandelier, his arm appeared badly broken and distorted behind his body, and he bled profusely. He was obviously cursing in Russian and was calling for the medics in his corp. Towards him ran two Soviet soldiers, one carrying a bag with a red cross on it. They laid him down on the steps of the Knesset and with Israeli assistance started to bind up his wounds as best they could. The blood seemed to pour from his body. His arm was hanging by the thinnest thread and had been dreadfully and agonizingly torn from his body.

Soldiers were runnning everywhere. The falling sparks were the size of the American softball. The white clad, turbanned Arab Chiefs and their aides were calling to Allah. They had fallen on their knees and were in the act of praying when the balls hit. Firey rocks smashed with terrific force into every car and jeep and truck in the area. Soldiers were knocked to the ground and the building was hit with tremendous force by the balls of fire. More windows smashed and debris was falling everywhere. To go out in the open fields round about the Knesset was to invite sudden death; to stay inside was better, at least the roofs and walls added some protection.

With the death agonies and indescribable screaming and din, coupled with the tormenting anguish of the soldiers outside, one could not hear himself speak or scream, nor collect his thoughts. It was horrible to watch the devastating destruction outside. No one could stop it.

The Israel Prime Minister, surrounded by four or five ministers, lifted up his voice like a Rabbi, and yelled at those around him.

"This is either the greatest act of Jehovah God we have ever seen, or I'll be damned!"

Wiping the blood from his cheek, one soldier called to the Prime Minister to come to the radio.

"Sir, the whole country is on fire. Houses are burning to the ground, factories, apartments, everything." He breathlessly recounted to the leaders. He told them that it appeared there had been an earthquake [7] over by the Mosque and the Intercontinental Hotel was apparently in ruins as well.

"It's made of thick stone. It won't burn." The Prime Minister replied hastily.

"It's not burning sir . . . it's split because of the earthquake and there are bodies of tourists all over. Some have been hit by the balls of fire," the soldier reported rapidly, while listening for the further communiques from Israeli detachments elsewhere.

The message came in Arabic over the wireless set. Probably either transmitted by an Arab or an Israeli, many of whom spoke perfect Arabic. "I am standing here on the other side of the Wall, at the Temple site. A terrible thing has just happened before my very eyes." The man was obviously thoroughly upset by it all. He was so shocked with emotion, he could hardly articulate.

"The Dome of the Rock Mosque has just been completely destroyed by an earthquake on the Temple Mount. There is not one stone standing on the other, only a pile of debris. It is all gone," the announcer wept. "And so is the El Eksa Mosque at the south end of the Temple sight. It has disappeared. Only fire can be seen burning where it was. All the Arab houses in this section of Jerusalem seem to be either partially standing or completely destroyed by the earthquake. Houses in the Armenian quarter are standing. Only the homes near the Temple sight are gone or are burning . . ." "We have just received word from the units in the Jordan desert and Judean Hills overlooking the city of Jericho and the Dead Sea. They say the earth opened up like a giant clam. Thousand have been swallowed up in a giant earthquake. It may be that the whole rift valley has opened up again. News is not clear . . ." "I have just been handed another report from Tel Aviv. Russians and Arab soldiers are running from the elements there outside the buildings. Many of them have been burned to death or killed. They are retreating to the beaches and are leaving the city as fast as they can. There is too much debris for them to use their armoured vehicles. They are abandoning them . . . Everyone, stay inside, stay inside . . . Do not go out in the streets."

It seemed rather unnecessary to tell the Israel population to stay inside, for everyone could see what was happening outside. Bad as it may seem to stay inside for fear of explosions and fire, that seemed the logical alternative to going outside and have certain death fall on your head in the form of a burning rock or meteor.

Soldiers were dropped in agony as they ran. Armoured vehicles were burning, and ammunition on board was exploding ferociously in every part of the country. Those Israelis nearby, in the shelter of their homes were blown to bits, as the tanks exploded and ammunition trucks rocked communities with the reverberation of their detonations. It was repeated in city after city, from the Jordan Valley to Tel Aviv, from the Gulf of Aquaba to Haifa.

All reports coming into the Prime Minister and his aides indicated complete annihilation of the Arab armies. The Soviet's position could not be evaluated as yet. Bethlehem was in ruins from the fires and the earthquake. Arab troops ran from that city into the Hills of Judea nearby, only to be overtaken by either the ground opening up to swallow them, or by the fire that fell from the heavens in dashing swiftness upon them.

"Haifa is being abandoned sir," yelled the radio man to the Prime Minister. "The Russians are running for their ships and can't even take their weapons or vehicles with them. There don't seem to be any Arabs left up there." He smiled as he gave the transmission. It was the first wrinkle of smile anyone had seen for nearly four days.

"This has to be an act of God. Nothing less than the divine act of the Holy God of Israel. No other explanation could possibly suffice." The Prime Minister elicited a joyous response!

Everyone muttered belief in what Prime Minister Uriah Daniels had spoken. It was an act of God. [8]

It was nearly five o'clock in the morning and soon the sun would be up and apart from the smoke rising in a thousand areas where fires were burning furiously, the land was quiet from the sounds of war. Not a shot was heard. No cannons or artillery fire could be heard. Just two hours before, it seemed that the whole country was one artillery battle after another, bringing the land to its complete ruination.

In utter and absolute disbelief, Israelis started to come out of their houses, their apartments, their stone places of refuge and even from the hospitals on crutches or staggering. They crept out, crawled over the fallen bodies smouldering, or near burning debris into the streets of every city in Israel, from Eilat to Haifa, from Tel Aviv to Beersheba. The latter had been badly hit and was almost totally destroyed.

They greeted one another in half-joyous, half-believing, half-functioning brains at the incredulous things their eyes were beholding. It was as if they were seeing but just could not believe.

The streets of every city were covered with dead Russians and Arab legions. Smouldering vehicles and their remains lay everywhere, with parts of them scattered as far as the eye could see. Tel Aviv was going to prove to be the worst damaged city of all. Haifa would be next.

The Prime Minister had gathered his wits about him and had organized Israel cabinet members, soldiers, and every citizen who could get to any hospital to distribute medicine and first aid to all injured.

Prime Minister Daniels came on the wireless to all who could hear. Every outstation was listening. Every military establishment heard it. Thousands of homes had wirelesses. The nation listened with great attention.

"There is no more enemy within our gates" . . . he said exaltedly. "God has sent Heaven's help and the enemy has been broken without the aid of any foreigners who are not here yet." The Prime Minister was obviously so shaken and so broken at what he was saying he had great trouble controlling his emotions over the broadcast.

Then with a loud voice, he shouted into the set . . . "Let all Israel rejoice, let all Israel shout for joy, let there be singing in our streets . . . for our Lord is One God and His mighty power hath gotten us in the miraculous victory all over the land. Rejoice you Jews, rejoice . . ." The Prime Minister was obviously weeping at that moment, for his voice faltered and you could feel the tears in it from one end of Israel to the other. Immediately music depicting a joyous Israel came on the air and ended his speech to the people.

Within two days the ingenious Israelis were making great headway in removing bodies from the streets, hospitalizing the injured and wounded, and were bulldozing out wreckage from one city after another. Families were informed of the living and dead in the military as the records were still pouring in.

Ya'er and David were alive, as were their parents and family members. That part of Jerusalem was hardly bothered at all.

How happy the Rabbi was to learn of his son-in-law's condition. Both families rejoiced over Ya'er and David being alive as much as they did over Israel and the death of the enemy.

When reports started to filter in two to three days later, everyone felt that a divine miracle had taken place. There was absolute awe in the land at what had happened.

Right when the entire country was inundated with Russians and Arabs an earthquake had struck and destroyed almost 80% of them within one hour. It was incredible. Just as the treaty of surrender was being signed, all hell broke loose in the land!

But what everyone found so unbelievable was that from the central countries of Africa, apparently right up through Jordan, parts of Israel, and on up through Syria, into Lebanon and up in Turkey and Russia, the Rift Valley, known for its earthquakes in the past since the days of Noah, had opened up again in violent eruptions. Mountains fell, valley floors fell away and cities, armies, villages, from Zambia and Zaire in Africa, north to Moscow, had been devastated in one swift overpowering earthquake taking millions of lives and creating billions of dollars in losses in those sections of the world.

Cairo lay virtually in ruins, Addis Ababa in Ethiopia was inundated. Only the oil wells of Saudi Arabia were intact with some damage. Mecca and Riyadh were shaken to the ground. Damascus would have to be totally rebuilt. Port Said was destroyed to the south of Israel, in the Sinai, and to the north only parts of Beirut stood. Istanbul and Ankara lay flattened in the wake of the earthquake and millions appeared to be dead in southern Russia right on up to Moscow, and Leningrad. Reports had it that Ural Mountains moved two feet and the Caspian Sea was a dry bed where the water had been. Something had swallowed up the whole sea!

When the city of Moscow, with the entire Kremlin, had been reported destroyed by the earthquake and the firey balls coming from some comet that must have encircled the area, the Soviet forces in the European area surrendered, and many rushed for home to find destruction and death. The military mop-up in Europe had begun, and the NATO forces there had things under control. The war was over—everywhere! Happiness abounded.

Israel is a land of bulldozers and had been for 35 years. Those bulldozers dug and removed more debris in 30 days than one could hardly imagine. In one month's time, more graves were dug than had been dug in 35 years of Israel's history, and still they had not buried all the dead Russians or P.L.O. The leader of the Soviet forces had been flown back to Moscow at his request. No prisoners were kept. All able-bodied Russians were needed at home to rebuild their countries and cities. They were immediately released without fanfare and shipped out.

Nearly 25 nations were ruined one way or another. They had all participated in the war against Israel. [9] Now, they either had lost their armies completely or were laying in virtual ruins from the earthquake. Much of their industry was in total ruins. The Warsaw Pact Nations had immediately surrendered and recalled their armies. They were under the surveillance of the Big Ten armies now. Stanos Papilos lost no time in sending his fully mechanized armies into the Eastern European nations, to take over the remaining wealth and leadership of these nations.[10] They were the victims now of war, not the visitors. He had all of Europe under his control. He even sent troops and aid to Russia. In one quick week he rallied his forces and swept into the Soviet Union and took over the government from the Ural Mountains in Russia south and eastward to the Aegean Sea, Black Sea and parts of the Middle East from Syria down to Lebanon, into Jordan down to Saudi Arabia.[11] He had encircled Israel himself with his NATO forces and immediately took over the oil wells from Kuwait to the Red Sea. It was the boldest and most aggressive move he had ever made since signing the treaty to protect Israel about three years ago.[12]

The United States stood in awe at the swiftness by which Papilos took over Europe without consulting the American President once. It shocked the world. But almost every nation, except the United States, voiced agreement with his sweeping takeover. Now, once and for all, the Soviet threat was gone. Gone were the mighty powers of the Kremlin. They were under Europe's democratic control and communism as such would be banished in all of the Soviet Union.

Papilos immediately proceeded to empty the prison camps and jails of all religious and political prisoners. That made headlines around the world, second only to the continuing stories of the "divine earthquake" as Israel continued to call it, and the nations picked up on the unusual description.

The leaders of the P.L.O. were all dead. Surveys had it that not one member of the P.L.O. executive nor one member of the Soviet Politiburo survived the earthquake and avalanche of cyclonic fire.

Little explanation was forthcoming yet, from anyone, about the phenomena. It was repeated in American scientific circles that "a celestian intrusion, such as a comet or group of falling stars, had come so close to the earth's atmosphere, that they disintegrated and triggered the earthquake." To date, no one had a plausible answer to the greatest phenomena since the Biblical Flood itself. Rabbis in Israel and ministers the world over of various religions hastened to attribute the entire act to God only.[13] No one denied nor ridiculed the theory. Anything was possible.

Three months went by and the mop-up had gone predictively if you knew the Israeli ability to rebound and work feverishly for restoration. In addition NATO troops, medics, nurses, engineers and builders had been sent from all over Europe to rebuild the houses, bridges, hospitals, synagogues, churches, apartments, streets, airports, harbors and all that had been destroyed by the Soviets naval bombardment or the acts of nature.

Stanos Papilos had personally been to Israel every month to see how the redevelopment went. He was pleased to be of help to this struggling, tiny nation and pleased that their enemies had been subdued forever. He said, ''Never again would the Russians rise to power. As the United States had overshadowed Japanese redevelopment after war Number Two and saw to it that Japan did not build militarily again for 30 years, so he would assure Israel that he would control development for the Arabs and Russians.''

His control over the oil of the Arab world and Iran brought great consternation to the United States and England, but no nations suffered for lack of oil. He made sure through his tight control that everyone had what they needed and that all supplies and parts to the oil companies themselves were delivered on time. ''America has no need to worry, Stanos Papilos will deliver all they need and is their friend . . .'' he repeatedly assured them.

But it was nevertheless a strange trick of fate, that from a tiny politician in Athens, Greece, he had been asked, yes, even implored to take over the struggling Ten Nations of Europe[14] after Greece had been admitted to complete the Ten. Now, to add to the irony of it all, he had been catapulated to a world power greater than the world had ever seen in Europe and in the Middle East. ''Not even the Emperor of Rome 2000 years ago had such power and so much territory under his jurisdiction,'' the newspapers explained.

It was true. In addition to taking over the Soviet Union he required every Eastern European country to knuckle under his control. He had swiftly moved into North Africa from Morocco through Algeria to Libya and had moved NATO troops deep into the African continent and had caused Zaire, Chad, Sudan, Ethiopia, Somalia on the Horns of Africa with Kenya, Uganda, Tanzania, Angola and Zambia to succumb to his dynamic control.

Each of the 25 nations that were involved against Israel found themselves under the control of Europe's "Beast of Brussels," whether they liked it or not. Their armies were gone . . . His move was overnight and he penetrated each country after announcing to them that he was coming formally and through diplomatic channels. No one resisted militarily for what could they do with only local and national police to resist. He was moving now to remove all leaders who opposed him and to replace them with "friendly cooperative leaders." Everyone in the Pentagon and White House and both Houses of Congress were worried about the spirited rise to power of this man in Europe. Now, they were petrified that he had swept into Africa, the Middle East and had at last united all Europe under his ever increasing iron will and hand. He had not seemed like such a tight-fisted leader to begin with. On the contrary, he had been soft-spoken and easygoing with all nations.[15]

Now he was the leader of Africa, Europe and the Middle East. The future presented a frightening spectre to world analysts in the United States. But there was nothing they could do about it. No man had ever secured this much power before in world history.[16]

Digital Monetary Inputs had been devised by world banking leaders in the late 1970's and implemented in the 1980's through New York, Chicago and Los Angeles. All the computers involved in this new government ratified banking and payroll system were hooked up to the largest computers in Europe which tied in international banking which facilitated the vast exchanges of funds daily across the Atlantic Ocean. D.M.I.'s could also be called "ECU," the new European Communities Unit for money.

It simply meant that all trade between the Common Market Ten Nations and North America could be transacted through the DMI's. Digital Money Inputs were used regularly across the nations and for employer-employee relationships for payroll and taxes. Governments could extract what they demanded by legislation in taxes from each person's account by having regional central computers to which thousands of small and hundreds of large businesses would be hooked into. Taxes for State and Federal governments came out automatically from a man's payroll check. Instead of getting the usual check, he was given, through the sophisticated computerized system, Digital Monetary Inputs, directly into his numbered account. This was the procedure throughout Canada and the United States. There was very little grass roots opposition to it, inasmuch as it meant little paper work for a company and all records were on the central computer and could be easily checked. All accounting could be done in-house by computers owned or leased by the management. Small business not requiring computers, had the service of the local central house for their computerized banking and recording needs.

It had taken millions and millions of dollars and hours to set it up in the United States. But when it was finally adopted, it was brought out that the US Government had computers from coast to coast already set up for the IRS and other Federal Branches of Government services. Consequently the computers that were only used a small fraction of their work time were used now for all businesses and even inventory records could be stored on them as well.

The big problem in the beginning was that a company's competitor could or would have access to another company's records of inventories or prices or returns on a product at the touch of a button. This was quickly controlled by changing certain numbers for competitive concerns making it virtually impossible for them to pick up the information unless they had a secret code that acted like a numbering code to open a bank vault. The secret numbers acted as a combination lock. You had to know the company numbers to open their ''locked computer file.''

Now, in Europe as in North America virtually all payments were made by computer even for grocery purchases and petrol or for almost every product within civilized areas. It had not reached outlying rural areas completely in the USA or in Europe. Canada had some back parts of each province that still dealt in cash as well. But if you lived in or near the urban areas, all transactions were done by your number being punched into a store's keyboard with the amount required to pay for the purchase. If the person had the money or the credit to buy the article or articles, the computer would kick out the affirmative signal in seconds. If he did not have the funds in his "computer bank," then a red light flashed quickly and somewhat privately to the clerk on his side of the counter. He would have to indicate privately to the customer that there was a problem.

It was being suggested in the western world of nations prior to the "Divine Earthquake," that all nations' currencies be dissolved and that the world use a newly devised currency fitting into the Digital Computer Input System called "ECU." It meant making everyone his own banker through computerization. No one needed a bank personally any longer for the transfer of funds from one city or nation to another. No one would need paper or coin money at all except in some more remote areas of the world and for certain cash transactions that presented problems not yet solved by the implementing governments.

American dollars, Canadian dollars, Mexican pesos, English pound sterling, Dutch gilders, German marks, Russian rubles, Swiss pounds, Arab pounds, Israeli pounds, Italian lira and so on would all be converted to the one kind of money called "ECU"—the new Euro-currency. It would solve a million problems, they said.

In spite of many pleas to the contrary the nations all met with their respective financial leaders individually and then came to a mutual point of financial agreement in Switzerland. They agreed on the values of each nation's currency in light of the proposed value of "ECU." After that time-consuming project was ended and by final vote each currency was valued in light of the value of "ECU" which was related and backed by the combined value of gold and silver at the time they set out. All countries were to have each family and each individual turn in his money—cash on hand for an equal amount of "ECU" punched into his number on the computer.

It has been readily accepted by some and totally rejected by still millions of others in Europe and North America.

Thousands of questions were asked. "Who would guarantee the value of "ECU"? Who could guarantee that the computer would always kick out the true amounts for each individual? Who was responsible for maintaining the computer money? How honest is the whole system? Could you not steal from one and give to another if you had mass control of computerized money? Why should anyone have to give up his savings for this unproven method?

Digital Monetary Inputs were one thing with your own money in your own hand so to speak, but the "ECU" idea was falling on stony ground everywhere.

However, within three months after taking over the oil wells of the Middle East, a report came out from Brussels that all nations wishing to trade with the Common Market Ten Nations and wishing to keep their oil supply uninterrupted would have to change to the new "ECU" system immediately or have their oil supply cut off.

It was the biggest shock of all. It was bigger in America than Israel's catastrophy or the attack by Russia in Europe. This message affected everyone in the western world, and there seemed no way to get around it all.

There was a Mayor and Governors meeting in the city of Washington DC. They were all stiffly resisting Washington's demands for the complete changeover. They had refused to vote on it.

Finally, after hours of debate and rangle, the President of the United States came to the meeting and took the podium. After a few moments of greetings and a slight preamble, he cleared his throat and looked up from his prepared text and spoke to the delegates from every city and state in the nation.

"Gentlemen," . . . and then sensing ladies present, "and ladies, of course. I submit to you this question only. Realizing you despise what has been ordered tyranically from Europe—and let me assure you I feel the very same as you do—here is the question. Which among us is prepared to go to war with Europe's head of state now and demand the oil and trading privileges without converting to the new money system. Who can fight this man?" • The President stepped down and ended the shortest speech in his record.

The United States and Canada sadly succumbed after heated debate and accepted the order to convert the money to "ECU." It was speedily implemented everywhere it could be, with many citizens secretly holding onto gold and silver coins and all of their precious stones. A buying spree on gold coins and silver coins was going on underground with the price of gold skyrocketing fifty times its original value. Silver did equally as well. Many felt that to take the new money was only financial suicide. The most moot point of all, was: Who controlled the computers controlling society's banking, commerce and trade now? The only answer was Stanos Papilos, the "Beast from Brussels."

---

1. Daniel 11:40-42.
2. Ezekiel 38:9-11.
3. Ezekiel 38:11.
4. Daniel 7:8,, 20-21.
5. Ezekiel 38:21.
6. Ezekiel 38:22.
7. Ezekiel 38:19.
8. Ezekiel 38:18.
9. Genesis 12:1-3.
10. Daniel 11:39.
11. Daniel 11:40-43.
12. Daniel 9:26-27.
13. Ezekiel 38:23.
14. Revelation 17:12.
15. Daniel 11: 21, 23.
16. Revelation 13:4.
17. Revelation 13:3.

Chapter

5

Stanos Papilos

Stanos Papilos

Stanos Papilos shocked the world by announcing he was moving his headquarters from Brussels to Jerusalem so he could "monitor world affairs," more securely and wisely. [1] He assured the Israeli Prime Minister he would not get in his way at all.

Dr. Steve Scott also shocked his family one evening around the table by announcing they were moving to California within one month.

Steve's decision did not rock the world, only the world of his family and that of Dr. Raymond Morgan. They had grown fond of one another and both families were together often, with or without Tonya Rae who was busy dating a lot in England's fashionable jet set in those electrifying days.

Raymond Morgan had gone to church many times with Steve, especially Sunday evenings. Dr. Robinson's talks on world prophecy were the hottest subject this side of heaven itself to Raymond and thousands of others.

The minister had to extend his lectures into Sunday afternoon and Tuesday night sessions in order to accommodate the swelling crowds who wanted to know his version of the "Divine Earthquake," and the subsequent world events surrounding "ECU" and Stanos Papilos.

A minister had to be careful what he said these days for police were everywhere. And certainly, London knew of this fashionable church center and what its good rector taught. Some said it was traitorous while others said it was the complete truth and loved the good doctor for opening his mouth.

What had alarmed Steve to the point of deciding to move was Dr. Robinson's statement that Stanos Papilos was the Biblically predicted

Antichrist and that he would soon take the world into the Great Tribulation Period predicted in Matthew 24 and Luke 21!

At first, Steve thought the minister was slightly mad. But in private consultation, Dr. Robinson had taken him through Daniel 2 and 7 and convinced him by the time Revelation 13 and 17 had been explained one weary night, that the prediction was right. Papilos was the Antichrist. Dr. Robinson explained to Steve that the world had less than a year to find this out, and that soon, Papilos would move to Jerusalem.

Three weeks later, Papilos made his announcement. He said he was moving because he liked the climate in the Middle East better than cold Brussels winters.

That had shaken Steve to the core. Raymond had also become a confirmed believer in it all. His wife, Charlotte made a confession of her faith, but Tonya Rae would have nothing to do with her parents' new found belief in Jesus Christ and basic Christianity.

After much thought and planning, Steve announced at dinner one night that they were moving to the United States—California in particular.

Steve had discussed it with Pamella Jean repeatedly for three weeks. She had been adamantly opposed to it at first, but had finally changed her mind.

The children were elated at the news. Jeff fairly danced for joy until he realized that he would be saying good-bye to all his soccer fans and playmates. Seriousness set in as Marsha Ann asked when the move would be made and how they were going?

Her father replied that they would fly to Los Angeles and then drive to their destination in California. He had been there many times before coming to England years ago. It was just a small secluded place called South Lake Tahoe in northern California near the Nevada state line. They had gambling casinos and a large lovely clean lake with beautiful mountains nearby.

"How long will we be there, Dad?" Marsha Ann inquired somewhat excited about it all.

"I really don't know, Marsha darling."

"Why are we going at all, Dad?" Jeff asked thoughtfully.

"I fear for your lives if we stay here in England, son. Things are going to happen soon [2] and I want all of us as far away to safety as possible. I can't go into detail concerning all the reasons now, but I promise you I will later.

Though his curiosity about it all was far from satisfied, Jeff knew his father well enough not to push the question any further. He was a teen-ager now, and Marsha was following hard in his footsteps academically and wanted to be just like him in every way. She admired her older brother very much. He was captain of his soccer team, and they had beat most of the schools in London lately.

When the Morgans found out about the decision there was much family discussion as to why they shouldn't go to California, especially because of the large chiropractic practice that Steve had built over the years. It was a wealthy one at that. Steve had acquired a great deal of this world's goods including over one hundred thousand in gold coins. He had seen the currency situation looming several years ago and had been buying Austrian coronas and South African Krugerrands for over five years. He kept them hidden at home in a secret safe.

Being conscious of world events [3] and somewhat cautious in his appraisal of the events coming economically to London and the western world, he had planned for some time to immigrate to the United States with his family. As a doctor, he knew he could get in immediately without difficulty. The necessary groundwork had already been laid through friends in government circles to get him certified as an immi-grant to the United States.

The house had been put up for sale quickly and all the furnishings would go with it, or be sold at a separate auction prior to them leaving. If there were any problems, Raymond assured Steve he would handle the affairs for him in his absence.

Raymond wouldn't think of leaving but understood why Steve wanted to go for the children's sake. "If I had little ones, I'd go too, Steve." He said. "We'll keep in constant touch. If things get out of hand here, I will join you in Lake Tahoe," he added resolutely.

Steve sold his business practice to three chiropractors who formed a consortium. They hoped that Steve's recommendation to the Princess at Buckingham Palace would enable them an entre in that direction. Steve felt sure it would.

The house sold quickly with all the trimmings. Steve netted a cool quarter of a million from it all after taxes and put most of it in gold certificates on South African mines. He would trade in the certificates for gold coins and silver coins and bullion later in California. Too many questions would be asked if he brought too much gold or silver into the USA. As it were, he would be smuggling some of it in through each family member. He had to trust God and good fortune to get him into the United States without the currency being found. Not that gold or silver was illegal yet, but it would certainly be recorded on a computer that he had it. So far, no one knew except Pamella Jean, his wife, that he had any.

With the house and business sold, they said farewell to all their friends and to Raymond and Charlotte and Tonya Rae in one big final dinner at the house. Many photos were taken of this stately old mansion for remembrances in the future. Everything personal was packed and ready to go.

In Jerusalem, while the Scotts were preparing to leave London, the Rosenbergs were having dinner in their second floor apartment. Their son Ya'er was there. David and Dianna were there with their baby along with Moishe and Sarah with Ruth by her side.

It had been three months now since the earthquake and the clean up was still going on. Family life in Israel had settled down to a degree, but there was an air of expectancy everywhere. The word was out that Stanos Papilos was coming to live in Jerusalem next week. All Israel was astir over it.

"It is not proper nor is it protocol." Moishe was angry.

"World leaders stay in their own territories and lead their own governments. Whoever heard of such a thing happening?" With strong feelings he went on to deeply criticize the move as politically unwise for Papilos. He did not trust the man at all.

"There has to be another reason for him to leave Brussels and move so much important and expensive equipment to Jerusalem . . . All those computer hook ups and stuff." Moishe recounted.

You must remember one thing, father," Ya'er chimed in interrupting his father's train of thought. "He controls more than just Belgium and the Common Market Nations now . . . This man has political and agricultural interests all through Africa. In this part of Asia he has the oil concerns, which are more important than most of his assets in Europe."

"Yes, I believe his interest in the African natural resources and

Arabian oil are the main reasons he is coming here, father,'' David added thoughtfully.

"That may all be very true." Moishe responded seriously to the boys.

But it was plain other things were troubling him as he contemplated the spectre of a very powerful world leader of various nations being welcomed with the red carpet treatment in Israel. He knew there was great consternation in the Prime Minister's mind over the unusual twist of events as Stanos Papilos tried to take some of the credit for Russia's defeat as he alleged his troops pushed the Russians back to Warsaw and Moscow out of Europe. Israel knew what had really happened—the Russians had no heart to fight on after their leaders were lost in the earthquake. It was that simple. Only about one sixth [4] of them had returned from Israel to Russia. The rest were all dead. And most of the survivors were wounded and were being shipped out to the Soviet Union as quickly as they recovered sufficiently.

Construction was everywhere since the earthquake. On the Temple mount new and exciting work was under way as the Chief Rabbi of the Knesset finally got passage of a bill enabling the Orthodox to recreate the Temple of Solomon's day, inasmuch as the Dome of the Rock Mosque was gone forever. The Arabs had lamented the loss terribly, but in the midst of all their other losses, these plans were inconsequential to the lives of the people.

The New Temple, as it was called, would be done in less than six months. The politicians felt that psychologically it would be good for the nations to have their ancient Temple back even though they were not in full agreement with the Rabbis of the Knesset that blood sacrifices should start again. [5] The Rabbis won this battle too. They had been training priests to function in this ancient Levitical capacity from the Mosaic economy for over fifteen years. They knew exactly how to prepare the Sin offerings, Burnt offerings and Peace offerings as they did in the days of the first and second Temple. Why not now? It was in anticipation of the Messiah's coming that they were adamant sacrifices should be included again in the Temple worship.

Great preparations for a massive feast and period of Holy Days was already under way. Israel needed a celebration, they had said correctly. And a celebration with a series of Holy Days they would have. The Temple was set up for a grand opening on the next Passover. That was less than six busy months away and so much had to be accomplished.

Workmen labored around the clock. There was never an hour when someone was not working on all points of this third Temple. They were patterning it after the size of the Second Temple with as much marble, gold, silver and specialized craftsmanship as they could afford and secure in so short a time.

Speculation had it, that orthodox concerns in the United States, in collaboration with the Orthodox Jewish leaders in Israel, had been planning this for several years and had some of the more expensive materials ready with literally millions of dollars set aside through donations for this magnificent achievement to be realized, that had burned in their hearts for centuries. Everyone wanted the Temple. Some for political reasons, others for religious. But, the hue and cry in the land was that it would unite all Israel again as they were centuries ago!

Stanos Papilos had ordered every phase of his government to help in the clean-up and had lent his able assistance by sending builders, cement workers and craftsmen from all over Italy and Greece. They were very accustomed to the stone architecture and would aid greatly in rebuilding. The United States sent more food than was necessary. Country after country was aiding. Some did so, to cover up their past alliances and to heal the breech that had come between them and Israel.

The Israeli army was turned into construction engineers and all civilians worked in one phase of the rebuilding or another.

Ya'er and David, along with their father, worked at the reconstruction of the hospitals and were later called in to do some of the work on the Temple.

That work was so fascinating to Moishe and his boys. He had instructed them on how the Temple did look, according to the best records of the past, through Flavious Josephus, a great Jewish historian and writer.

While work went on at a feverish pace everywhere, Stanos' men found a suitable older hotel and proceeded to buy it and remodel it sufficiently for their leader's residence along with his entourage of employees and much equipment. The hotel had not been badly damaged in the earthquake and was at the extreme western end of the southern section of West Jerusalem, occupied by the Jews of course. Within a month it would be painted, decorated and furnished according to the plan and ready for occupancy. One central computer hook-up was also under construction, having been shipped in from Rome. Israel was apparently the busiest, biggest little nation on earth in anticipation of Stanos Papilos' arrival and the building of the New Temple.

The important official was counting the days until he could move to the "Center of the Earth," [6] as he had called it in one interview. It was certainly the center of his multitudinous activities and interests as one looked at the map and could readily agree.

Tonya Rae Morgan was an exciting woman. Though never married, it was not because she was unattractive to many men. Her hair was light blonde and her eyes hazel. She had a strikingly beautiful figure that caused men to look again and again at her at parties. Invitations to dance came instinctively. While other girls far younger maneuvered for invitations, Tonya could have been out every night of the week partying or theatre-going somewhere in exciting London.

She landed a delightful position as Executive Director of the Marine Insuring Department for a large insurance company with the greatest of reputations in the business. She had endeared herself to all the chief executives by dancing with them all at their London parties, and knew all their wives by name. She was careful to pay proper attention to each of the spouses, while dancing with each of their husbands, virtually with the permission of all. The executives knew her to be efficient, unassuming and unexcelled as a department head. She entertained their clients so proficiently that she was called on many times to escort the management to client dinners and evenings out on the town, in group fashion. She was not opposed to taking the arm of a rich potential, and wining and dining him throughout London, in order to help secure the account for her company. She was rewarded amply in the Digital Monetary Inputs the next day. It was always of interest to her to check the computer division, punching up her number to find the amounts accumulating in her "ECU" computerized account. She was becoming rich without spoiling her reputation.

Dr. Raymond Morgan, and her mother Charlotte, loved her dearly as their only child and were shocked when she once moved out to her own apartment in order to be "free." They were both delighted beyond words when, just before Christmas, Tonya Rae turned up one evening and said, "Merry Christmas everybody." She was wrapped in bright red and green velvet ribbon with a card attached neatly to her side. It read "To the Greatest of Mothers and Dads."

When they gleefully unwrapped the velvet and opened the card it read, "To the dearest and the most patient parents ever. You now have me back . . . till I marry someday!" Tonya Rae promptly and happily moved back home into her lovely suite of rooms and was her happy self again. She couldn't have made her parents happier.

Once, the French came out in her mother as she and Tonya Rae were alone in the kitchen fussing over some chocolate fudge. While Tonya was acting up, talking about a dance she had been to the night before with some very French clients, mother asked in a very casual, secretive manner . . . "Tell me about the great love of your life darling . . . I'm dying to know." She dropped her eyes and continued to stir the chocolate.

Nothing bothered Tonya much so she took her Mother at her word and replied . . . "Mother, he was the dreamiest man I've ever known and he was German, would you believe." She answered honestly.

"Did you love him deeply?"

"Yes, I thought I did at first, and then it wore off, and I was disillusioned and disappointed, so I left him and came home to you."

"Did he love you?"

"He said he did, and I believe he still does. He never ceases to call me and is now asking me to marry him." . . . And while gazing straight at her mother's quivering eyes at that last remark, simply and reassuringly said, "But I will not be his wife." Charlotte had known in her heart that Tonya was having an affair, but felt it not her place to enter into the situation at all, 'till now. After all, she sighed, Tonya is nearly 26. Goodness!

Then a strange event, calculated to change the lives of the Morgans completely, happened to Tonya while on one of her business appointments one evening in a very high class restaurant in London with management and two clients present. She had not been told who the clients were, only that it was top brass, and they had the potential of being the largest account ever if this deal went through. She was to come and add her usual exciting sparkle to what might turn out to be the toughest sell yet. She met her boss at the door and the whole restaurant seemed to hum with excitement when she alighted out of her London cab.

"Whew, you have managed to do it again. You look ravishing tonight," her employer said with a smile.

"Thank you, Mr. Ratcliffe, you do know how to make a lady feel fantastic" . . . She realized something different was up, for he was in a dither while taking her white full-length mink fur from her shoulders and muttered in her ear while standing very close . . . so close she could easily smell his cologne . . .

"Tonight we have the top client to sell . . . Are you ready for this?"

She looked surprised and smiled saying, "Have I ever let you down before?" Recognizing he was nervous she said, "Who in heaven's name has you so up tight?"

"Stanos Papilos, that's who."

"Stanos Papilos . . . My God in heaven . . . What . . . Who . . . brought him to us?" She exclaimed in disbelief.

"He called today, out of the blue, . . . sometime this morning and said he wanted the best company for insurance. We would be his guest at a dinner party tonight for introductions of his closest associate also interested in a large personal policy." Mr. Ratcliffe pointed the way for them and merely said . . . "Go to it, darling. We need all your charm this night."

Stanos Papilos saw Mr. Ratcliffe coming his way. He calmly rose, stared at Tonya Rae and held out a chair for her to be seated, while nodding in answer to introductions of all concerned. James Hunter was the handsome gentleman with Mr. Papilos.

She always ordered rather simply. An end cut of prime rib with baked potato and creamed corn. Salad with oil and vinegar, and she usually declined bread of any kind. Her exquisite figure meant more to her than bread. English Trifle was always better than fattening bread at the end, anyhow. She enjoyed a dry wine, and if possible, a French dry wine which pleased Stanos, and he ordered a chilled dry wine that he knew she would appreciate.

With an appreciative glance at her now and then, the conversation turned to business. The rest of the patrons were very aware of the elegently dressed world politician in their London restaurant.

It appeared that in his position, he had acquired several yachts from Arab and European leaders. They had heard of his love for boating and the sea life. At least four Arab oil tycoons had honored him with ships running from 75 feet to 250 feet, each one trying to outdo the other, jealously bidding for the favors of the new leader of many of their affairs. As a consequence, he and his business associate wanted insurance and rather than leave this personal matter to staff members to decide, they thought they would take the matter in their own hands.

"That is now a decision that indicates I have great wisdom, Mr. Ratcliffe," Stanos announced as he smiled at Tonya Rae, indicating her presence was the reason for the remark.

She blushed and indicated her pleasure at being with him tonight, for it was not often she dined with such a man of world renown . . . she had said admiringly.

The amounts of coverage and the costs for the same, on an annual basis, were openly discussed over English Trifle and cognac as the men lit their pipes and sat back. The music started up louder and the evening of dancing was underway in a beautiful setting dimly lit with multi-colored fixtures of crystal flashing through the room as the full orchestra played.

Before reaching any definite conclusion, Stanos put his drink down, looked over at Tonya and said softly with apparent admiration in his eyes . . . "Would the young lady with the exciting Russian name dance with the Greek tonight?"

Tonya smiled her approval. He moved his chair with a graceful sweep and stepped behind her as she rose, moving her red velvet, high backed chair, as they both headed for the dance floor.

The restaurateur gazed at them exceedingly pleased that every patron saw him there. They knew that by morning the papers would be full of it and the advertising would be worth a million dollars. Even the BBC would pick this one up. Already photographers were impatiently waiting outside. The BBC had a small television camera on hand as well and were setting up lights for some footage for the late news or early morning London broadcast of the BBC to the world. Never were two restaurant owners happier than that night.

Tonya had been on business dinner dates before, but nothing ever like this. This man instantly put her at ease on the dance floor. It was majestic, the way he handled her and himself, gliding across the floor as though he were made for dancing.

His cool, smooth manner and warm charm cast something of a spell over her momentarily, as he drew her close to him for a very romantic old song. She lost her breath as he pirouetted her over the floor so gracefully. She felt light as a feather. With his hands on her waist, they danced like both of them had been melted together by the music of the gods. Never before had she felt like this dancing with any man. She had been with the best of dancers before, but this . . . it was indescribably wonderful!

When his piercing black eyes peered into hers, she felt her heart would burst. He would not take his eyes from her lovely face. She found it superlatively exhilerating as they danced on affectionately. Then he pulled her to him in a warming embrace that sent a chill through her body like no man had ever done.

Was it because of who he was or what he is? She didn't know the answer then, and for the moment it was totally unimportant. She was electrified by his manner, his being and his eyes . . . Yes his eyes were so strange . . . deep . . . but oh so cold, and then so very strangely warm . . . The contrast bothered her. He seemed both divine and devilish!

The music ended on that song for a short break. They returned to their seats casually, laughing at themselves being the last ones on the floor, not noticing that nearly everyone had left the floor when they first danced over 20 minutes ago!

Business talk resumed. The deal was firmed up, to be finally transacted at his hotel in the morning after breakfast.

They quickly turned from business to talk more personal of where had Tonya Rae been all his life, while looking for a good dancing partner.

She was ecstatic that he thought of her as she had of him . . . the best partner she had ever danced with. She subsequently proceeded to tell him a little about the family . . . Vienna, . . . Her father's psychiatric career and current prestigious practice. He was impressed and asked her about Vienna.

Abruptly, the musical instruments sounded and struck up familiar notes. Tonya was invited to dance again, no one else at the table dared to ask her.

"This cannot be our last evening for dancing, my cherie," he whispered in her ear as they danced the lovely tune, softly gliding over the parquet floor, just perfect for ballroom dancing.

She smiled her assent to his remark, humming the tune with the band as they played on, and the two of them romancingly lit up the floor.

"When will it be possible for us to continue our dancing again?" His dark eyes penetrated to her very soul, she thought.

She fell silent for a moment and said nothing, but then looked up and said, "I doubt ever . . . You are moving to Jerusalem, I hear?"

"That won't be tomorrow, however, and tomorrow night I shall be the loneliest man in the world unless you join me for dinner, dancing and English Trifle" . . . reminding her of her fancy for the continent's number one dessert.

Trifling with him openly, Tonya whispered . . . "I really can't think of anything else to do tomorrow night . . . I'm available."

A broad smile revealed glistening white teeth. He was so handsome, she thought to herself . . . "Why does he have to have such a terrible reputation . . . maybe it just isn't true!" But even then, a twinge of doubt hit her conscience.

Lights flashed and cameras clicked as they walked outside, arm in arm, laughing together. The BBC reporter had waited five hours for a short interview. . . . He walked forward only to be stopped by three men who had also been outside waiting until their boss came out from the evening's dining. They were obviously Papilos' personal bodyguards and looked the part. They were impeccably dressed, but looked very tall and muscular.

He motioned for them to let the reporter through to him, while holding Tonya's arm tightly. Flushed with his victory, the BBC reporter came in for a close shot with his small TV camera and thanked Mr. Papilos for the pictures on behalf of the BBC.

"Is it true, sir, you are going to move from Brussels to Jerusalem soon?" He presumed Papilos would allow him at least one question . . . He had asked a loaded one, and one which the whole world would be extremely interested in.

"Yes, as far as I now know, I will be in Jerusalem before winter sets into Brussels. I get so cold there and it's damp. But, also I like the Middle East. It is close to my oil interests, and if you look at a map, Jerusalem is the center of the earth and Israel is the bridge to three continents; Africa where I have interests; Europe where I have my Presidency; and now the Asian continent where I also have great opportunities.

That was the end of the interview, but it was a startling one and one that Tonya felt he would not have given had she not been on his arm and had he not been in such good humor.

They said good night and she stepped into her employer's limousine which whisked her away, leaving Stanos standing wistfully looking at the black sedan as it sped off into the London night.

"Wow!" she fairly screamed her delight in the car as it turned the nearest corner and headed her home. "What a night, boss."

"You really turned on the charm tonight my dearest. Never have I seen you so radiant."

"Who wouldn't be radiant in his arms on the dance floor for nearly an hour. I may not make it for nine in the morning."

"Take the day off. You earned it and besides you will be better prepared for tomorrow night's rendezvous . . . will you not?"

She thanked Edward Ratcliffe profusely. He knew she was thrilled as they parted, each very happily.

When Dr. Raymond Morgan read the early morning London Times and saw his glowing daughter on the front page holding the arm of the man who was called the "Beast of Brussels" he was absolutely speechless. He excitedly motioned for Charlotte to come over quickly, showing her the pictures while reading the write-up with such astonishment that he lost his breath reading out loud.

The papers had all the names and places correct. They even played up the one hour part on the dance floor and named the tunes Papilos had danced to. A full outline of what the guests had and who they were followed on an inside page of this front page scoop for the London Times.

Charlotte took a look at the article almost forcing disbelief at what she was reading about her adoring daughter hanging onto Stanos Papilos' arm!

There was a mixture of amazement and then pride in Charlotte as she looked at her darling on the front page again and again. She felt a surge of elation and yet found the whole thing quite traumatic when she thought of who Tonya was holding onto. Her daughter had dinner with the President! It was overwhelming. She sat down feeling her heart pound.

"Just act normal when you see Tonya. She's obviously sleeping in," Raymond cooly cautioned.

"What's normal when your daughter is out with the man purported to be the coming antichrist, for heaven's sake?" She was aghast at the thought.

"We're not sure who he is going to be and besides we know it was business. It's over and don't worry about it, or worry her either."

Charlotte thought a lot about it that morning and decided she may need a psychiatrist herself if she didn't put it all out of her mind and get on with the day's chores.

When Tonya came down at noon, her mother had gone shopping for a new dress, the maid said, while serving Tonya brunch in the garden, as the fall weather had not yet penetrated London as severely as it would when the rains came. The sun was shining on the chrysanthemums and Tonya couldn't remember when the flowers looked so lovely as they did then. Bees buzzed in the foliage as the day was relatively tepid and the sun felt so warm and pleasant on her bare shoulders. Lunch was served and the maid smiled excitedly as she brought her the paper to read. She placed it square on her awaiting plate, just before serving her piping hot eggs and country ham that smelled so good.

With a radiant glow Tonya read of the activities so fresh in her mind, of last night. She knew she wanted to see that man again and it wasn't just for the dancing. It was so intoxicating to see herself on the front page of the London Times, with the President of the United States of Europe, as they called him in the report. Europe's most powerful leader, the report had stated. The Times went on to list the countries President Papilos influenced or directly controlled around the world.

"Whew," exclaimed Tonya as she showed her maid the list of countries under his jurisdiction. "I have never known such a powerful man, Mary Ane, and was he a doll to be out with! She smiled broadly, stretching her awakening limbs, feeling such lovely emotions about last evening.

Mary Ane brought the phone to Tonya. She had not heard it ring inside the spacious house, but saw by Mary Ane's flurry and fluster with a sparkle in her eyes that someone important was on the line.

"Ah think it's him, ma'am!"

With an immediate sense of titillation she took the phone and discovered to her great delight it was Stanos, calling to rearrange the time for the evening date on the town and to explain to her the unusual train of events leading to the change.

"Buckingham Palace?" she wildly screamed with a sudden sense of delicious delerium.

"No, I have never been there, ever. . . ."

Feeling as though she might faint with excitement, she told Mary Ane to bring her more coffee quickly . . . immediately after terminating the call with the timing set for 7:45 to be picked up by Stanos. They would proceed immediately to a party being thrown in his honor by the Queen of England, in Buckingham Palace.

"What a night this will be! Help me get ready, Mary Ane—Dear Lord, What will I wear?"

The Scott family of four had arrived safely in Los Angeles and met with old friends while staying in a downtown hotel on Figueroa Street. All arrangements had been made by their travel agent in London to secure them space in Los Angeles for at least two weeks in order to show the children the sights of Disneyland and Knott's Berry Farm, Universal City and so much more in exciting California. When that was done, they were to rent a car and drive to the area of their destination, South Lake Tahoe, high in the Sierra mountains, which were most beautiful, Steve promised the family. All personal gear would follow along with Emily, who was still with them, faithful till the end.

Jeff and Marsha loved every moment of it. If this was like what America would be . . . "Why hadn't we moved here earlier Dad?" Marsha beamed.

Steve suddenly broke the silence at the breakfast table on the top floor overlooking the city while the children slept late that morning. He was omnivorously devouring the Los Angeles Times and couldn't believe the news.

"Well, I've been shocked before in my life. But I am flabbergasted, honey . . . absolutely flabbergasted!" He looked aghast, as he turned the paper for Pam to catch a quick glimpse while he read the account of Papilos and Tonya Rae, the food, the dancing and the dinner dance appointment with the Queen to come that night.

"Tonya Rae." Pam gasped, somewhat in pleasure and somewhat in just plain shock.

Pam immediately sprang up, came around behind Steve while they both poured over the account, stunned as they read on, especially of the Times picking up the fact that tonight they were all to dine with the Queen at a dance thrown in Stanos' honor.

"My niece will be dining with the Queen of England tonight." Pam sighed. The thought of it put her in a dizzying whirl of imagination as to how they dress and how they would love Buckingham Palace, as she had on one formal night several years ago.

Steve finally read the whole article and put the paper down, requesting more coffee from the waiter. He just stared at Pam in deep meditation, looking far beyond her in his mind.

"I just find it all so uncanny and impossible to accept that Tonya Rae met Stanos Papilos, sold him insurance worth millions on his yachts, danced with him, and is going out with him again tonight . . . and we are sitting here six thousand miles away reading about it! Our niece!"

"It's a small world with today's communications . . . You have often said it yourself." Pam answered reaching for the cream.

"Imagine how Raymond must feel! His daughter is going out with the antichrist!" His voice lifted slightly as he clenched his fist in a short burst of anger, unaware of staring eyes about him.

"For Heaven's sake, keep your voice down Steven. You'll have the whole restaurant looking at us . . . most of them are now!" Pam retorted, embarrassed.

After a moment of cooling down for Steve and severe embarrassment for Pam, she went on to say, "Raymond will be upset but I can guess that Charlotte thinks it is the living end . . . Her lovely daughter out with one of the world's greatest politicians and leaders."

Steve looked angrily at his wife and replied with quivering force as he leaned across the table, lowering his voice as cold as steel.

"She is out with the wickedest man imagineable, Pam . . . not the world's greatest leader!" He was visibly angered at her paying Stanos any kind of compliment.

"There is no point in us getting angry at one another, dearest," she said with sarcasm in her voice, as she uttered dearest.

"You're right, and I'm sorry, but, but . . ."

"I understand your negative emotions over it . . . I feel heavy inside myself . . . I wish I had never read it."

Steve went back to the article, drank more coffee and finally after putting the paper down, discovered Pam had excused herself. Her purse was gone so that probably meant she had gone looking at the many shops downstairs under the main dining room she had spotted yesterday. She had planned to stroll there this morning, he remembered.

He proceeded to the hotel pool, to contemplate the bombshell news that had jolted him into a state of mental despair and rage.

If Steve had been jolted into rage by the morning news, then the evening news would have been much better not read or heard at all, according to Pamella Jean Scott.

She had been shopping most of the afternoon and happened to hear over the radio an announcement encased in the news that the United States was resisting all efforts by leaders in the Common Market to speed up the transaction of converting all monies in the United States to the Digital Monetary System, now being called "ECU." As a result of this patriotic resistance movement, sponsored by conservative elements who were growing in strength everyday in North America, the switch was not coming off as planned. They did not want to lose their own currency under any circumstances and were resisting this movement.

"So now it is ECU for the States." Pam thought to herself. These Americans are not going to lose the good old American greenback or gold . . . I can feel it in my veins," . . . she thought as she bought a paper.

When Steve got to reading it that evening before going to dinner with the family, his face dropped and he became very sullen.

"They have threatened in Brussels to cut off all oil within two weeks if a decision is not implemented here in the States."

"What will that mean, Dad?" Jeff asked.

"It really boils down to an energy crunch in this country, son. That means gas rationing, less driving and less industry and less of everything we use . . . cause it's all related to oil as a base for most products in the homes and factories." Steve attempted to make it plain to Jeff's teenage mind. He was not nearly as mature as Steve would like him to be.

"If only these Americans had developed nuclear energy when they saw this coming ten years ago, they would not be in this pickle today." Steve reminisced about the London newspaper revealing how Americans were going to save the environment and not develop nuclear power. It had been a ridiculous item to Britishers, and was the talk of Steve's church circle of friends at the time. Dr. Robinson had commented on it from the pulpit, stating that the day would come when American dependence on foreign energy would cripple the country politically and might put it under a dictatorship.

Just then his eyes alighted on a third page column write-up that suddenly caught his attention. As he read it, the hair on the back of his neck seemed to rise up as his excitement arose.

"Pam . . . honey . . . come here . . . You won't believe what's in this paper fulfilling prohecy just like we said."

"What is it darling?" . . . she called from the bathroom, while hastening to come out, wondering what disaster he was going to read next.

He read excitedly, "Reports from all over Israel have it that as a result of the phenomenal salvation of the State of Israel in the last war, a great surge of religious interest has come to the somewhat secularistic minded youth of the tiny State. The rebuilding of the Temple came as a result of this interest within the ranks of the orthodox and conservative Jews of the land. But now, a new rift in the religious revival had appeared and is stirring all of Israel. Many are being stirred to anger over it, especially in conservative circles, but nothing they can say will dampen the enthusiasm of the new religionists. It is a revival of the Christian cult among Jews. They simply call themselves Completed Jews and testify to believing in Jesus Christ as the coming Messiah, and their Savior." . . . "Can you believe this Pam?"

"All over Israel" . . . Steve hurriedly read on, "Jesus groups are springing up among the youth . . . This is fantastic, honey . . . The Bible says that as a result of the great war with Russia-Magog, many Jews would believe and turn to God. [7] This has to be the fulfillment of those predictions." Steve smiled ever so largely.

"Judaism's most powerful leaders are stirred up about it" . . . [8] Steve laughed and read on. "But there seems little that can be done except persecute them with certain sanctions if it persists. [9] 'The increasing amount of youth turning from old Judaism to become Jesus fanatics is most alarming,' the Chief Rabbi has said to the Prime Minister. They are making new converts every day, teaching that the New Testament fulfills the Old Testament and doing it with the State of Israel textbooks in Hebrew!''

"That is fantastic . . . fantastic. . . . . It's happening now in Israel.'' Steve was elated. It brought Jeff and Marsha Ann into the room.

"What's made him so happy, Mom?'' Jeff asked his mother.

Steve tossed the paper to Jeff, and told him to read it to his sister while his father put the finishing touches on his wardrobe for the evening. He would explain at dinner later. . . .

Later, at a lovely French restaurant in Beverly Hills, while looking over the establishment for some Hollywood stars, Steve related to Jeff and Marsha Ann how there were to be 144,000 people in Israel[10] turned to Christianity at just about this point in time. He explained that Israel and many Christians in it, but they had not been accepted by the government for the most part and were considered renegade Jews that should be punished and brainwashed back to the faith.

It was another fulfillment of the fantastic prophecies of the Bible, meaning they were close to the end of the age when the Messiah would return to bring peace to the earth.[11]

It turned out to be a fascinating study of Hollywood personalities at the restaurant and an intricate analysis of prophecy at the same time. Marsha Ann really got involved in it and was shocked to learn that Jesus could return within five years.[12]

"But Dad, I thought the Bible said no man knows the day nor the hour when the Lord will come?'' She asked inquisitively.

"No man knows the day nor the hour when the Lord will return, but we are not ignorant of the times and seasons of His coming, Marsha. Jesus comes to have the battle of Armageddon[13] after certain prophecies are fulfilled in the Middle East, and they are rapidly being fulfilled.'' Steve answered excitedly.

"It's really quite exciting for us as believers, because we know that God will take care of us through all that is coming,''[14] Pam injected encouragingly.

In spite of his two teenage children's strong protests, Steve said, "No more prophecy tonight . . . When we get to Lake Tahoe I'll fill you in on the whole mystery of why we are here and what is going to happen.''

That night, long after the children had watched some television, Steve and Pam lay in one another's arms contemplating the trip to the Tahoe area that weekend, but more importantly, at that moment, they thought and talked about the marvelous fulfillments of prophecy that were taking place since the war with Russia ended . . . They rehearsed all that Dr. Robinson had taught them, like the end of various money systems . . . Getting the world ready for the universal credit card on the back of the hand as predicted . . . The war with Magog-Russia and the King of the South-Africa rising up. . . . The neutralization of the Arab nations and the takeover by Stanos Papilos of the Ten Nations, and now his move to take over the oil of the Middle East and his desire to live in Jerusalem.[15]

Steve had pointed out to Pam all the places where the prophecies were listed and found in the Bible, they jointly used for prophecy study.

"With the formulation of the 144,000 Jews for Christ, we are now ready for the biggest prophecies of all to take place, darling."

"Bigger than the ones we have already seen with Russia and Africa and Israel?" She yawned sleepily.

"Bigger than all of them put together. . . . Wait till you see the Antichrist in power in Israel and what he is going to do there."[16] Steve turned off the light, rolled over and dreamed all night about money and gold.

---

1. Daniel 11:45.
2. Luke 21:9-36.
3. Luke 21:36.
4. Ezekiel 39:2.
5. Daniel 9:27, 12:11.
6. Ezekiel 5:5.
7. Ezekiel 38:23.
8. Daniel 11:35.
9. Matthew 24:9-10.
10. Revelation 7:4-8.
11. Matthew 25:31-46.
12. Matthew 24:36.
13. Revelation 19:11-21.
14. Revelation 3:10-11.
15. Daniel 11:45, Revelation 13:1-18.
16. 2 Thessalonians 2:1-10.

Chapter
6

The Man
Of Power

The Man Of Power

Stanos Papilos was right on time to pick up Tonya Rae. Five jet black limousines stopped simultaneously outside the Morgan residence and an aide went to the door to inquire for Miss Morgan.

The maid answered and said she would be right down. Five minutes passed and Tonya appeared. She took the gentleman's arm offered her and was escorted to the second car in the procession, a sleek, shiny, black Rolls Royce limousine. It was the largest Rolls she had ever seen!

Stanos removed himself from the chauffeur driven car and awaited her with his door opened by another aide, holding the car door for them both to enter.

He greeted her warmly and quickly took her hand as she entered the most luxurious car her eyes had ever seen.

It was all upholstered in tufted white and pale blue velvet, with jet black, tight curtains on the windows, keeping peering eyes out and the lights of the city from piercing in. Facing her was a beautiful car bar, filled with all kinds of wines and liquors and fresh ice, recently taken from a small built-in refrigerator. Two small glasses were ready for whatever their owner wished to pour into them.

Immediately, Stanos reached over while still holding Tonya's hand tightly, and kissed her on the cheek. He told her how stunning she looked for the occasion and proceeded to pour two drinks.

Tonya did look stunning. She had carefully chosen a dress she had worn only once before in Vienna to a ball, thrown by one of the Counts. This occasion called for just such a dress with a man like Stanos Papilos.

It was an expensive long, black, silk dress that clung to Tonya's figure as though she had been poured into it, and yet with exquisite taste. The long sleeves were beautifully matched by Tonya's black leather, hand-sewn gloves from Rome.

Her carefully chosen plain black suede shoes matched her elegant dress and made her look like the most stunning woman Stanos had ever been out with. At least this is what he said, after viewing her full attire within the dim lights of the limousine, while they both casually sipped their champagne.

Stanos prepared her for the Queen's dinner and dance evening. He assured her that after the formal introductions were over, she could relax and act normal with royalty and high officials. He assured Tonya they were as human as she, and would love dancing with her. But she had to promise that only one or two dances would be given away to the queen's consort, or guests. After all, how could she refuse the Queen's husband, the Prince of Wales? She joked with Stanos that he would have to stand in line with the other princes.

The entourage surrounding Stanos that evening was a retinue of body-guards, secret service police and one or two political favorites that he wished to expose to the press. The press were always lurking somewhere in the shadows, looking for news concerning this powerful world leader.

When the cars pulled through the tall iron gates leading to the Buckingham Palace, colorful guards stood everywhere. They were gayly decked out with the large bear-skin hats, and red uniforms trimmed with gold tassles and white fringe. Their swords hung at their sides, adding to the grandeur of their impeccable dress, as they opened the limousine doors and beckoned for Stanos and Tonya to enter the large ornate Palace doors. They mentioned quietly, ''Good evening, Sir and Madame; Her Majesty awaits you inside.''

When Tonya entered the immense entrance to Buckingham Palace, she drew in her breath so sharply that Stanos placed his other hand on her arm calming her momentarily while she gazed at the majestic decor and beheld the sheer elegance of the Palace housing Britain's Kings and Queens of the past, and now Queen Elizabeth with the Prince of Wales and their family.

Aides immediately took their coats, which both had brought as it was a cool evening in London and rain was predicted. One handsome butler took Tonya's white mink coat from her shoulders where Stanos had placed it.

As the butler took her coat, Stanos stared again at his delightful companion of the evening and thought how ravishing she looked and how appropriate the single strand of beautiful pearls looked on her open necked dress. You could read admiration in his adoring eyes as his eyes met hers. He smiled broadly, taking her arm as they were ushered into the room where royalty awaited. The room was already buzzing with the excitement of chatter as soft music was playing in the background by a full orchestra.

They were immediately led to the central area occupied by the Queen and her handsome husband and entourage. As Stanos led Tonya, two of his men followed hard at their heels, while the others remained outside, chatting with the Queen's own regiment guards of the evening.

The Queen rose from a large royal blue velvet chair, with gold tassles hanging from its very large arms, and smilingly extended her hand to Stanos for him to kiss.

Stanos Papilos bowed, slightly tipping his head, while taking the Queen's hand in his. He kissed it gently and said, "Your Majesty, it is so lovely to see you again, and I am so indebted to you for this thoughtful gesture of friendship and kindness," . . . he paused . . . And I do apologize for not calling you, but I did not, knowing how busy you are these days. I did not want to bother you."

Stanos had held the Queen's hand the entire time he spoke. Now he dropped her hand gently, as she replied with equal warmth and with great gentility, "You are always welcome in my home and should always let us know when you come to London for a visit. It is never a bother to see you and to discuss what we have in common . . . She paused and smiled, pretending to be indignant with him, as her head went high. She slowly peered through her hand held glasses while placing them in front of her momentarily serious eyes . . . She continued, "I did not know whether you would get a royal pardon for not calling me this time until now, but fortunately for you," she smiled and turned, "your taste has bought you my pardon." She looked at Tonya as she continued, "but only if you hurry and introduce to me the lovely creature in black you have brought with you tonight. She is your redeeming quality this evening." The Queen was so gracious, while beaming with apparent pleasure at Tonya, who flushed as never before in her life.

"May I present to your Majesty, Miss Tonya Rae Morgan, of London," Then looking at Tonya, "Tonya Rae," Stanos said rather formally, "Her Majesty, Queen Elizabeth the Second, and Prince Phillip of the British Empire."

Tonya stepped forward with her heart pumping so hard she knew they could hear it. She curtsied to both the Queen and Prince Phillip, looking beautiful as she did, but feeling faint.

She lifted her eyes to look at the Queen while glancing to the Prince, and managed to utter with choked sounds, "It is such a pleasure, Your Majesties, and I thank you so much for my invitation, to come this evening."

Tonya felt faint as she gratefully took Stanos' arm and was led away to be seated. While he busied himself meeting other personalities and personages of the occasion. He had left her with the two gentlemen who had come in with them, whom she had just now met. They were "two of his closest associates in political affairs, Mr. James Hunter of Paris, whom she had already met, and Mr. Aubrey Miers of the United States, former Secretary of State for the American government several years ago.

Both men told her immediately to call them by their first names.

James sat on one side of Tonya and Aubrey on the other. They made her comfortable while explaining to her they too were both wet with perspiration, as if they'd been in the rain, over the formal introductions themselves.

"As the Secretary of State for the good ole U.S.A." Aubrey said, "I never got over my nervousness meeting royalty. I guess because I came up from such a poor European family background financially before going to the United States for my education as a teenager."

James merely reiterated the same thing. He could meet Prime Ministers and Presidents easier, he said, because most of them came from the grass roots of society into their elected office. But royalty threw him a curve, realizing they were really the only bluebloods left in this world.

"This lady is real royalty." Aubrey hastened to add and then launched into an extensive conversation with Tonya over what her role in life was, about her parents and what her father did.

The conversation went most pleasantly, while the Queen was meeting other guests of honor and introducing some of them to Stanos. Tonya was glad not to be near, so as not to have to go through that nerve wracking episode again. She decided fraternizing with royalty was not her cup of tea.

She enjoyed conversing with James, and with Aubrey about his family, who were in Brussels and were all looking forward to moving to Jerusalem. James appealed to her greatly that night. She found herself occasionally looking over in his direction admiringly, smiling softly.

Suddenly, her Uncle Steve Scott, popped into her mind, and something he had said about Stanos was coming back to her . . . something about Stanos fulfilling a prophecy somewhere in the Bible, about being a powerful world leader, and that he would move to Israel some day if he were "the" man. "What a strange thing to think of," she said to herself, while gazing beyond Aubrey as he spoke on of his wife and children and their happy anticipation over the move to Israel within a month.

The contrast of Tonya's striking blond hair and deep blue eyes with that of her black silk dress was so impressive, as Stanos caught her eye across the room, that he could wait no longer to come to her side once again. He quickly whisked her away from his associates and introduced her as his guest for the evening everywhere, and then shocked her thoroughly by simply mentioning to the Ambassador of Belgium that shortly Tonya would be his executive in charge of computerization in Brussels.

Before she could utter a word, he led her to the table to sit by his side, as the Queen had summoned all to join her at the loveliest table Tonya Rae had ever feasted her eyes upon.

As Stanos gently held her chair out for her, her eyes alighted on the luscious roasted lamb in the middle of the most lavish table accoutrements she had ever seen. The cutlery was all gold, with enormous decorative plates of gold, under the finest of English bone china, awaiting her first course. The table was set so beautifully on a Belgium lace, full-length tablecloth that it defied description.

Each serviette was wrapped individually in gold foil, and placed so neatly next to the gold under-plate, by each service. Gold trimmed crystal water glasses, shimmered in the reflection of the candles that lit the table from one end to the other. The table had to be thirty feet long in Tonya's estimation. She quickly counted the guests, including the Queen and Prince Phillip at one end, with Stanos next to the Prince and then Tonya by his side. There were fifteen guests per side making thirty in all, in addition to the Queen and her consort.

Sitting next to Tonya were James and Aubrey, happily for her. Opposite her was the Ambassador from Belgium and his wife, and several other Ambassadors and their wives from various European countries plus the United States and Canada. She knew France was represented and thought of her mother, and how she being from Paris would love this night. She purposed in her mind to remember as much as she could to relate to her on the morrow.

With the elegant dinner nearly over, Prince Phillip rose to his feet, champagne glass sparkling in the candlelight, and said, ''This evening was hastily called in honor of President Stanos Papilos and his marvelous achievements of cementing our Ten Nations together. I ask you all to join me in a toast to the happiness of our President in his new home in Jerusalem as he oversees all his worldwide concerns from the Holy City . . . He lifted his glass as all joined in the toast to Papilos. Tonya beamed at him as she participated in sipping the loveliest champagne she had ever tasted.

''To the President in Jerusalem. . . .'' The room rocked with joyous congratulations from one end of the table to the other and, just as the chatter lessened, music was heard as violins began to play his favorite Greek tune.

The Queen arose with the Prince and walked over to Stanos as he was helping Tonya from her high back velvet chair. The Queen extended her hand and said, ''The Prince will not mind at all dancing with Tonya . . . as she smiled at her, while I have the first Greek dance of the evening with the Greek God of the night.''

The Prince took Tonya's hand, while the Queen was escorted to the floor by Stanos and they danced at first, lightly and serenely, and then as the music quickened right where Stanos knew it would, he took the Queen in a gentle twirl of her graceful body as they picked up the pace of the Greek dance. The Prince and Tonya looked on momentarily, both deciding whether they would try it or not.

Before they both knew it, the tune had ended. The musical accent changed and the Prince beckoned for Tonya to follow as they danced their first dance of the night to the orchestrations that set Tonya's head humming with ecstacy.

"I can't believe I am dancing with the Prince of Wales tonight." She said smiling ever so beautifully. Her full head of shimmering blond hair falling across her shoulders virtually danced with her as the Prince whisked her across the floor as other Ambassadors joined in. He was a marvelous dancer. He held her so erect and danced with the ease of a ballet specialist. He knew exactly how to lead her and only smiled slightly in response to her gracious remarks.

Tonya had never seen such beautiful surroundings. Black velvet chairs, red velvet chairs, each room was done in velvet decor, but in differing yet marvelously matching shades. Some rooms were brighter and some shades darker and in more somber tones. Brilliant chandeliers bedecked every room and candlelight had to be a first love of the Queen, for of the four rooms they had been in tonight, each was illuminated not only by the elegant Austrian crystal chandeliers turned down, but with a hundred candles on and in the most ornate gold and silver highly polished candelabras, such as Tonya had never seen before.

Long flowing silk and velvet drapes caressed the windows, keeping the ugly darkness out and the beauty of each room in. The lounges that each one languidly relaxed on, were the most comfortable Tonya had ever enjoyed. The beautiful delicate patterns complemented the elaborate draperies, while the whole of the ballroom revealed the very utmost in contemporary yet British taste so pleasing to the eye, and so relaxing to everyone, while dancing, that no one noticed the evening had passed, and it was now one o'clock in the morning.

Stanos took Tonya by the hand as he thanked the Queen for the incredibly wonderful evening and the lavish dinner in his honor. As they left, they started the procession of dignitaries happily waving goodnight to everyone as they too left, one by one. James Hunter held Tonya's hand momentarily, smiling warmly, and very admiringly at her, as they parted. He couldn't remove his eyes from hers, or her, as she vanished out the doors.

The black Rolls was at the door. Two aides assisted them into the jet black limousine again, and with a final wave to the others and a nod to the chaffeur to drive on, the Queen's own Regiment opened the gates and let the stream of black limousines out, as though it was a royal funeral headed off to the final commital.

Tonya was snuggled next to Stanos Papilos, world government leader in the back of his sleek Rolls limousine and she couldn't believe what was happening to her.

Stanos immediately kissed her at first gently, then somewhat passionately, in the back seat as they raced for the Dorchester Hotel where he had the Presidential suite and his men occupied most of the rooms on the top floor nearby.

Before she knew it, he had her out of the car and onto the private elevator to his suite. She was relaxed in sumptuous surroundings in a moment, while coffee was poured by a middle-aged butler, obviously with Stanos' group of men. His men had not come into the suite, but said goodnight and winked at Stanos while smilingly going in their own direction, murmuring to themselves about something that seemed to humor them.

The coffee felt so good and helped bring Tonya back to reality. She looked at her watch and discovered it was two forty-five—nearly three o'clock. It had been ages since she had stayed up this late, she told Stanos as she sat very close to him on a luxuriously comfortable couch. He was looking at her completely sober with piercingly deep black eyes and said, "I want you to head up the most important department of my government and come to Jerusalem with me to do it next month." His eyes were warm, but she could see the businesslike expression on her countenance, though he spoke in somewhat loving tones. He was asking her at nearly three o'clock in the morning to leave London, move to Israel next month and take over a position she knew absolutely nothing about! She could not believe it. She thought he had been joking.

"You cannot mean what you are saying, Stanos." Though she knew he had and felt the impact of it with her heart pounding like a machine gun again.

"I know what I am asking. I know you can handle the position, though you think you can't. I also know I will make you very happy with me, in Jerusalem. You shall want for nothing." . . . his eyes lowered and he leaned over and kissed her once again, taking her into his arms as they lay back on the sofa. It was a long penetrating, passionate kiss. It had been so long since she had felt anything like this—it seemed that heaven was closing in.

When he released her, they both reached for more coffee. Tonya slowly and thoughtfully weighing out her words, said—"You want me to work for you in this totally foreign land and in a totally foreign area of responsibility to me. It hardly seems logical."

"What is logical in life anymore? The only things that are logical in this world are what you make or do for yourself. Life is full of disappointments, cruelties, incongruities and contrasts that defy the age of reason. I believe in making what I want to happen and taking advantage of every opportunity for happiness and success that passes my way. You know I am extremely fond of you. I like your manner, your business acumen, your record is excellent . . . I ought to know, I read most of your life history today from your firm, compliments of your boss!" he laughed.

"Yes . . ." he said quickly, with a large smile . . . you will fit into Jerusalem and the government officials with me beautifully. You and I will fit like hand and glove" . . . reaching over for her again, he quietly whispered, "Don't turn me down." . . . She was kissed with a fire and passion never felt before.

She stayed another thirty minutes and between sips of coffee, and the tingling embrace of his arms, she whispered, "Yes, I accept, with your help to acclimate me to the job. When do I leave?"

"I leave London early tomorrow . . . well, today really," he said, realizing the time. "I will call you with all the arrangements made for you, this week sometime. You can plan on meeting me in Jerusalem in about a month. You will be paid exceptionally well," he smiled knowingly . . . "Five times what you are earning now. You will live in a giant hotel suite in Jerusalem with everything you need, plus your own maids and all expenses paid as well. But for now, just pack what you would like to have with you of a personal nature and we will have it picked up by the end of the month, and soon you will know exactly when you will be flying in one of my planes. My jet will pick you and your luggage up here in London when we are ready there in Jerusalem.''

The night ended after a few more questions were thoroughly answered and he took her home, just exactly as he had picked her up, only this time there were only three limousines . . . Two others were tucked in for the night, just as she would be momentarily. But she knew sleep would probably evade her for several hours, if she ever got to sleep this night-of-nights. This night topped it all.

Needless to say, there were several lines in the Times, on the front page, of the Queen's activities the preceding evening including a list of her ambassadorial guests plus Tonya Rae Morgan. The house of Morgan was astir the next morning. Charlotte was all a dither reading of the Ambassador of France having been there with her daughter and the long list of notables with the Queen and Prince Phillip. They could hardly wait till Tonya got up. But wait they had to, inasmuch as Tonya was still daydreaming all that had so suddenly transpired in her life—within the short span of three days or less!

When she came downstairs, both of her parents awaited her in the large, casually appointed outer kitchen where they often ate breakfast or other meals when it was not comfortable to eat outside, or when they didn't desire their charming dining room with its richly appointed Viennese suite all cut and polished in the eastern European styling.

As she ate her brunch of ham and eggs, hardly thinking of what she was eating, she proceeded to tell the events of the fantastic evening in the illustrious Buckingham Palace.

''Mother, when I met the Ambassador from France and his wife, I knew you would have been proud of your French heritage all over again. He danced like a gazelle on that shining floor with me. He beamed with happiness when I told him I was half French, and half English. Did that ever draw him to me.'' . . . she mused . . . ''All the Ambassadors of the Ten Common Market Nations were there and the Ambassadors from Canada and the United States, though I hardly remember them . . . and all their wives came too. Not one wife missed that party. It was fantastic.'' . . . She related the whole evening in detail, as best she could, savouring the best till last.

When the last question had been answered with both her father and mother relishing every morsel of her answers, she said she had a surprise for them, that they may not like totally, but that it made her very happy.

''Stanos asked me to move to Jerusalem with his inner staff and take a very exciting, responsible position overseeing his computer division handling each nation's inventories of total goods and foods. It is just one division of computerized control and supervision that he has over the various nations he guides and controls.'' Tonya shocked her parents while looking at both with a serious, but happy expression on her face, awaiting their response.

They were both stunned and speechless. Raymond had to sit down and have another cup of coffee. He could not believe what he was hearing from his one and only daughter. She was going to work for this infamous scoundrel—and leave him, and London, and home. He choked on his coffee. Charlotte brushed tears from her eyes as she saw her daughter's intentions were to accept and go. She was virtually wordless, not from a theological or prophetical point of view—that hadn't occurred to her as yet—but just from a mother's point of view. She was leaving and it sounded so final . . . Sadness crept over her rapidly while Tonya got up and hugged her mother who stood by the window, looking but not seeing, as the tears freely coarsed down her cheeks.

Raymond had a constriction in his throat. When he tried to speak he coughed and his fingernails were cutting into his palms with pain, as he broached the subject with the most sickening sense of dizziness entering his head via his queazy stomach.

''I know you are serious, you always are, and I sense your great desire to do this thing . . .'' He felt like he had just heard God announce that the world was ending today. ''But the seriousness of what you are about to embark on needs much consideration, and frankly, you do not know what you are getting yourself into.'' Raymond paused, not wanting to say too much, lest he alienate his daughter at this sensitive moment. But he went on to say, ''You know of your mother's religious convictions and mine, since coming to London. I know you do not share them with us, but you do respect them, and we are grateful for that. We have been praying for you to see things as we do prophetically . . .'' Her father coughed again, paused and with great difficulty, pushed out the sentence that was the most difficult of all for him to say.

"This man, Stanos Papilos, has all the power and all the ingredients politically, to make him the greatest predicted world leader who will conquer most of the world and become the most ruthless dictator of all time." [1] He lifted his hands in desperation and futility, as though to shout—"Please, darling, don't!"

Tonya Rae understood what he was saying and had heard enough conversations over dinner tables to be aware of the prophecies of the Antichrist. She was fascinated with those prophecies and rather enjoyed debating at times with Uncle Steve about them, but had never really seriously entertained becoming involved with really believing them. It was enough that her parents were becoming religious and that filled such a void in their lives . . . She knew it, and saw it, and was inwardly happy that it brought a new dimension to both her parents' lives and happiness. Whatever it was, they were happier than she had ever seen them anywhere.

She came to her father gently and lovingly. He had been so good to her, all through her varied experiences. He had financed every endeavor she entered into. She took both of his hands in hers, stood squarely in front of him and looked at him so lovingly, while saying, "I respect and appreciate what you just said, and I know it came hard for you Father. I love you for the way you feel for me and about me. I do not believe for one moment that Stanos is the man predicted, but . . ." she paused for her genuine, honest sincerity to impress her father. "If I ever discover, that he is the man that you think he is, or could become that man, I will leave him and his government position immediately, and come home to you and mother without hesitation. I could never work for a tyrant. Please believe me, and give me your blessing, as I at least try this new endeavor. It will pay me five times what I am earning now . . . over one thousand pounds a month!"

She looked lovingly at both her parents and said, "It is not just for the fantastic increase in salary and expenses, or fine living, but I will see Jerusalem, have a chance to meet many important people and world leaders and climb to a very important position in life. I cannot turn this opportunity down . . . Besides, I am very fond of Stanos, and he is of me, as you have surmised. I feel I want the opportunity to be exposed to his world if not for him, then for someone else in that upper echelon who may come along and sweep me off my feet. I've changed my mind about always wanting to be a career woman . . . Some days the thought of marriage and having babies really appeals to me deeply. I need this, father. And I promise you, I will take care of myself and will watch for what you think might happen." Tonya looked lovingly at her father and mother.

She dropped their hands, threw a kiss at her mother and ran out of the room with obvious breathless excitement saying, "I love you both so much, be happy with me today!" She thought, "How strange it was to think of James Hunter simultaneous with thinking of home and babies!"

Raymond knew as soon as he heard from Steve that he would write him and get his advice on this, the most sensitive, serious matter ever popping into his life as a father, and now as a believing Christian. "What would Steve do in a case like this?" . . . he thought to himself and resigned himself to the fact that little could be done. She would have to see the light herself. Any antagonistic browbeating, he knew, from his profession, would drive her further away from him and from God. He felt like he had to pray as never before and went to do so in the privacy of his room.

Stanos called as he said he would . . . and called and called and called. It was almost a daily event. Especially after Tonya quit her position and was spending her time packing, selecting this, discarding that and reading every book she could get her hands on related to the climate, topography, politics, styles and even of the government of Israel. She knew she would eventually meet Prime Minister Uriah Daniels and his ministers in the Israeli Knesset. The very thought of what was coming made her heart race and when she allowed her mind to drift to Stanos and the kind of man she thought he was, she could hear nothing but her own heartbeat until the day came when tearful good-byes were spoken with her father and mother. She was off in a waiting limousine to the London Heathrow Airport where Stanos' private jet was waiting to whisk her away to her new apartment suite in historical and exciting Jerusalem nearly three thousand miles away from London.

Hours later, Stanos met her at the newly built extended Jerusalem airport. For three decades big jets did not land there, but now they could and did from all over the world.

As the plane landed, amidst the Israeli music being played over the intercom on board for her delight, she felt the tingle of superlative excitement grab her every nerve. Jerusalem at last! She was ecstatic.

Stanos took her in his arms in front of everyone and kissed her warmly as he led her away to his limousine while smiling at well-wishers and waving to friends who had come to welcome her. He had paused to show her off, and had waved his hand in a gesture saying . . . "Look at her . . . Look at her . . . This is the reason I am happy today. Thank you for coming." And then they screeched away from the busy airport.

"You look so adoringly gorgeous. Why did I ever wait four weeks to get you here, I will never know . . ." He beamed.

He kissed her again. "It is going to be the greatest test of my self-discipline to keep business and pleasure apart from one another now."

"I will help you from the very start." She replied, smiling at her new-found happiness, but wanting to impress him with some ability to separate business facts from the dizzying effect he had on her. She swallowed hard and said, "I would like to get busy immediately, if you will show me what you want me to do."

"Time enough for that. You must be tired. You have had a five hour trip. It is later here than in London and you can rest and get ready for dinner and some fun tonight as I show you the Old City, when the special lights illuminate it as it once was centuries ago."

The sights enroute to the hotel were so unique to her. There were mosques, dome shaped homes, and stone—white and greyish stone—everywhere in the buildings. Nothing was built of wood or brick.

The Arabs, with their regalia so common to them, were such a different sight from the straight cut Englishmen's business suits she had just seen that morning.

The Jews were everywhere. They were so easily distinguishable from the Arabs in their relatively modern dress, except the orthodox, which

Stanos pointed out to her.

"They live in their own sector and dress according to their own primitive code. They wear black. And if you and I were to drive near their section of the city on their sabbath, they would stone this car and us, as readily as look at us. No girls can wear mini-skirts in their section and only at certain times do tour buses go through the Orthodox quarter. But I will show it to you one day. You have so much to see and learn . . ." He smiled and laughed so broadly. He was obviously happy as they sped along towards his own hotel in the Jewish quarter of Jerusalem.

Their hotel was lovely. It lay in the midst of a valley surrounded on all sides by gardens of freshly painted trees of every nature and beautiful flowers, some of which were totally new to Tonya. They walked through the gardens smelling the distinct aromas of the red and pink oleanders and the yellow flowering gentia gave off a delicate fragrance. They walked slowly, arm in arm, taking it all in, occasionally stopping to catch the scent of garlands of bougainvillea surrounding the archways leading to their private entrance. It was all so breathtakingly lovely. The air was warm . . . so much warmer than London.

With great pleasure, Stanos led her by the hand to the elevator and they got off on the eleventh floor. He took her to the right, pointing out that his own suite of rooms was to the left, down where two men stood guard.

He opened the door to her suite of rooms and her breath left her. It was like a dream. Obviously an interior decorator had done a superb job. She was speechless, as Stanos led her to the dining room, done in English style heavy mahogany wood, with eight high backed velvet tufted chairs in deep crimson. The crimson was such a delightful constrast to the off-white carpeting, she was thrilled. The kitchen was like any other kitchen, except this one was nearly country size, fitted with every convenience, even a dishwasher, which Stanos said, was unthinkable in Israel. He mentioned that maids would be in tomorrow to cook, clean or do whatever Tonya wished to have done. They were superb cooks, whenever she wished to dine here, rather than downstairs where all of the staff would eat. Hers was the only suite outfitted with its own private kitchen other than his own.

She turned to him, her face covered with a delighted smile and unanticipated joy.

He was thrilled with it . . . but said, "You get some rest . . . I'll call for you at sevenish . . . Tonight you can meet some of my special friends and associates here in Jerusalem."

She could not get over the elaborateness of the lovely suite of rooms she was to occupy in Jerusalem. Little did she know at the time how special these rooms were compared to the somewhat barren way of life for the average citizen in Israel. It was a no-frills country, as she would soon learn.

After a luxurious bath and a short rest, she dressed for the evening, having taken an appropriate dress out of her suitcase and hung it thoughtfully in the bathroom while she bathed, letting the hot steam take out the wrinkles.

She wore a street length dress of soft brown colors which contrasted so elegantly with her long blond hair, falling gracefully over her shoulders.

At seven he called, dressed in a very business-like suit and together they entered the dining room filled with executives, secretaries, wives and even a sprinkling of children, here and there.

It was a gracious room done in ornate Israeli style, with oriental tapestries bedecking every wall between the windows. The floor was a series of beautiful persian rugs, thrown here and there beside the tables which were on hardwood floors, reflecting the age of the building.

As they entered, the buzzing of busy voices stopped, the waiters paused, and all eyes were on Stanos and Tonya. She felt exceedingly embarrassed again.

Stanos lifted his hand, smiled at everyone and politely said,

"This is Tonya Rae Morgan, whom you have heard much about. All single men here ignore her; all married men gaze at her . . . when your wives aren't looking. You gals will love her, and so do I!"

With that he waved at them all to go back to eating and led her to his private table for two. While passing, she smiled and said hello to James Hunter, and to Aubrey Miers and his wife. They all responded politely—the men rising as she paused—then they went on to dine.

She purred at Stanos with her heart pounding as they finished their meal and set out to have a romantic, relaxed, beautiful evening. Her first night in the Holy Land was going to be a smashing success.

Tonya's thoughts drifted momentarily to her father and she thought, "If dad is right about Stanos, I have yet to see one thing about him, except his world power, that would indicate he is a ruthless, terrible dictator. On the contrary, he is warm, loving, affectionate and extremely thoughtful.

Her first night in Jerusalem was thrilling as he showed her the city.

The ancient wall was a sight to behold. It contained the Old City with its strange sights and sounds emanating from camels, Arabs, donkeys and exotic looking little bazaars.

Stanos insisted on her going to bed early that night . . . At least midnight seemed early. Stanos proceeded, after breakfast the next morning, to take her to the Mount of Olives where she could see the ancient city in the light of the golden rays of the morning sunshine, . . . brilliantly illuminating the city of gold. She loved every moment of the tour. He took her to the Temple site where they were putting finishing touches on the grandest edifice she had ever seen in her lifetime.

"This Temple will be dedicated within a month," he said, pausing for her to bathe in the glory of it all, as they walked momentarily inside a portion of it. With workmen everywhere getting ready for the festivities of Passover, she overheard two men speaking fluent German. Tonya paused and smiled at them speaking in perfect German herself, asking them if they were from Germany. One of them, the older, answered and said he had been born in Germany, but had come to Israel over 35 years ago. His son, whom he was conversing with, had been born in Israel, on a Kibbutz in Galilee. When she asked what that was, they all laughed and told her it is a communal farm where immigrants often go first to get acclimatized to the language and land of Israel. The government puts them up there, allowing them to work for their keep, while going to school and furthering their Israeli indoctrination, while attempting to blend them into their new social culture. She asked the man his name and that of his son . . . only to find out that he was a Rosenberg and that Moishe was Israeli, for Moses. His son's name was Ya'er and they had been working on the Temple for almost six months now, and they were anxiously awaiting its formal dedication next month at Passover.

"The Jews want their Temple worship so badly now to cement the people together and stop the Christians' revival here," Stanos said.

"Thousands of Jews are becoming Christians, feeling their own religion has disappointed them, and done nothing for them and that God miraculously saved them in the war with Russia seven months ago." Tonya merely nodded and listened appreciatively to all that he taught her as they walked and drove watching the mixture of cultures go by.

In the afternoon, after lunch at the lovely hotel, they went to Bethlehem, and saw the ruins of the great church that had been built there over the supposed sight where Jesus was born in the manger with Mary and Joseph that night a long time ago.

They drove down the 35 miles to the Dead Sea and saw where the city of Jericho had been before the great rift in the valley had swallowed it up.

Finally, her education for today in the land and its religions was through. She was thoroughly tired, sweaty, thrilled, happy and dying for a hot bath. She marveled at Stanos' knowledge and patience with her, and reveled in the thought that he enjoyed teaching her and most of all, being with her, as he said.

After a delightful dinner alone in his lavish suite, fitted out so masculinely, the maitre d' left.

It was their first romantic evening with soft lights, beautiful music on his very expensive stereo import, with no care in the world, except for the two of them, sequestered away, while passionate hunger arose in both of them. Their union seemed to be a symphony of perfection. Tonya was powerless to resist his advances, even if she had a thought to, which she didn't. She yielded to his experienced, passionate lovemaking as though it were the most natural thing for the two of them to do.

The days that followed were days of education and enlightenment concerning her new responsibilities in a nearby large cement building that had been reconstructed after the war seven months ago. It had been wired precisely as Stanos needed, and he was having his master computer control set up now. It would soon be completed, enabling him to punch into every computer he had in Europe and Africa. He had installed computers in every cooperative country in Africa and Europe with his paid technicians programming and controlling all that went in and the valuable information that came out of these powerful beasts of man's invention. He had a master control that monitored all entrees by the moment. Each country fed vital statistics to the technicians locally. His men would then feed the data into the steel beasts with electronic brains, as they watched from Brussels and Luxembourg. Now Jerusalem would soon be complete. All that went on in the nations attached to the Common Market Ten Nations, with other nations participating in the trade benefits set up, had their vital statistics fed into the computers.

He knew the gross national productivity of every nation every day if he wanted to monitor it himself, and often did. Any day of the month, he could punch into the master control and know exactly the wheat surplus in the Ten Nations and their associates, including the wheat fields of the United States and Canada, who had allowed themselves to be connected into this deal, needing oil guarantees so badly. Stanos had the oil; they had the wheat and many foodstuffs in abundance that he wanted. He had already started draining the North American continent's food supplies to help poorer African countries. He was taking from the rich and giving to the poor. [2] In addition, he had set up educational reform programs for greatly increased agricultural production in most African countries and was assisting in the redevelopment of the Soviet Union as well as other Eastern European countries.

He had his supervisors working out a crash educational program in Africa, teaching the illiterate to read, write and do simple arithmetic. His program of education was being endorsed by various religious bodies of Europe and even North America supported him in the educational endeavor.

The World Council of Churches, a basically Protestant organization, backed his humanitarian aims at feeding and teaching the poverty pocket areas of the world. The Roman Catholic church with the Pope in Rome, backed his efforts at rechristianizing Africa and parts of Europe now that communism was dying in the eastern bloc of nations.

Stanos was being backed by some who hated him, but they got on his bandwagon realizing that it also furthered their own causes for the world. It was a strange merger of religions, politics and the strangest of all a mixture of politicians who backed his varied program of world education, feeding of the hungry and political control of the natural assets in each of these countries in return. [3]

Consequently, nation after nation found themselves easily coersed into signing agreements entitling him to have control over their natural resources in return for fair prices, educational benefits and a large initial give-away program. All the data from their constant development went into the Master Control. Stanos knew of every drop of oil produced; every bushel of wheat in the Nebraska breadbasket; every ton of coal in Newcastle and every diamond in Africa, and of course, every ounce of gold in Russian and South African mines. Atomic energy, nuclear power and military development were all under his personal supervision. The only part of the world he had trouble controlling was the Far East, which to date had not knuckled under at all, stating they do not need his help, oil or science. They had developed their own.

Stanos had control of world production of goods. He had complete knowledge of inventories for large and small companies, all over the western nations. With other computers staffed by his organization, all banking was monitored by his men. They knew of large loans to companies and for what reason the loans were granted, via "ECU."

They monitored large and small transactions in America, Canada, South America and Central America, along with Africa, Asia, and Europe. Virtually nothing went on in international trading, commerce, banking, or in any other field of endeavor, whether industrial, energy, finance, food production, precious metals, mining, births, deaths, transfers of properties or persons, aerospace development, natural catastrophies, total inventories of companies and governments, regardless of products, nature, political maneuvers, even down to salaries of most officials. He had not yet perfected inventory controls of small stores, warehouses and small businesses or radical elements who opposed his control in the more remote areas of the world, but he was working on it feverishly, and had thousands of his agents out every day tracking down the insurrectionists.

He was beginning to feel the powerful opposition of Orthodox Jews and so-called born-again Christians. They were against everything he wished to do, even if it were beneficial. They spread nasty statements and allegations about him everywhere. Underground presses were starting to call him a world dictator. He was to be watched constantly, stopped at all costs, or he would control their very life breath. He was aware of world movements against him, but only discussed them with Tonya Rae after he had a few drinks. He would break down and talk at length of his desires, only to help the world. Why did the Christians and the Jews oppose him so?

Was he not a man of peace? [4] Was he not vitally interested in the welfare of the nations, under his supervision, since the terrible catastrophy of their unsuccessful bid for world power? Had he not elevated their position in terms of wealth and well-being? Had he not guaranteed the United States oil in exchange for their food, for the hungry millions that had increased in the aftermath of the war and the lack of agricultural development? Had he not kept his bargains and been a peaceful negotiator to benefit the world with his benevolence?

These and similar questions kept Stanos and Tonya Rae up many a night as he could not sleep worrying about his opposition and thinking of how he might crush or silence it. She was a good listener and seldom offered any suggestions. It was all too much for her. Just learning about his master computer control of inventories of countries alone was enough for her to learn in six months. It had been six months since she left London. Letters had come back and forth, and occasionally she longed to see her parents and the life of London. Israel was nothing like the sophistication of the Europe she had grown up in. It was still so primitive in a way, and yet the people were very warm. "Had it not been for the war, perhaps Israel would be more developed," she thought occasionally. They still found the bodies of Russians from time to time, as bulldozers unearthed those buried in the war and earthquake rubble. "Here they were, six months later, still sending Russian bodies home to Moscow!" [5]

The New Temple was almost complete and only the architects and engineers knew where it had to be finished after the festivities. The Rabbis and Prime Minister decided to go ahead. "Israel needed this, Judaism needed this!" The Chief Rabbi flatly stated. He was feeling the opposition of the newly created Christian Jewish Party that had been allowed entrance to the Israeli Knesset, after a vote enabling them to do so as law abiding citizens of Israel. Israel had allowed the communists in as a party before the great war; now they must allow the Christian Jewish

Party in. They caused much trouble and were evangelizing everywhere, making proselytes of everyone to Christianity.

Thousands were joining their ranks. They opposed the presence of Stanos Papilos, for he represented a world power that they could not cope with. Even the Orthodox and the Christians had joined forces on one rally occasion and paraded with banners in front of Stanos' hotel-home, inviting him to leave the country.

He told Tonya he would not forget them in this opposition and breathed out his wrath upon them one day in a moment of weakness. One day he would teach those Christian rebel-rousing Jews, and the Orthodox ignorant who he was, and what they were . . . He swore to it by all the gods of heaven in front of his staff and Tonya. Many of them agreed with him that something should be done. He had left the table muttering violently angry with them, to the point of not returning to his office for the day.

Walking as quickly as he could, James came over to Tonya as Stanos left. He sat down at her table and while ordering more coffee started to apologize for his boss' bizarre behavior.

"You don't have to explain to me James . . . I think I am beginning to understand both sides of this leader of ours. One is gentle and peaceable, and the other is a distinct ruthlessness, reaching almost to the extremes of murderous hatred. I've seen it already!" She related quietly, but seriously, all the while staring deeply into Jim's eyes.

"Never mind." James quickly changed the subject, having been watching and waiting for this moment to come. "We are going out today and I will show you the sights and sounds of Israel . . . maybe some Stanos has overlooked. Would you like to go with me?" He looked so excited with his eyes dancing as he smiled ever so adoringly at her.

For a moment he made Tonya's heart absolutely flip and her stomach twist in delightful anticipation of the afternoon.

"I wouldn't miss this for the world Mr. Hunter. Let's go before Stanos changes his mind!" She hastily agreed.

It was two in the afternoon when they left and eleven at night when she eventually, unhurriedly returned to her apartment with James by her side.

James had shown her parts of Tel Aviv that afternoon and evening, with dinner in the city of fun to top the evening off.

"You go to Jerusalem to pray, Haifa to stay, but Tel Aviv to play," he had said. They had played, eaten, danced and sipped their wine till both were a bit light-headed and amorous.

James was invited in for further cocktails and maybe a song or two. He accepted, of course, and while topping their drinking off for the evening with more imported French Champagne, Tonya sang three love songs with such charm and grace that even James began to sober, listening enraptured to her. She was gorgeous and sang like a nightingale as she played her white baby grand piano.

Then she popped off the piano stool, downed her last drops of champagne and standing before him impudently and voluptuously, she said, "It was a terrific day . . . You are a terrific guy . . . I like you too much for my own good. Please leave me now as I slip into nothing and go to bed. I have a big day tomorrow . . . and besides two more drinks for both of us, and you will never leave . . ." She smiled and looked so demurely at him . . . "and I won't want you to either." She barely whispered her affection for him as he rose, took her gently into his arms and kissed her lightly, then passionately for a long time. She clung to him like a drowning sailor to his life preserver. He held her tightly and they both stared deep into one another's eyes, realizing that if Stanos knew, he would fire them both on the spot. She was his girl and James knew it and so did Tonya. . . .

But what they both were saying with their adoring eyes, but without a word, was that they knew they both felt very deeply for one another, and perhaps had begun to feel this way back in London months ago.

"We will find our moments, darling." James whispered in her ear, as though the very walls were bugged for Stanos.

"If we do, God help us if we are caught or even suspected." Tonya grimly replied in his ear, while feeling his pounding heart against hers.

"I'm not quite sure what's happening to me, Jim." She continued, nervously. "But I like what I feel when I'm with you . . . I'm relaxed, yet excited and tingle all over . . . I know . . . I feel that . . . uh . . . maybe there is something for us in the distant future. . . . Do you feel it too?''

''You know I do. . . . You know I do.'' He drew her so close to him, while burying his face in her beautiful hair.

''Our day will come . . . soon!'' He kissed her lightly, dropped his embrace and strode quietly out of her apartment, not looking back.

Tonya had learned quickly and was soon Minister in Charge of Affairs for World Inventories. It was a title indicating that all those under her were working to secure daily information on all products produced; farming, industrial, scientific, energy products, etc.

She had known about Digital Monetary Inputs in London, and now had the pleasure of seeing her own ''ECU Account'' grow to sizeable proportions as she was earning over five hundred English pounds in the equivalent amounts of ''ECU'' weekly. And she had no expenses that were not covered on top of that.

Tonya's refrigerator and cupboards were kept full by her two maids. All expenses incurred in the apartment never came to her. It wasn't that she completely felt like a ''kept woman,'' but at times the luxury bothered her as she realized she paid out nothing for all the services she received. Even her cleaning was picked up and delivered back to her without charge.

Occasionally she tipped her maids the best they had ever seen. They were cute little Arab girls from the West Bank that had survived the War and the Earthquake. They talked incessantly about both and how it was so miraculous that Israel had been saved by God from both. They liked the Jews and both had Jewish army boyfriends.

Tonya learned a great deal of both languages the first six months. She had majored in languages in college and found them fascinating and rewarding when she could converse in the native tongue. She was doing quite well in both Hebrew and Arabic.

Her trips to the Old City fascinated her, and she often went alone. Once she visited the Rosenbergs at their invitation, after their chance meeting in the Temple. She enjoyed the two families and their Jewish traditions, and had dinner with them all.

The day of the Passover Dedication soon came. It appeared that all Israel was present, along with thousands of Jews from virtually every country in the world. It was the greatest Passover in two thousand years because it was their land at last, and they were dedicating the New Holy Temple, as it had come to be called most affectionately.

One thousand lambs were slain on the outside brazen altar by the Priests of the New Order of Levites. All over Israel, literally millions wept beside their television sets, in the courtyards of the Temple and Wailing Wall, and throughout the world, as they opened the Gates of the Temple and the Chief Rabbi, who was of the Tribe of Levi became the Chief High Priest of the New Holy Temple. He was annointed with oil, sprinkled with blood, and then he only went into the Holy of Holies to offer atonement to God for the national sins of Israel and for Jews the world over. He took the blood of a perfect lamb with him and offered it to the Lord, in accordance with the Book of Leviticus and the Old Testament Mosaic Economy.

Simple blood sacrifices were established for the nation. 6 It was not going to be a daily offering, but a Sabbath Offering each Saturday for the nation. Each Sabbath at high noon, the Priests would offer the sacrifices to atone for the sins of those present and those wishing to be represented. On any given Sabbath you could be included in the number represented by the sacrificial Lamb simply by notifying your Rabbi. He would put your name on parchments to be hung together with thousands of other names on the Wall by the Temple, entitling you as a Jewish believer to absolution from your sins as Jehovah God forgave you on behalf of the shed blood of the lambs.

"It was the holiest week in Israel's two thousand year history," said the press, and all Israel agreed. For the first time in two thousand years they had a Temple and sacrifices regularly for the sins of the people. Millions were planning pilgrimages to Israel now for the festivities would last eight days in all.

Tonya received a long distance call from London. Her parents were coming for the Dedication of the Temple. She was elated.

The Morgans arrived, were picked up in the style, complementing Tonya's own way of life and that of her employer. Her parents loved every minute of staying in her suite of rooms, meeting Stanos and many of his staff members.

Tonya, after the initial Dedication, had shown her father much of her new responsibilities, and they chatted amiably about a thousand things that happened to all three of them in Jerusalem and London in the past seven months.

It was a great week of reunion, pleasure, eating out, sightseeing, and observing the Dedication of the Temple. Raymond was ecstatic over seeing it all in his first visit to the Holy Land.

Charlotte was more caught up with the beautiful hotel and gardens, and especially with Stanos.

Then one day shortly after the Dedication, Israeli naval intelligence began monitoring the presence of many warships in the Eastern section of the Mediterranean Sea, north from the coast of Alexandria in Egypt and south of Athens, Greece, and Istanbul, Turkey. They came suddenly and without any warning or explanation on Stanos' part. They anchored offshore of Tel Aviv and Haifa, waiting for orders. Israeli leaders were extremely concerned as the Prime Minister called for an emergency meeting with Stanos Papilos regarding the presence of so many ships lying offshore. They were inside the limit of two miles—a limit that had been set by Stanos himself regarding the sovereignty of waters for each nation. No foreign powers were to inject themselves into the private waters of any nation without permission to do so. Friendly nations and ships would not hesitate to comply, and therefore enemy ships could be monitored and stopped. In this case, it was friendly ships from friendly nations in Europe that were anchored just offshore the State of Israel, without permission granted, or even requested.

Stanos walked up the steps to the Knesset to be greeted by the Prime Minister and the angry members of his Cabinet. Television cameras were taking the appropriate shots and world press was standing still for an explanation regarding this naval intrusion into national waters.

The swift and shocking answer stunned the world and brought Israel to her knees. It was far worse than the Soviet war or the ''Divine Earthquake!''

1. Daniel 8:23-27.
2. Daniel 11:39.
3. Daniel 11:24.
4. Daniel 11:21.
5. Ezekiel 39:12.
6. Revelation 11:1.

Chapter
7

The World Dictator Appears

The
World Dictator
Appears

The nation of Israel was stunned! No one could believe what they heard. The birds had not stopped singing nor the air moving, the mountains were not removed into the Sea, but everyone expected each of those things to happen any moment now. The shock waves of Stanos Papilos pronounciation caught the world off guard.

Stanos proudly walked into the Prime Minister's presence and handed him a formal document to read. It startingly stated that he, Stanos Papilos was taking over the State of Israel, as his home and his nation. His armies were at the gates, his atomic weaponry trained on the citizenry, and he would either wipe out the inhabitants and mop up the land afterward, or he would take the reins of government and control without the firing of a shot—depending on the actions of the Prime Minister.

The Prime Minister and all Cabinet Members would remain in office under his guidance and administration. They could run the country for the most part, but he, Stanos Papilos, would set down the guidelines for them. They were thunderstruck! His boldness overwhelmed them.

His power stretched over Europe, Africa and the Middle East and into parts of Western Asia, he now became a self-proclaimed, "World President." [1]

When the sputtering was over, Israel surrendered and signed the document within sixty minutes. Within two hours after Stanos Papilos had entered the Knesset, seventy-five thousand of his fully armed soldiers came swiftly from the anchored ships and speedily started to take over the land from the borders of Lebanon to Egypt in the south. They were everywhere. By nightfall, fifteen thousand Israeli families had been dislodged from their homes, told to leave and to find friends or relatives to live with. Their homes were confiscated by the armies for billeting of the soldiers on a round-the-clock basis.

Small pockets of armed resistance were quickly squelched and those involved were immediately shot by firing squads, quickly set up in the main streets and squares of towns, cities and villages. [2]

Within twenty-four hours all was quiet, except for the pounding in Tonya's heart . . . and probably three or four million thoroughly saddened Israeli and Arab hearts in Israel that night.

The news had not only been broadcast to Israel, but every nation heard the command to surrender or be annihilated. World leaders were indescribably shocked, especially in the United States and Canada.

But who could or would resist him. [3] He had the power and total control, and he had peacefully offered benefits for all who complied and still promised aid to all cooperating with his "benevolent dictatorship."

Stanos changed overnight. While ignoring Tonya for several days, it seemed he had at last stripped away his own masquerade of warmth and charm, and had become a mad dog. His first move after everything was quieted down, was to swiftly round up as many of the "Christian Jews and Orthodox Jews" as possible.

While gathering them together the first day, the news went out everywhere that they were going before the firing squad. Great appeals from the Knesset to Stanos Hotel Headquarters accomplished nothing. He could not be found and no one would answer for him.

By nightfall, three thousand women, men and some children of the Orthodox quarter were rounded up, but less than one thousand of the Christian Jews could be found. Thousands had hid and were leaving the country over the rugged mountain terrain for anywhere, rather than be shot. [4] Fear and panic broke out.

By morning Stanos called over the radio for all Orthodox Jews to turn themselves in, and for the Christian Jews to do the same. If they would not, their brothers would be shot. No one turned up for the word had leaked out that all were going to be killed immediately.

At high noon, over four thousand Jews and Christians were murdered by firing squads in the streets of Israel from Dan to Beersheba, and there was nothing anyone could do about it; unless he wanted to be immediately shot himself. The cries of anguish were going up from everywhere, including Tonya's bedroom. She wept in anguish for these people. She felt only hatred for this terrible mad man.

When Stanos finally took notice of Tonya and wanted her favors one night, she locked him out and would not open up in answer to his knocks. He could have smashed the door down, but elected not to. He decided to leave it till morning, when he would work out a reconciliation with her—she would understand then why he was doing what was only necessary and expedient.

When they finally met in her office, she was ice-cold to him and told him exactly how she felt about the merciless killings, and that she preferred leaving his employment and life as quickly as possible; never wanting to see him again. It was over.

Nothing he could say would endear him to her. However, he would not give up on her completely, and she was forbidden to leave the country or his employ. She knew too much about the internal workings of his specialty computer control of inventories the world over, and he needed her to work now, more than ever. His greatest world program was ready for implementation.

She knew her duties and she would do them well, he had said. And then, for days she didn't see him hardly at all, only as he passed in the distance, but each day she heard of more and more of his attrocities.

Then, the most incredulous, unbelievable act of all took place. Stanos suddenly marched his men up the great steps to the New Holy Temple and forcibly ejected every Priest there, and threw out the sacrificial lambs and cleaners who worked there. He raised his Imperial Flag of Nations over the Temple and proclaimed it his. [5]

Within a day he had the Temple "cleansed," he joked—like Jesus once did—and took over the New Holy Temple declaring that it would be his own new home forever. [6] Within three months he was living in the Holy of Holies, claiming to outsiders that the Holiest Place was his giant bedroom and laughingly quipped that if they wished, they could all come and worship him! [7]

Reaction in the Knesset was just less than violent the day he took over their New Holy Temple and profaned it by marching into the Holy of Holies, as only the High Priest was to do once a year on the Day of Atonement. Stanos had committed the unpardonable act of the age to the Jews. Nothing he could do now would ever atone for his wretchedness and their misery.

For Stanos to take their Holy Temple would mean a planned war of attrition. They knew they could not conquer him overnight or in an out and out confrontation; so small bands of Israelis were now attacking at night, sabotaging his efforts in various places. They would not attack the Temple, as yet, but would wait till he was more vulnerable. To get near the Temple took passes; you had to go through heavily armed militia and were searched completely even in your private parts! He was guarded by the best of his soliders and the most loyal of his European armies.

Communications were set up in the Holy Temple, so he could broadcast to Israel and telephone to anywhere in his empire.

A large kitchen and several adjoining rooms for guests and consorts were set up to accommodate world leaders who visited him, many of whom were most reluctant to do so, fearing the wrath of the Jews for even entering the Holy Temple area. But they came and in vain implored him to give up the Temple as he could have any building anywhere in the world for his headquarters, or Palace. World press reaction was extremely violent over his usurping jurisdiction over this holiest of places for a "house."

The President of the United States cabled him to remove himself from the Holy Temple or suffer the consequences from the people of North America. The President did not threaten Stanos; he just flatly called him a "Devil of a man" and told him to "extricate himself from the Temple within twenty-four hours, or the United States would send no more food stuffs, and would cut off all communication with Europe and the Middle East. If that led to an all-out war, the North American continent was ready. It would use their nuclear power against his!"

When the message hit the press and television, it was as though the whole world shouted with joy over the strength of character manifested by the newly elected President of the United States.

Canada's Prime Minister joined the American President in the revolt against Stanos and told him to grow his own wheat and beef! There would be no more supplies sent from the Dominion of Canada until he was out of the Jewish Holy Temple.

Stanos was violently angry. It took his associates several hours to calm him down, and then only with large doses of alcohol which they let him drink until he was in a stupor. They finally put him to bed like a child.

It was fifteen hours after the communiques from America when Stanos woke up. He immediately called for the Ambassadors from the United States and Canada to appear before him in the Temple.

They sent word they would meet with him anywhere else, but refused to meet him in the Temple.

Stanos shocked the world once more by sending a detachment of his own personal guards in plain clothes over to the Embassies and promptly blew them both off the face of the earth, along with all the staff members and Ambassadors inside!

When the news reached Washington and Ottawa simultaneously, it was broadcast over all the media with headlines screaming "Murder in Jerusalem!" Both the President and the Prime Minister of both countries took it as an act of war, and consequently called in their cabinets and Joint Chiefs of Staff to officially declare war on Stanos Papilos and his entire regime!

All communications were cut from the North American continent to Europe, except for telephone lines. All computer hook-ups were severed and no further inputs came to Europe from America or Canada.

There was jubilant shouting in the streets—from New York to Los Angeles, from Halifax to Victoria . . . Never had the two nations been more united and friendlier in their mutual decisions than today.

They knew the oil would be shut off, but Venezuelan and Malaysian oil would keep coming faithfully, as long as they were not bombed by Stanos. Neither country by itself could stand up to him or his forces . . . who could?

It was the boldest move in modern history. Both leaders were aware of it. But they were backed unanimously by their Cabinets and Parliaments.

Military preparedness was under way for it had been the biggest gamble any two nations had ever taken. So far it was working.

Papilos had to think first, "Would he want an all-out war now with North America—with Jews against him in Israel? Great council meetings took place. His associates advised him to move out of the Holy Temple, and stop the world reaction and hatred. He bitterly and wordily resisted their advice, storming out of the council chambers.

On the fourth day, he strode into his executives' session and told them he had decided to do nothing for the time being, except cut off all oil to the U.S. and Canada. [8] All oil tankers enroute to North American ports must turn around and immediately return home. He would tend to the leaders of these two countries later.

The two greatest democracies left in the world rejoiced, and yet were constantly on their guard. They knew that combined they both produced seventy percent of all exportable foods in the world. Europe had needed the States very much for many goods. It would work a terrible hardship on all of Europe, though they could survive with some immediate switching of emphasis and priorities to agriculture.

Much of Stanos' European budget would have to be diverted from the military to civil defense and to agricultural and industrial development. His program in Africa would have to be stepped up for agricultural development. He would have to beef up imports from Australia and New Zealand, where up to now he had exercised little control because of the distances between them and his sphere of operation.

The threat of international war hung over the whole world as never before in history. Never had one man with so much power made so many enemies overnight as Stanos Papilos, the "Jerusalem butcher."

Chinese leaders had let it be known from the outset of his adventures into the Middle East that neither he nor his military minded executives would be welcome east of the Euphrates River, and that he should keep himself where he belonged—out of the "yellow empires."

Stanos knew the day would come when he would have to reckon with "Yellow Power." He dreaded it for the Chinese now possessed nuclear power of their own. Their oil wells produced all they needed and had some left over for export. They had a standing army of over two million fully trained men, representing over one billion in Chinese population alone! Add to this ominous amount of men India's eight hundred million people, who despised his autocratic rule to the core, and you could see why Stanos was cautious. If India joined the Chinese in a "yellow and brown revolt" against white supremacy, it would be the war of all wars 9 and Stanos knew it. He would let sleeping dogs lie for the moment.

His day would come, he had told his closest associates; but the game would be played by his conniving rules. He was too clever to court probable disaster at this point.

America might have won the war of words, but the Jews were losing their war of attrition. They were being slaughtered everywhere for resisting Papilos' men and orders. He was ordering innocent Jews to be butchered in the streets for any act of war against his authority. Women with children were rounded up and shot in large shopping malls and squares in front of screaming and crying thousands, as punishment for the actions of the "Jewish Underground," as the armies of resistors were labelled.

Any Christian Jew was shot on sight, without mercy. Trials had never been ordered nor did courts have any jurisdiction over the military. Jews were searched anywhere and everywhere, and homes were constantly raided to search for arms and weapons. Upon finding them, the owners were killed on their front lawns as an example to others.

Stanos made an official pronouncement that any Jew finding Orthodox Jews or Christian Jews for him would be granted permanent protection from death or imprisonment and would be summarily rewarded plentifully.

From that point on, households were divided against households, and even some parents turned against their children and sons and daughters turned against mother and father. [10] It was a scene of miserable confusion and terrifying circumstances, constantly surrounded by Stanos' European henchmen. They were wickedly brutal and many Israeli women were beaten and raped and left to bleed to death as soldiers searched for the two hated sects. [11]

The despicable treatment of Jews who cooperated lessened and their reward for turning in the "conspirators" was extra food, money and the blessing of Stanos Papilos upon their families.

Moishe Rosenberg and his family were still alive and living fairly modestly off his living as a builder now, since tourism had died completely. Ruth still made good wages working for the government in Gordon's factories. Both David and Ya'er did odd jobs of clean-up for the government or rebuilding, but were ordered into their homes most of the time by the troops patroling the streets of Jerusalem.

The Rabbi Perla and his kindly wife Miriam lived in constant fear that they would be destroyed or imprisoned because of his religious profession. Had they originally chosen to live within the Orthodox Quarter, they felt quite sure they would be dead by now. Living in the Jewish section in Jerusalem had saved them, even though the Rabbi always dressed the same in his blacks.

David and Dianne's baby was just over three years old. They lived in fear daily. So much morbid fear had fallen on all Jewish households with respect to when they might lose their own lives, that you could hardly trust anyone anymore. There was a strange feeling of sickness and evil creeping all over the country. Happiness was not seen on faces anymore; in its place was a sick look of incredulous unbelief at all that was transpiring in their homeland. So much had happened so soon after the hilarity of the Feast Days and the Passover Dedication of the Holy Temple it was unbelievable.

Moishe called the family into a private conference one night including Rabbi Perla and Miriam. He told them they would have to leave Israel.

It came as no shock to Sarah, who had discussed the possibility of escape with her husband more than once. They had pondered many an early morning hour on how to get out of the country, swiftly, silently, and without any neighbors' prying eyes catching them and subsequently earning rewards for themselves by turning them in.

All the shades were drawn with only one light on as they gathered quietly around the kitchen table with little Joel Rosenberg fast asleep in his mother's room.

"I have made a plan for all of us." Moishe said as he looked at each one soberly. His mind flashed back to Germany and Poland years ago when he and Sarah had escaped the cattle car that night of destiny.

"Once before I had a plan for Sarah and I as teenagers, on board a German train in Poland headed for Treblinka, and it worked. We escaped and God was with us then. He is with us now, Rabbi." Moishe smiled encouragingly at the aging Rabbi and his wife, who looked so frightened at the spectre of escape.

"What is your idea Moishe? We are all anxious to go over it with you." Rabbi Perla said as he stared deeply into Moishe's serious eyes.

"Well, escape by air is impossible. We have no access to planes. Escape by ship might be possible, but we have no access to anything bigger than a fishing boat up by Joppa, and we would be caught perhaps by shore patrols and we couldn't go very far in such a small boat anyway. Therefore, escape by land is our only hope." He looked squarely at each one in the room while unwinding a cloth map he had drawn of their proposed escape route.

"This is a route of escape that takes us right through the center part of the southern areas of Israel. We might not be noticed too much there, as we would be going by night in ground familiar to the boys, having fought in that region.'' He looked at David and Ya'er, who both nodded their knowledge of the topography of the Sinai and lower regions of Israel, going towards the Gulf of Aquaba and Eilat, on the Red Sea.

''We could travel by night.'' Moishe was almost whispering the scary plan, while looking from face to face for reactions in the quiet shadows of the room.

''It is almost three hundred miles, maybe less. We cross over the Israeli Jordanian mountains of Edom here.'' He pointed to a point slightly above Eilat, near where many high mountains were.

''At this point there are accesses to the high mountains of Jordan. Being that it is summertime, we can make it over them or around some of them, carrying what we can take on our backs, and we can gain access to an ancient city fortress here.'' He pinpointed their ultimate destination, which to them meant nothing.

''There is an old mountain city carved out of the rocks there. I have been there on tours many times when they allowed us over the Allenby Bridge. It is capable of housing hundreds of thousands of people with fantastic protection from almost everything that would try to get us, except maybe bombs. But even then they would have to get direct hits and bomb us out of deep caves in the mountains, and it could not be easily done. We could live there indefinitely with much water available, and we would only be thirty miles from the Red Sea for fishing. There are some wild animals in those mountains and we could hunt and eat them. Plus one or two armed guards could protect us from the enemy as there is but a narrow pass ten feet wide at the only entrance!'' Moishe exclaimed.

''What is the name of the place?'' inquired Rabbi Perla anxiously peering over his black spectacles at the map.

''Petra, or the Rock.'' Moishe replied.

Suddenly the Rabbi burst into tears in front of everyone. His wife in absolute bewilderment attempted to comfort him.

''What is it father?'' Dianna whispered in his ear softly with her arm around her weeping father. She had never seen him cry.

He composed himself in a few minutes, wiped his eyes, blew his nose and reaching for the Bible, turned quickly to a passage from the prophecies of Isaiah:

"Let the wilderness and the cities thereof lift up their voice, the villages that Kedar doth inhabit, let the inhabitants of the *rock* sing, let them shout from the top of the mountains. Let them give glory unto the Lord, and declare his praise in the islands. . . . I will bring the blind by a way they knew not; I will lead them in paths that they have not known; I will make darkness light before them, and crooked things straight. These things will I do unto them, and not forsake them." He stopped reading and looked excited.

"The prophet foresaw this day and this move of many, to Petra, the "Rock." Rabbi Perla gently put the Bible down and again wept under the impact of the prophecy. Leaving the table he gave silent consent to the plan to evacuate as quickly as possible to the "Rock."

He turned to add, " 'Deliverance will come from Israel's God while we are in the rock city.'[12] Let us know when the plan is complete."

Moishe wiped a tear from his own eye and looking up while leaning back in his chair said, "Isaiah the prophet is full of references to Israel being saved while safe in the Rock. This may be it. I have always wondered what it meant. But one thing is for sure, we could hold out for a long time with just a little help and a few guns and ammunition. I really don't think anyone would bother to come and get us anyway. We aren't worth the bother to them. But we are worth everything to ourselves. So we must get out!"

"We have our guns and some ammunition, Dad," Ya'er injected quickly. "We must plan quickly and thoroughly on how we will leave, and what else to take with us."

An extensive list was prepared, from water purifying pills to the basic needs of medicinal aids. They stayed up the whole night planning the venture. David realized he would have to have a chest carriage for their son to ride in, while carrying a pack on his back as well. Ya'er offered to share the baby load at times.

They would be travelling by night and would need flashlights for occasional use as well as a strong radio to hear what was going on behind them and in front of them. Ya'er had an army model, capable of picking up the military maneuvers of Stanos' men. The next day would be a day of quiet preparedness for a journey, no neighbor would know anything nor suspect.

The next day Jerusalem had a torrential rain, which made it easy for the boys to hide various items of necessity under their large army issue raincoats. Bulky items were well concealed as they came and went unsuspectedly.

Bread was freshly baked and smelled so delicious, coming hot out of the ovens for the trip. They were to have one large meal before leaving, cleaning up everything edible in the apartments. It would be a long time before a square meal was set before them again. After eating, without cleaning anything up, they would leave. They never expected to see this apartment or their furnishings or personal belongings again! Only God knew their future.

Nightfall brought them together for the "last supper." It was a table to behold. Sarah and Miriam both had prepared it, in addition to the food stuffs they wanted to eat on the way.

They gorged themselves, on fried fish, roasted chicken and broiled pieces of tender liver. The Rabbi and Miriam refrained from the liver, but all ate hearty portions of everything as if they would never eat again!

Sarah had outdone herself on this meal, and a rich red robust Israeli burgundy wine was served to everyone reminding them all of the feast days, when they usually partook of such a delicacy. Everything was succulently delicious.

Roasted potatoes and a host of vegetables from the roasting pan accompanied the chickens, as they went from one course to the other, with great delight, smacking their lips and happily licking their fingers like they had never eaten before. It was a happy time, though all were filled with a sense of sadness at leaving home and possessions and were dreading the trip into the darkness and unknown, especially the women.

It was an early dinner starting at four o'clock in the afternoon, providing them time for enjoyment, resting and final moments of organization.

Everything was packed securely. Each man had his gun holstered under a heavy jacket. The women, were armed, the guns being strapped on their waists under outer garments.

They were all set. Without cleaning up the dishes or washing a thing, they proceeded to hoist the packs in place. It would soon be midnight, the selected hour of departure through streets lightly patrolled that time of night.

With the lights out, they prayed for safety and crept out of their apartments, down the front stairs, glancing in every direction for movement of hostile human bodies.

Stealthily moving through back alleys and yards, furtively glancing down every corridor, they made their way to the outer limits of Jerusalem and in the moonlit distance could see the "Shepherds Fields" in the area of Bethlehem, less than five miles away.

Once into the fields, they picked up speed though their trek was difficult and the land foreign to the women. Many times the women stumbled, but regained their footing and composure quickly thinking of the fury of the hated leader should they be caught.

To the obvious displeasure of Rabbi Perla, they had chosen a Friday evening for the departure from Jerusalem, as many Jews would be preoccupied with the Sabbath. And knowing Jewish observance of the same, the patrols would be less likely to bother them, though they were out beyond curfew time.

Arabs journeying during the day with mules and camels had worked paths into the sides of the Shepherds Fields and the surrounding hills around Bethlehem. This made their journey easier as they made their way downward past the Dead Sea, working south at the same time, just missing the thirty-five miles of rugged mountain terrain directly east of Jerusalem.

The boys knew the way through the mountains they were traversing now. Military maneuvers had taken them this way often. Jeeps and tanks and other armored vehicles had cut a path over these hills, but they were no longer used by Stanos or his men, for they were out-of-the-way and there was no reason to patrol them now. No one lived in them.

The journey at best would take a week, at worst, two weeks or longer, depending on the women enduring rugged mountain terrain. They had to walk by night and hide in caves by day, drinking from streams that flowed through the mountain valleys. They saved as much food as possible, eating whatever fruits they could find here and there growing wild, or in some remote farm area. They were the strangest looking group you ever saw. Their clothes were dark browns, blacks or dark greens, so as to be somewhat camouflaged with the night.

Now, after three days, they were many miles from Jerusalem and south of Beersheba. Civilization was sparse, and they could walk by day and sleep mostly at night. It had taken them four days to slowly creep from civilization over the rugged Judean mountains by night and not be seen at all. So far, so good. To their knowledge, absolutely no one had noticed them. They were safe, but so dirty, dusty and tired. Their bones ached from sleeping out in the dampness at night. Baby Joel fared best of all, thinking it was great as David and Dianna made a game of it for him.

By the sixth day, after much of the danger was apparently over, they were suddenly accosted by a group of Christian Jews hiding in the hills themselves from Stanos and his men. They must have seen them coming at twilight and hid. They were suddenly surrounded by the Christians, aiming guns at them, who immediately interrogated them as to why they were there, and what had happened. They were all happy to meet friendly faces.

There were at least fifty Christians. They immediately took Moishe and his family to the hidden fires in the hills for warmth, rest and a rabbit stew.

It had been the first warm food any of them had had in almost a week. It was so delicious and the new found friends were so eager to hear of what was transpiring in civilization, for their radios were useless by now.

They had left months ago and were living here in the mountains in caves, hunting and fishing and never hearing a word or seeing a soul, except for an occasional plane overhead. They had fled because of Stanos' persecution of their sect.

Upon discovering that one of the small family was a Rabbi, several set about to convert Perla to Christianity, arguing as only Jews can over the Messianic claims of Christ. They found him a worthy opponent and a knowledgeable man of the Scriptures, not about to be easily won over to their point of view.

Night had fallen quickly over the Jordanian mountains, and with their stomachs full once again of beets, rabbit and weak coffee, they turned in for the night.

The delicious smell of fish frying and the chattering of friendly voices awakened Moishe's cave early the next morning. They stretched and smiled at one another, while chatting happily, having found new friends, and then went to wash in the icy mountain water while a beautiful sunrise brightened their spirits.

Moishe discussed with the Christians' leader Ehu about Petra.

"Some of my partners wish to see the map and would like to study the possibilities with you this morning, if you can stay with us another day?" Ehu said seriously, earnestly imploring them to rest one more night.

"I have no special time that I have to get to Petra." Moishe smilingly answered, and spread out the cloth map on the ground, going over the journey they would take to the "Rock."

"It is a virtual fortress and will protect all of us. They have used the caves since before the flood of Noah's day and have carved the most beautiful cylindrical columns."

He went on to explain to the whole group, who had by now gathered to hear the exciting proposal, that the caves had been dug out centuries ago before King David's time, by the Edomites, who were the Arab nomadic descendants of Ishmael, Abraham's other son.

"These mountains were here when Moses led our forefathers across the Red Sea into the Wilderness. Moses knew of Petra. This is where Aaron, his mouthpiece died and was buried. This is where Moses struck the rock twice in the wilderness and the water came out. I have drunk water from that well by that rock at the mouth of the entrance to Petra. It is there now and the caves will accommodate thousands and afford us protection from every kind of pursuer except an atom bomb."

He added, "They will not drop bombs on us, for we are not that important."

Assuringly, Moishe went on to add, "We will be safe indefinitely, until deliverance comes one way or another, or until we can devise a further plan of escape somewhere else. It will give us safety and time to make our plans. We might find ourselves going out to Sea someday from Eilat or Aquaba, but we need time to plan it, and get us a ship. We have friends in the outer world who would help us if we can communicate with them."

They spent the day discussing it, eating again at the time of the evening meal. As supper ended, they began to sing softly and hum the nostalgic songs of Israel. Soon the whole encampment of nearly sixty persons was singing the national songs they loved so much.

Within a few moments several young former Israeli soldiers that Ya'er and David had become acquainted with, were up dancing the dances Israel is so famous for around the world. Soon two dozen were dancing around the fires, falling down over the uneven terrain and laughing and chattering in complete happiness, almost unaware of the circumstances that had brought them to the hills of Jordan outside their own country.

The next day, it was sixty people crawling, walking around mountains, down into valleys, foraging for food in the earth, and following Moishe as he led them further and further away from any known civilization. They were a peculiar, if not funny sight to behold. They had packed up frying pans, large water pots and were carrying these on strong backs for the next meals.

The Old Rabbi was bent low carrying his heavy load. No one suspected that he had over five thousand Israeli pounds in silver and gold coins, weighing nearly eighty pounds, hanging from various portions of his clothes. He had suspected long ago that the only money that would buy anything extra someday, would be silver or gold coins. He had no faith in "ECU," despised its usage and while being paid a pittance from the Israeli government for spiritual services rendered, had been saving for over six years all the gold and silver coins he could barter for or buy. He had scrimped, gone without clothes, and even cut down on their daily diet, to have these valuable coins that most people felt were worthless. He had convinced Miriam that these would save their lives someday and the lives of others. He was right.

Suddenly it happened. Stanos Papilos put forth a new edict from the Holy Temple, via his broadcasting facility, to all of Israel, the surrounding Arab states under his control, and to Europe. The essence of his new delirium was, "Take my new insignia upon your hand in order to secure your 'ECU' rights and savings." It was a tattoo for everyone.

It was a strange edict. Most had a very difficult time understanding what he was talking about, or why it was being presented so quickly and with such fierce determination. His men were everywhere, lining up "stamping stations," for Israelis and others to take an insignia mark, or emblem as he called it, upon the back of their right hand or on their forehead. It was a small prearranged number tattooed to either of these parts of the body. It meant you had then pledged your cooperation to his program, whether you liked it or not, and that you had been searched, your identity screened, and information gleaned from you as to your relatives, names and addresses. And finally, it meant that you understood that to withstand the orders or edicts of Stanos Papilos was to predict your own demise as soon as you were caught. This was your pledge of allegiance to the regime and rights of Papilos!

Taking the insignia mark or emblem, meant you have access to your ECU funds at any time, as usual. Not taking the emblem, meant you were in opposition to Stanos Papilos and his government, and you would not only be denied your rights as citizens, denied your savings or earnings, you would also lose your job, for no employer could employ anyone without the mark.[13] Anyone employing a man or woman without the emblem would be shot and his business given to relatives. That put relatives against relatives in some cases where there was little love and much to be gained by spying on one another for Stanos.

Everyone had sixty days to comply or be shot when found without the emblem. In this way, Stanos would round up all the underground Jews working against him who were still living in the cities of Israel, but mingling among the people as the P.L.O. had mingled among the Arabs in many sections of Israel prior to this time of Stanos' rule.

Within three days, hundreds of thousands of Israelis were lining up for the emblem. They were tattooed quickly and painlessly with an electronic device that did one person every minute. It was a black mark on your hand. You had your choice of the name PAPILOS to be marked there, or a number containing eighteen small digits, the last three digits being 666, or you could have the picture of a lamb on your hand, about one inch long and a half an inch deep. Each mark, name, or emblem measured the same. He had given everyone their choice, but you had to take one or the other.[14]

It would take weeks to do all Israel and then Papilos wanted all of Europe and Africa to do the same; but that could wait for now. His first intention in doing so was to round up the terrorists and their friends, who out of principle would not take the mark of pledging their allegiance to Stanos.

The mark was accepted by many as a "credit card" enabling them to buy or sell and enter into business. Without it, after the allotted time had elapsed, one could not do any kind of business. Eventually everyone had to have this mark to pay his rent or even have his utilities kept on. Stanos was thorough.

Thousands were rebelling as well. They had nearly two months to make up their minds, Stanos said. No violence till then . . . unless he changed his mind again, . . . Something he was not adverse to doing quickly these days as power went to his head and he seemed possessed by devils. Some of his men had said this quietly to Tonya, during her working hours at the computer center.

"He is mad," James Hunter said, sitting in Tonya's office early one morning. "I do not understand the boss any longer." He was obviously worried for himself personally and for everyone involved in the buildings.

"It seems like he is a possessed man. . . .15

"Possessed by what?" Tonya inquired with her brows knit in unbelief at what she was hearing from James.

"Possessed by demons, that's what. The man seems so normal at times, and then turns from a Dr. Jekyll to a Mr. Hyde—he's mad. He looks mad, his eyes are mad and he paces up and down his office like a panther in a cage, waiting to burst out with some new venture of evil like you wouldn't believe." James admitted.

"I have never disclosed this to anyone and only Aubrey knows, for he is constantly by his side these days," James confirmed.

"My mouth is shut and always has been." Tonya whispered. "I'm walking on eggs myself, for having turned him down for over two months now."

"He has other women to sleep with. Don't worry about his passion not being satisfied." James injected, knowing it wouldn't hurt Tonya any.

"Thank God he's leaving me alone." She answered with a gesture of thanksgiving with arms raised towards Heaven.

"The other night," James said, "I walked in on him. He was drinking heavily, walking up and down the Temple and yelling . . . "Where are you God? Damn you, God, anyway. There is no God. No God but power. Almighty power. My power. My power is God. My power is the only God!"

"You have got to be kidding!" Tonya shockingly replied.

"I wish you could see him in one of these fits."

"Does he have them often?"

"An average of . . . oh, say, once a week." The conversation ended abruptly, James spotting Stanos at the end of the long hall, just entering the office building.

Stanos walked straight into James Hunter's office and without smiling said, ''What's good for the mice is good for the cats . . . all the fat cats in here, I mean. Make sure they all know that they take the emblem right away, James.'' He walked out, leaving James terrified at what else he might have on his mind for them all.

When James reported the command to everyone that day, Tonya flew into a rage and went screaming down the hall into his office, slamming the door open. She found Aubrey and James sitting together shocked as she stormed in so unexpectedly.

''What the blue blazes are you yelling about?'' Aubrey sprung to his feet, angrily confronting Tonya with his hands clinched into fists.

''I am not taking that hideous mark on my body anywhere, not even there'' and she pointed to her rear end! James burst out laughing at her, happy that her anger wasn't over some other anticipated surprising danger that most of the time he expected to happen.

''God almighty Tonya,'' Aubrey said. ''You can con yourself into and out of more things than I have ever dreamed of with that man. If you don't want to take it, tell him . . . He lets you get away with absolute murder anyway!''

It ended with that, with James still laughing at the idea of having Tonya tattooed on her posterior. Before she left he said, ''Now about that location for the mark, . . . How in heaven's name do you plan on showing it in stores and gas stations to get petrol or groceries? Let me know when you do . . . cause I sure do want to photograph you doing it.''

She thumbed her pretty nose at him, smiled and walked out, somewhat cooled down by what Aubrey had said. It is true, she could pretty well have her own way over things. She would see to it this time, more than ever. . . . ''Seems like I was told something like this would happen in a letter from good old knowledgeable Uncle Steve living in Lake Tahoe, California. Lucky dog . . . Sure wish I was there.'' . . . Her mind drifted to the letter and she went and read it again. She read about the Mark of the Beast, a credit card that Steve suggested would come from Stanos or a compatriot. She was not to take it under any circumstances, and when she wanted to know why, she was simply to ask him or her father and they would tell her. [16]

It was time to call her father again. Calls had gone through rather regularly in the past three months, about once a week. She had said just enough to let him know all about the troubles firsthand, although most of what Stanos did was in the world press and Raymond and Charlotte knew what was going on daily. The London Times had arranged a "Government Column" and one of Stanos writers wrote for it daily, telling quite frankly what Stanos expected from England and her associated commonwealth nations.

"I'm frightened to death about the emblem, Dad." Tonya rapidly explained to her father during the call. "Yes, I am going to try to put it off and maybe I'll succeed. If anyone can, I think I can, but maybe not for long. Then what?"

Raymond felt that the day would come when this question would be put to him or Steve.

"Then you get out fast and furious, and don't worry about anything else. Just flee to the hills somewhere, or if you can, arrange to come here, it is safer than there for sure." Raymond expounded.

"Take some of your 'ECU' now and convert it to gold and silver coins quickly and unnoticed . . . do you understand?" He asked quietly.

"Yes, and I know why, too. I will . . . I will, Dad . . . quickly."

Raymond offered as much advice as he could risk on the phone and ended the conversation with the thought that he might come down and see her soon.

Tonya felt so much better. Just to talk to her father gave her strength— strength she was going to need.

Down in the valleys of Jordan's southern wilderness, nearly sixty souls wearily wended their way through desert land and tough mountainous country, enroute to the mystical and ellusive Petra. Twice they had thought they were there only to be disappointed. One night, an old Bedouin tending his flock of sheep was startled by their procession. They had heard the sheep in the distance and the thought of lamb cooking in their giant pot gave everyone goose bumps just dreaming of it.

After a short period of convincing the old shepherd they meant him no harm, he told them how to get to Petra, twenty miles to the southeast. They were too far west!

He also informed them there were Bedouins living there, with horses and food and water. They were to tell them that Taleb had sent them from the hills to the north. They would be friendly and would welcome them, especially if they would pay for whatever they received in coins.

Rejoicing, they bought a fatted lamb from the Arab, prepared it, and cooked it skewer style over the fire. Singing and dancing followed, scaring the sheep half to death, Taleb said. But he danced an Arab dance with them and shared his hatred for Stanos with Moishe.

By late afternoon, the next day, just as the hot summer day sun was slipping behind the Jordanian Mountains for another day leaving the valleys cooler and darker, they came to the Rock. The water was flowing, just as Moishe had said. They could see Bedouins in the distance watching them as they approached. They were cautious, wondering who might be lurking among the Arabs feeling totally antagonistic toward runaway Jews. But their own guns were showing, automatic rifles slung over shoulders, as they approached the wall.

A tall dark, swarthy Bedouin surprised them as he stepped out from behind a mountain crevice and motioned them to come and drink.

"Drink." He said it in Hebrew, smiling, knowing how thirsty and tired they were.

Ehu spoke to him in Arabic and discovered that Petra was still two miles inside the canyon, and motioned for Moishe to come and get further details from the friendly shepherd.

Just as he did, everyone heard a sudden roar of engines at the same time. They looked up, and to their shock and amazement discovered two planes circling above. They were Israeli jets, obviously being flown by Stanos' men.

Screaming at everyone to take cover in the many crevices in the mountain beside the well, Moishe and Ehu pushed the women out of their petrified state and Moishe virtually threw Ruth, Dianna, Sarah and Miriam out of the way of the plummeting plane spitting gunfire as it came plunging out of the heavens with a thundering roar.

Machine gun fire was everywhere. It kicked up the stones and shot them in a thousand directions. The dust rose fifty feet in the air from the pressure of the bullets ricochetting in every direction of the hard packed ground, hitting the mountains around all of them.

The second plane followed repeating the same movements. Miraculously, no one was hit.

The women screamed in terror, feeling that all was going to be lost as they were attacked again and again, but each time the pilots could not penetrate into the mountain crevasses.

It took darkness to send the diving planes back to Jerusalem. Stanos' men knew of this little band of nomadic Jews now, and might even send others down with heavy armour to get at them.

"It would take some time for them to route us out, and they know it." Moishe comforted all. "We have time and God's mountains on our side. Let's go." He led the way into the mountain crevasses no wider than a car in most places as the evening darkness fell.

No sooner had they entered the canyon way then they heard the sound of horses hoofs on rocks, coming hard and fast right at them! Three Arabs on fleet-footed steeds reared up and stopped. Everyone was surprised. The Arabs were shocked at finding Jews and the Jews looked petrified at this new unexpected event. They were wary of everything by now. The men had their guns down and pointed at all three Arabs. It was a sight to behold!

The Arabs threw up their hands in surrender and immediately prayed to Allah to preserve them. They screamed, "Don't shoot us . . . we mean no harm. We have come in peace . . . Don't shoot!" They said it in clear Hebrew.

Moishe motioned for them to get down, which they did. He explained they were coming into Petra for refuge to the caves and needed food and horses. He informed them he would pay in gold and silver.

He motioned for them to turn and lead the way, expressing to them, that if they cooperated, no one meant them any harm. They would and could work together.

It was almost another forty-five minutes before the canyon broadened and the exclamations of delight and bewilderment from the Jews brought pleasure to the Arabs.

The Bedouins laughed as they walked their Arabian steeds, pointing and shouting all manner of names for the caves and carvings surrounding this pathetic group of tourists. They stood with eyes beholding, but minds unbelieving the modern-like structures of the carvings in the red-rose mountain walls. It went as far as your eye could see. There were marvelous carvings everywhere. Whoever had accomplished such a feat, did it forever, and though it was certainly not like home in any way, they discovered they could climb up the rocks easily and enter the dark caves carved out by hand. They had found the place where humans had dwelled in the "Rock Fortress" before.

At that moment, Bedouins came out of the rocks everywhere. They had been watching all that was transpiring, but were frightened seeing the Jewish guns.

The Jews waved to them and told them to come—they had nothing to fear. It took but a few minutes to let these understanding people know what had gone on. They were told of Stanos' latest move. They knew him alright.

Silver coins were brought out and laid on the ground. It surprised the old Rabbi how many people had coins. But he kept his to himself for the time being. Even Moishe and Ya'er were carrying a heavy load of them, believing that someday man's intrinsic love for gold and silver would help buy them whatever they needed in an emergency. They were proven right on this occasion. "ECU" meant absolutely nothing to these people—they wanted nothing to do with it.

Moishe wasn't bargaining to buy the caves, but for the Bedouins to get them some food and water quickly and build fires for the wanderers, also for them to tell him where the good caves were.

Immediately, they dispersed, travelling fast on horseback and running in several directions while the Jews made their way down through the canyon floor as it broadened out.

In less than two hours, everyone was situated temporarily for the night, and a great fire was roaring at one end of the settlement— where the Arabs were cooking for the nearly sixty newcomers to Petra.

They were safe at last, and on the morrow would discuss sustenance, living and protection with the Bedouins, whose presence so far was certainly a blessing to all concerned.

After a night on some old army cots, the women couldn't believe how wonderful they felt not having to sleep on the ground. The men had been given blankets for a price in silver equal to many times their value. But at least they had proper coverings and were warm.

The next morning the Bedouins were back with a sloppy creamy-like substance in a milk can that you ate cold. No doubt it was something mixed with goat's milk, for there were hundreds of goats to be seen everywhere in the Arab section.

They were trying now to get Jerusalem news, or any news they could understand on the radio they had brought with them.

With a series of crackling noises and then a loud crack, it died! News from the outside world was out, unless they could repair the radio.

Dependence on the Arabs for news would be their only hope. That too would cost money. There was no love here on the part of the two groups, but money would keep them together.

---

1. Revelation 13:1-6.
2. Daniel 8:24.
3. Revelation 13:4.
4. Daniel 11:33.
5. Daniel 11:31.
6. Daniel 11:45.
7. 2 Thessalonians 2:1-8.
8. Revelation 6:6.
9. Joel 2:1-11.
10. Matthew 24:10.
11. Luke 21:12-13, 16.
12. Revelation 12:13-17.
13. Revelation 13:16-18.
14. Revelation 13:18.
15. Revelation 13:2.
16. Revelation 14:9.

Chapter
8

Lake Tahoe

Lake Tahoe

Steve Scott and family, with their maid Emily had moved to South Lake Tahoe. For some time, while all the excitement was going on in Jerusalem, they had lived in a lovely rented house fully furnished, right on the gorgeous lake itself, so pure you could drink it anytime. They loved it.

Steve bought a boat, large enough for them all to sleep on if necessary, with a small inside cabin, head, cooking unit and a fly bridge. The boat was twenty-four feet long and the family loved to ski or just ride, exploring the lake. It was all so beautiful.

But as world news got steadily worse and Steve knew what was coming, they searched feverishly for some suitable spot away from prying eyes, where they could live at peace and be away from coming anarchy and violence in the streets of America.

They found their spot hidden just inside a section known to boaters as Emerald Bay, where there was an island in the middle of the bay. Boaters ski there often in the shelter of the cove.

Steve and Jeff gave it a thorough going over from every vantage point, before unanimously deciding this was it for their future.

They showed Pam and Marsha one day and told them of their plan to build there as quickly and quietly as possible, away from all prying eyes and would-be government interlopers.

The girls did not see how they were going to have anything to live in there, but the two men, father and son, set about getting the job done.

They had discovered an access by road in the interior part of the forest, through the mountains north of Emerald Bay. It had been a road cut primarily for forest fires and protection. They would use it to bring in the necessary lumber, furniture, and other belongings.

Renting a dump truck and buying lumber cut to size was not necessarily what Jeff had in mind working with his father, but they plunged into the tremendous task of cabin building and enjoyed it.

Load after load of lumber, shingles, insulation, roofing, nails, sink, pipes of steel and plastic, were dumped at the campsite away from the main road by at least two miles, and away from the lake shore by three hundred feet. It was nicely hidden in the thick foliage and tall trees.

It seemed like nature had already carved out the spot in the midst of some giant oak trees. Within one month everything visible was done to the outside and three quarters of what had to be done inside was accomplished.

No wiring was required in the cabin but the plumbing was in, as primitive as it was. The men had built a large water container at the edge of the roof, but placed just below it. Nearly all the rain water from the roof would pour into it. Melting snows would fill it, too. Steve placed a large mirror there, to help melt the snow.

"Ingenious honey!" Pam smiled at Steve . . . "I'm going to love bathing in dirty rain water." she laughed.

"Better than going dirty, my love, or washing in the snow."

The work proceeded nicely, and while the men put the finishing touches on their woodsy cabin, the women put away the many non-perishable food stuffs they had brought in rather large quantities—several large bags of flour, sugar, powdered milk and cream, powdered eggs, dehydrated meats, beans, fruits, vegetables, and so on.

Within two months the food was in place, the cabin relatively completed, the beds were in, along with odd pieces of furniture. Steve had turned in the rented truck and bought himself a large four-wheel drive station wagon, which had a tremendous ability to navigate through almost any amount of snow or sand.

The boat was safely moored behind a wall of brush and wooden planking the boys had built out into the water, completely hiding it from anyone passing by, close or far. It formed a boat garage on the water.

Their next task was to run a water line into the lake, hidden in the underbrush, where they could pump water into the house and reservoirs when needed with Steve's new diesel motor.

A separate shed had been built for the wagon, motor and two skiddos, which they felt would give them some fun in the cold winter.

Pam had magazines, books, games, peanuts, and dried fruits put in for the winter.

They finally moved in, with enough oil for the fuel burning unit in the middle of the cabin to last the winter, along with plenty of wood. They had saved all the shavings and had built a small fireplace of cast iron into one of the walls for a little atmosphere and additional warmth from freezing cold nights.

"We have enough toilet paper to wipe the town of South Lake Tahoe," Jeff said jokingly, "and enough toothpaste and aspirins to clean our teeth for five years, and drive out headaches for ten!" He exclaimed laughing at their inventory of goods and things.

"We'll need them and maybe more." Steve looked at him frankly. "We might have company, or who knows what might go wrong."

"I love our television, Father." Marsha Ann beamed.

"Well, we cannot watch it all the time. The batteries will give out. I have others, but that is the one thing we want to keep alive so we can keep in touch with the world."

"What do you think will really happen, honey?" Pam asked honestly, as much for the children, as her own sake.

"There will be a depression, and then much hunger, unemployment, maybe even starvation, and then robbery and stealing. No one will be able to trust anyone and the old and infirm will be the worst off.

"I expect that Stanos could attack here in full force and if he does we might be safe and we might not. But, we have the greatest chance of survival away from the busy inhabited, populated areas. It will be a long time before we are even spotted here, and chances are, we are so remote no one will ever bother to come after us, even if some guy in a plane does see our smoke curling up in the winter." Steve assured them.

Christopher Columbus, what a story this will make someday!" Jeff chimed in. "I hope I live to tell the story to my grandchildren, Dad!"

They were set for the winter with all supplies in. It was now time for Steve to go to town for perhaps the last time and phone Raymond in London.

Shortages were evident everywhere, and the casinos had closed down. South Lake Tahoe was looking more and more like a ghost town everytime he drove in. The snow was falling lightly and the weather was getting colder every day.

It seemed like the place was almost deserted today as Steve and Jeff drove into town to make the call. It had to be collect now . . . No one was receiving silver or gold coins much for phone calls, and he couldn't charge it to his room or home phone. He didn't have any. To use his "ECU" account would reveal where he was. That made Steve feel strange.

He finally got through to London catching Raymond and Charlotte in bed for the night. A sleepy Raymond answered and bolted up out of bed as soon as he heard it was collect from Steve.

"Where are you, old man?" he affectionately called Steve.

"In South Lake Tahoe calling you . . . Sorry for the collect call. I'll have to do this from here on in, for I have no phone. I'll pay you later for the calls."

"Don't be ridiculous, man. I want to hear from you as much as you want to call me. I'll pay for the calls; you just make sure you call. What is happening in the States?"

"Not a lot yet. There are shortages everywhere, and the beginnings of a terrible depression, as you know. Everyone is out of work, it seems, or maybe about one quarter of the population anyway, and there is already a lot of violence. We are lucky, we are hidden away and hopefully God will protect us during the terrible time coming. What is happening with you, and what about Tonya . . . I am dying to know what is going on with that niece of mine."

"We are safe here in London, so far. Stanos is trying to make us all here and in Europe take his insignia mark, as you heard. It is not going well. The English people resist being branded like cattle. The Queen is leading the revolt with all Parliament agreeing. I am not sure that armed resistance won't spring up here keeping the British, Scots and Irish from taking it. [1] The Irish are indignant at the very idea and scoff at the soldiers in the streets. They went on a murdering rampage yesterday and killed every one of Stanos' soldiers in Belfast . . . It was beautiful." Raymond chuckled.

"Tonya is safe, but she's in the lion's den every day. She called two days ago and may run away any time now. She got your letter and, of course, will not take the mark at all. She really doesn't understand the danger, but says she hates Stanos, and won't take it for any reason. Jews are fleeing all over Jerusalem to the surrounding hills and she might have to go to. I told her about your gold and silver coin idea. She's getting some in Israel through the black market.

"If things get worse there, I'm going down to get her out somehow. I may have to send Charlotte to you. Would you mind?" Raymond asked politely, but the tone of his voice indicated he was worried.

"I wish you both would come and bring Tonya Rae as well." Steve answered hurriedly and excitedly. "We have food, a lovely hideaway that I built with my own hands, and you are all welcome."

They chatted on for a few moments about the rapid fulfillments in prophecy, and promised to pray for one another. Steve would call again in perhaps another two weeks about the same time.

Steve and Jeff drove back to the cabin in the first snowstorm of the season.

Within another two weeks, unemployment was at a record high. In the North Eastern sections, where the heaviest weight of the unemployed was felt, there was not a street where anyone felt safe. It was every man for himself. The President declared martial law, and called out the National Guard. There was violence everywhere, with the elderly not going out of their homes. Grocery stores were constantly robbed and thieves were smashing into every conceivable type of food establishment to get food for their families and friends.

The press couldn't keep up with the home news. If Stanos had wanted to attack this would have been the time. But he was waiting for America to destroy itself. He had cut off all oil from the Middle East.

Those who had heeded warnings before and had gotten out of the big cities were making it the best. Some had gone to well-stocked mountain and desert retreats. Others had taken to their boats and were living safely offshore or on the high seas.

America was in a deep depression, brought on in less than four months after Stanos cut off the oil supply.

The government had confiscated most of the available oil for military and government usage. "The military came first," they said, and mentioned that preparedness was mandatory for the well-being of all citizens, especially if Stanos' armies and navy attacked the U.S.A.

Within a few short weeks, industries were clamouring at the government to release fuel, oil, and natural gas, for industrial purposes. They refused. Powerful lobbyists pressuring friendly congressmen and senators in Washington got nowhere.

The government was adamant. They were saving the energy sources on hand in case of an all-out attack against America. They would not budge.

The richest of the countries' insurance companies that invested heavily in large industries were getting it in the neck both ways. Millions of dollars of interest was no longer coming in from billions invested in American industries, and literally hundreds of thousands of insurance purchasers were cashing in their policies just to live! Insurance giants lost capital, interest and now the investors.

Central computer houses could not keep up with the workload of bankrupt businesses, nor could the courts process the papers for businessman and householders declaring bankruptcy. Confusion reigned supreme, and the theme of the hour was not making money or having a job, it was "How do we eat this month?" For many, it was "How do we eat this week?" For millions more it was, "How do we eat together, today?"

Families in America were living on one meal a day by the time seven months had passed. The American dream had vanished in such a short time. It was unbelievable.

Cars were abandoned as people walked where they wished to go, which usually wasn't far. Hotels and motels closed by the thousands, as vacations and travel became a thing of the past. Beach resorts and Nevada gambling houses closed until further notice.

Every industry you could think of was affected drastically. Only basic food producing and processing plants stayed open, with government inspectors and the National Guard protecting them. It wasn't the employees anyone would hurt, but the food they wanted so badly would be ripped off.

That was a strange phenomena. If you worked in a food production plant, you were considered extremely important and everybody respected you, and wanted to be your friend! I wonder why? . . .

Unions lost their power and tried to suave the feelings of their men by dolling out millions of union dollars to keep them alive. But that money was running out fast.

Coal miners were working long hours. Jobs were being created in related energy industries, and oil companies were drilling as fast as possible everywhere oil or natural gas might be!

If the nation could survive this year or maybe eighteen months, nearly everyone in political power or important energy sources felt they could recover. If Stanos did not attack, and they could keep some semblance of sanity on the streets and cohesiveness in the country's people, America would make it.

Steve Scott felt terrific about the decision to live where they were. Lost in their little beautiful wilderness of Lake Tahoe, they had peace of mind, good food, uninterrupted quietness, lots of good books to read and games to play with one another.

Charlotte had finally flown over from London and Steve found himself picking her up in the San Francisco airport. It was one of his few, brief glances at civilization since the Great Depression had struck. Charlotte was hostile at first to the idea but finally had agreed when Raymond said he had out-of-town work to accomplish. He would be away from London periodically, leaving her alone. She quickly fell in love with the Lake even though it was deep in snow late this spring.

They had survived their first winter. The fuel lasted well; they even had hot baths twice a week, and that was an accomplishment for cabin dwellers without electricity. The oil pump never stopped.

The occasional times Steve drove around the lake in their four-wheel drive wagon with the family that spring was a real delight for them all.

Then one day Steve and the family went driving up the east shore of Lake Tahoe toward a look out point they had picked as a favorite to stop and look at the beautiful mountains and snow contrasted with the serenity of the deep blue lake reflecting the blue of the sky that day.

Just as they pulled up they saw in front of them a gang of about twenty motorcycle riders with their typical black leather jackets and long straggly hair hanging everywhere and the longest beards he had ever witnessed on young people. They had all packed their bikes heavily with sleeping gear, cooking utensils and fishing gear. Girls were enmeshed in between the hair and beards on the bikes. They all pulled up together and when Steve's lonely wagon pulled in, they encircled it immediately.

"Everybody stay inside and lock all doors . . . Jeff make sure the twin back doors are locked and bolted from the inside." Steve took control of the situation as readily as he would a patient in an emergency. What his family didn't know about his heart beating like a machine gun at that moment wouldn't hurt them. Perspiration immediately popped out on his brow as the apparent leader of the group got off his bike and nonchalantly walked over to Steve's side front view window and motioned for him to open it and talk.

Steve hesitantly cracked it two inches and waited for the bushy haired freak to speak. He was covered with ice particles hanging from his beard and long hair and was a mess of filth and grime.

"Get out, we want to talk to you." He gruffly commanded.

Steve snarled an angry, "No way!"

"I don't want to have to pull you out of that wagon man, but I will if I have to!" He screamed his fury at Steve's non-compliance. He motioned for his accomplices to move in closer.

Now they were all staring in the wagon trying to see beyond the quickly fogging windows to see what supplies or whatever else they could find of value inside.

"Ain't nothin' in there." One bearded bike rider, slightly shorter than the leader, complained.

"So what, this wagon will bring us a pretty piece, you fool." The leader was looking at the wheels of Steve's wagon, and the chains he was wearing to get them through the unplowed roads he had to go on.

"Get out now!" The burly one screamed getting angrier at Steve. He cursed with excellent proficiency and banged on Steve's door suddenly trying to open it.

Suddenly, without a warning emanating from his lips or a change of his expression, the doctor went into action.

He swiftly released his left foot on the clutch and slammed his right foot to the floorboard spinning the wagon's wheels and twisting the wagon's position. The wheels dug in and feeling the chains grappling with the loose snow getting down to where the well packed hard snow was, he yelled, "Hold on tight everybody . . . we're getting out of here and this mess now!"

"Blackbeard" fell tumbling in the snow piled high round about—obviously hurt and shaken by the wagon knocking him head first. He was lucky the snow was there.

Four of his gang were sprawled out in the banks of snow trying to clean off their goggles. The girls screamed obscenities at Steve as he drove right for them frightening them to death that he was going to kill them. Steve slammed on his brakes, skidded the wagon to a stop, twisting it again as he made a complete turn before any of them could even reach for their guns or bikes.

In moving as fast as he had, they had sprawled themselves into the deep snow to avoid being hit and had literally dove out of his reckless way as he spun the tires and twisted his steering wheel to throw the wagon completely around on the icy snow.

It took less than five seconds to gain momentum. The chains grabbed the hard packed snow again, and Steve was off down the hill gaining speed while trying to hold the wagon straight.

Cursing him madly, the group leaped on their bikes and came screaming after him, snow blowing everywhere, bikes slipping out from underneath them in their hurry to catch him.

Steve had noticed guns stuck in their belts, and that had motivated him to action. Prior to that, he was going to try to talk them out of it.

The dangerous chase was on. Jeff was up front with his father. Marsha Ann clung to her mother on one side, and Charlotte lunged for Pam's free side as they slid from side to side in the wagon clutching one another for anchorage. They were now screaming, frightened out of their wits.

"Shut up everybody." Steve grimaced loudly overriding their screaming with his powerful voice. The wagon careened wildly down the snow covered roads. Snow was blowing twenty feet high outside the windows, and to make matters worse, it started to snow and was blowing wildly in front of them. Steve had to slow down to see where he was going and where the road curved. It was all he could do to go twenty miles an hour. The snow was coming down heavily.

The gang had one advantage over him. He was breaking the trail in front of their bikes. The girls started shooting, while the guys did the treacherous demanding two-handed driving of those big bikes which also had chains on.

With the bikes swerving and bouncing on the snow, the girls couldn't get a straight shot so far. Steve was counting on that fact. They were gaining on him quickly as the road was a maze of twists and turns worse than Steve had ever remembered. But you don't think of those things when driving leisurely.

"Everybody lay down on the floor." Steve screamed as they carved out another treacherous curve. The gang was closing and so were the shots.

"Jeff, you are going to be the rear gunner man . . . Shoot their bikes, rather than them if you can . . . But don't worry if you hit them . . . Try not to kill them . . . aim low . . . hit their legs . . ." Steve was breathlessly giving Jeff orders while Jeff was reaching for the automatic rifle laying between them on the floor. They always had it in the wagon loaded.

"Hand me the other gun, Jeff." Jeff handed his father a handgun, fully loaded, from the glove compartment.

"I'll roll the window down some, you lay the gun over the back seat and fire when you think you can hit them. If they aren't stopped, they'll kill us for sure." Steve started to slowly activate his back window button on the panel.

The bearded leader was pulling up close. Behind him came the angry gang—slipping, sliding, cursing and shooting as rapidly as they could reload their handguns.

A bullet crashed through the back window into the front window shattering it slightly on Jeff's side. No one was hit. They were closing the gap. Bullets were coming steadily closer, hitting various parts of the wagon.

Jeff started to fire nervously, but cautiously. He blew one gang member clear off his bike and the girl went with him spinning and crashing into the snow and off the road. Blood covered the girl's face sitting behind him.

Suddenly, the leader closed the gap from him to Steve's side at the front of the wagon and pulled out his gun crazily attempting to control his bike with one hand as he shot at Steve simultaneously. He missed, but the shot was close to the top of the wagon. Steve sweat badly.

Steve eased the pressure on the accelerator and then swerved the wagon hard to the left just as the leader of the gang pulled up for a close shot in the raging blizzard by Steve's left hand. The wagon hit the front wheel of his bike sending it left and the leader right. His body crashed into the wagon with a dull thud, and his cycle sped down an embankment smashing below. Steve could hardly hold the wagon. The rear end was equal to the front end on the road. They were sliding sideways facing the gang on their right side which was the passenger side. Only the momentum of the car was keeping them moving and from going down the steep embankment themselves.

Jeff turned the gun and fired another round hitting two of them in their stomachs dropping them into the snow as their bikes collided with one another. "Four down and about sixteen to go!" He yelled wildly!

The gang had to slow down themselves or hit Steve's wagon. Then with a twirl of the wheel back to the right and slapping on the brakes for a second, then speeding up, with massive bursts of acceleration Steve turned the wagon frontwards again amidst the screaming of women and slamming of the bullets from the gang through the car smashing windows and hitting the post over Steve's head.

Jeff opened fire again downing several in the sprinkle of sporadic firing. He watched them topple to the road to be hit by a couple of bikes right behind, all of them spinning into the snow.

Five more were still coming, cursing and determined to avenge the action against them.

Just as they burst ahead and had almost overtaken Steve—their guns aimed at his gas tank area—Steve slammed on his brakes full force holding the wheel while the car spun again in a complete circle on the snow and hard packed under ice. All five bikes hit the car at high speed. They hit with such an impact, the occupants of the wagon thought they were coming through right into their laps.

With screaming everywhere, the bikes crashed, then slammed to the snow and slid in every direction with their cursing, bleeding occupants doing the same.

Shots still rang wild around them as they managed to get the wagon moving again. With nearly every window knocked out by gunfire, and the wagon riddled with bullets, they drove to the main road leading from Reno to South Lake Tahoe, not stopping to analyze the damage. They were headed home, laughing and crying—wiping tears mixed with sweat, thanking God they were all alive but still scared to death.

"My son! Oh God, thank you for helping him be a good shot!" Pam rejoiced hugging him so lovingly. They all hugged one another and fell on their knees after that battered, beat up wagon, pulled into their partially snow plowed drive . . . safe within the warmth of their home fires.

As Steve hugged Jeff, he drew his arm away staring at his hand covered with blood.

"I know, I've been hit. It isn't fatal . . . I'll live, mother! They hit me in the shoulder, but I don't feel a thing right now. I'm alright."

Raymond heard about the rendezvous with near death for his wife and the Scott family two nights later in a long distance phone call.

Learning that all was now well there in their hidden seclusion, he said, "I am leaving for Jerusalem in a week or two to see Tonya. She called last week and all is fine with her for the time being. Tell Steve Tonya's too smart to take the insignia but that it is being enforced slowly but surely here in England and in Europe. I will not be available after two weeks from tonight for about a month. I want to spend that much time in Jerusalem with Tonya. We have much to talk about—something I am planning."

Raymond had been scheming for some time. "There must be a way to get her out of that fiend's clutches before it's too late," he muttered to himself.

Water had to be the answer, he reasoned. If you could only get a small inconspicuous boat and follow the coast line down the Mediterranean Sea from Tel Aviv or some other port city or town, then with enough food and fuel you could arrive at Alexandria in Egypt, and either take a larger boat out or fly home from Cairo with some gold coins to black market the provisions and passage.

Sixteen days later he was safely in Tonya's apartment, having a lovely dinner served by two waiters in deluxe fashion.

They talked way into the morning hours after Raymond checked the rooms for wiretapping and hidden microphones, but found none.

"He wouldn't do that to me . . . not yet anyway." Tonya assured him. "Stanos feels I am with him to an extent and so far trusts me to do his bidding. I have never done otherwise, and I work hard for him. No one has ever kept him so up-to-date with inventories of the varied national productions as I have.''

''What is he going to do about the American idealist President?''

''So far as I know now, nothing.'' She answered. ''He has all he can handle with Africa, Europe and parts of Western Asia. He cannot control the world overnight. My opinion is that he will do nothing about America until all is really under his control here . . .'' He frowned and looked surprised.

''Everyone is supposed to take the emblem or insignia, and I have acted too busy till now. James Hunter hasn't either, but everyone else in the employ of Stanos Papilos has, and they are beginning to look at the two of us like we are weirdos.''

''Why hasn't Mr. Hunter taken it?'' He asked inquisitively.

''That is a good question. I have never asked him why, nor he me. But I will one of these days, if we last much longer.'' She laughed nervously.

Late that night and on into the morning hours, Raymond discussed his plan of escape with Tonya. He told her of his idea to buy a boat and hire a crew, slip down the coast unnoticed, and escape through Egypt. She went for the idea, but wanted to wait as long as possible before doing so. For the more she worked, the more gold she would have to leave with.

Raymond told her of Charlotte's being in Lake Tahoe and the terrible encounter with the gang. He also said he felt the safest place for them all to go apart from the United States with Steve, would be, in his studied opinion, Australia, New Zealand, or as a last resort, Tasmania, lying off the south coast of Australia. They could be safe there until the time was up, or the world recovered. According to the prophecies in the Bible, Stanos had but two years to go and maybe less, depending on how you chronicled the timing of prophecy. He was only to reign as dictator for three and a half years, and was either two or two and a half years into it now. [2] The end was to bring the return of Jesus Christ as the world's Messiah. [3]

To this Tonya could only reply, . . . ''Pipe dreams, Dad . . . Let's be realistic. You believe in a mystical Messiah, I believe in me and you. If we get out of here, then maybe I'll think about religion. This man Stanos doesn't evoke any religious conviction in me at all.''

Tonya finally disclosed to her father why this was not the time for her to leave. She invited James Hunter over for a late dinner. When James arrived, dressed beautifully in his American silk suit and matching ensemble, he was pleased again to meet Raymond Morgan. The evening progressed very nicely through dinner.

When the stewards had departed, Tonya unorthodoxly put her feet up on the coffee table while relaxing after dinner and proceeded with her fascinating secret disclosure.

"We are going to blow up his international computers and sabotage the entire National Inventory Division, leaving him without a clue as to what is going on in every one of the twenty-five nations he controls. It would smash his plan to take over the world. We have carefully laid out how James and I and one other person can do it. You could be that other person Dad, if you care to" . . . She paused hopefully . . . "And I know we can trust you never to divulge what you have heard here tonight."

Before his shocked but controlled expression, they disclosed the actual plan enthusiastically, like two kids excited over a new discovery, and they stunned him with the enormity of it all . . .

"I'm interested, go on!"

"Here's how you fit in, Dad. We need special plastic explosives brought here of a very sophisticated nature, but with the capabilities to do the job. The center is over one hundred feet long and the same wide. It will take powerful small explosives that neither James nor I can get our hands on. They have to be brought into the country, or gotten somewhere within this country without anyone knowing. We cannot trust our own shadows!"

"I know absolutely nothing about explosives." Raymond sighed dejectedly, while leaning back staring wishfully at the ceiling dreaming for a moment.

"But I am darn well going to learn," he confirmed determinedly. He walked over to Jim shaking his hand. "I'm with you all the way, partner . . ." He hugged Tonya as they rejoiced in their new found relationship to complete the ambitious program of disassembling the total computer network of this world dictator.

"We need you, Mr. Morgan, . . . Raymond, if I may call you that" . . . James added assuredly. "We need you because you have access in and out of here as her father. You can be legitimately visiting your daughter for any reason, and each time you come you bring plastic explosives hidden somehow on you. Not even the scanner x-ray machines at the airport will pick it up on you.'' He explained logically.

''The plan might work.'' Raymond reasoned. ''But I would first go back and give up my practice and set my house in order there. Secondly,'' his systematic mind was in focus now. ''I'll have to learn all I can about explosives, systems, wiring, detonating . . . I know absolutely nothing . . . but I will learn.''

They talked three more nights at length about the plan, the needs, how to communicate on the phone without ever mentioning it. Their secret word for explosives would be ''your practice.'' How is ''your practice'' going Father. ''Sounds very realistic to a doctor from his daughter.'' Tonya laughed. No one could ever pick up on that. An affirmative answer would mean he was gathering fuel for the fire, and a negative one meant he had not succeeded yet . . .

Raymond left and went back to London. He could easily turn his practice over to his subordinates who loved him for what he was trying to do for the needy in England. He would close up the house when necessary, and in the meantime, try through British military contacts in England to discover the most practical method for blowing up a multi-billion dollar kingdom of the ''Beast from Jerusalem'' without disclosing why.

Tonya and James kept up their daily responsibilities. Only once had Stanos approached her about taking the insignia. It was on one of their infrequent dates, and while holding her hand after dancing and dining out at one of his favorite Tel Aviv establishments, he commented on it.

She shrugged very unhappily, trying to cover her intense nervousness over the subject. She didn't think he cared about it, as long as she was doing a good job for him. It was those he couldn't trust . . . the Jews, that he was trying to ferret out. Not her, she argued quietly.

He became very angry with her, to the extent that they promptly left the restaurant without finishing the next dance. While in the car, she attempted to assuage him by becoming amorous. She succeeded.

Tonya spent the night with Stanos in the Holy Temple, dreading every moment of it, and not sleeping one wink after he was through satisfying his own intense hunger for her.

She could not believe she had succumbed to him again, having vowed never to do so again. But if the plan was to succeed, no sacrifice would be too great. This was her way of getting even, it was her revenge and a revenge the whole world could enjoy once they had accomplished it. She would actually be freeing nations and turning Stanos' wicked dictatorial control upside down. It would take armies months to reestablish control once the world knew and the word was out that his computers no longer bullied them. It might mean war . . . big war . . . for him to conquer all that he stood to lose, should they be successful. "But, how could he ever put such an operation back together again without losing billions of pounds . . . dollars . . . ECU . . . and support? . . . The immensity of the consequences of the destruction was incomprehendable . . . and worth her night of infamy," she thought as she lay there next to the "Beast."

She evidently spared herself the problem of Stanos worrying about her not taking his emblem. He never mentioned it again though he expected more from her from that point on, and most of the time, for fear of him, he got what he wanted. She hated this "Man of Sin." [4] But her inner feelings were rising for James. They had only managed to meet three times thus far, but each time it was beautiful, and he made no physical demands on her.

Moishe and his "children of Israel," were safe and in Petra for the time being, as long as their silver coins held out. They had brought many with them and of course, Moishe and the Rabbi had pooled theirs, laughingly.

Suddenly one morning, an Arab came screaming into their mountain pass down to where the Beduoins were working near their caves. He seemed frightened to death. Moishe ran over to listen, understanding most of what they were saying. He paused and waved to Sarah and the boys to stay back where they were. He finally ran back to the encampment of Israelis.

"We may have a lot of company here." He shouted to everyone. "Several thousand Israelis appear headed in this direction. Stanos has a new proclamation out in the country. Everyone was to come to the Temple to worship an idol creation [5] of his. Some religious leader in Europe had a statue presented to Stanos of himself and they placed it in the Temple Court on behalf of Stanos and his marvelous accomplishments. [6]

"Now, everyone is to pay homage to him by bowing in front of the statue. [7] Those taking the insignia are doing it alright, but the others fled overnight.[8] That was about five days ago. They are headed in this direction through central Jordan." Moishe explained excitedly. [9]

"What do you think is going to happen?" Ya'er asked his father with a worried expression.

"Where? Here?"

"No, in Jerusalem." Ya'er pointed out.

"He's going to have a nation of robots serving him as a God, that's what's going to happen. Those opposing him will be killed or will get out. And they will have to get out fast."[10] Moishe said grimly.

"Would they know about Petra, Moishe?" Rabbi Perla asked compassionately.

"We knew about it because of my tours down here. Others would have to know about it for the same reason, or have read about it in some of the journals or papers telling about the "Rock." Lots of people would know about Petra, without ever having been here." They took five hour shifts on the mountain top from that hour on.

An electrifying shout came on the third day. In his binoculars the man on the peak shouted down, "They are coming. They're about a mile away and there are thousands of them. It's a long line and it never seems to end. . . ."

With Moishe and the Rabbi leading, they went out to meet the weary travelers.

It was a tearful, yet happy meeting as they jabbered to one another in Hebrew, hearing the story of the proposed idol worship set for the day after they left the Holy Temple. The news had gone out that day over radio and television that all Jews were to start coming to the Temple by their names in alphabetical order the next day to worship and pay homage to Stanos.

"He's gone stark raving mad!" Their exhausted leader had said. "He is blaspheming the God of Israel.[11] He killed a thousand Arabs praying in their mosque on the West Bank with machine guns as they came out on Friday night."

Stanos had chased them for three days with his soldiers looking everywhere and finding some. They immediately shot them. But as they melted into the mountainside during the day in caves, they had been safe, and in one case literally hundreds of Stanos' men in the valley had been covered by a landslide of rock and sand, as an avalanche hit them from above.[12]

Another man said the soldiers had to be blind; they had walked right by them in their caves and never once ventured in nor looked in their direction. It was as if they had not seen the opening of the caves at all, and inside were over five hundred people packed like sardines!

Other miraculous stories of escape filtered out,[13] but time enough for that later, Moishe said.

They asked for a joint session of all that night early after dinner. Thousands came and milled around, after their meal, by the giant fires.

Happy songs were struck up and all joined in. Then Uri asked everyone to be as quiet as possible as he interpreted what he felt was the answer as to how long they were going to have to stay here.

He plunged into the book of Daniel, chapter twelve and Revelation, chapter twelve, and shared with the whole rapt audience, how that Stanos was the predicted Jewish persecutor, the Antichrist.[14] He revealed to them, both from the New Testament and the Old, how that Stanos was to take over the Ten Nations out of the Old Roman Empire,[15] and lead them into being world conquerors. He had done this several years ago. He pointed out how the prophecy in Daniel states, in chapter seven, that this man would rise, and how in chapter nine, he would make a covenant with Israel[16] for seven years, and in the midst of the seven years march on Israel,[17] breaking the covenant with the Holy People and then subsequently take over the Holy Temple,[18] which was also predicted to be built by Daniel,[19] by Jesus,[20] by Paul,[21] and by John.[22] He took time to present all passages clearly and distinctly.

Uri was so gifted in articulation and so unoffensive in how he presented these thoughts, that even Rabbi Perla and his family, finally listened with rapt attention, following along in his Hebrew Bible, as did some others, who had them.

"Stanos was to rise." Uri remonstrated gently. "He did. He was to take over the Ten Nations. He has. He was to sign a covenant which we know to be history. He was to march on Israel after the miraculous defeat of Russia,[23] which now, we know all about. He was to take over the rebuilt Temple. This is all history to us now. And" . . . he topped off his remarks to this point deftly, "He was to issue a new kind of credit card buying power on the right hand."[24]

Uri showed them the passage in Revelation thirteen, where this was to be found. He proceeded, to let them know that full given name of Stanos Papilos, added up to six hundred and sixty-six[25] in the ancient Greek numbering system, for each letter of the Greek alphabet also meant a number. This was indeed the clincher of his entire message.

"Here we have conclusive proof that both the Old and New Testaments prophecies were predicted by the true prophets of old, of God."

"Uri brought in the New Testament prophets with the Old very cleverly," Moishe thought to himself.

"They say that in addition to persecuting the Jews and the Christians for believing in their religions, the Antichrist would set up an image of himself in the Temple, for all to worship and bow down to. It is called the 'Abomination of Desolation' in the Bible . . . both New and Old parts.

"He has now done this, as we all know. And Jesus said, 'When we saw the abomination sitting in the Temple, to flee Jerusalem and all of Israel.' Exactly what we all did and you did not know that it was predicted! You also have to hear the rest of this fantastic prophecy . . . It is so exciting!" Uri was chuck full of the thrill of it all. Everyone enjoyed him so.

"In the prophecies, it says that we would "flee into the wilderness," to be taken care of by the Lord for a time, times and half a time.[26] That means a year, two years and half a year! It must mean that for it talks of the Antichrist coming and taking over Israel for the same amount of time and in another verse says he will reign for twelve hundred and ninety days.[27] But that we will be gone for three and a half years. This does coincide with when some of the first groups left Israel and Jerusalem. Moishe" . . . he asked pointedly, "you and your group left even earlier. We are part of this prophecy, and the prophecies of the city of Petra are clear. We are the children of the Lord praying to God and praising Him out of the Rock in the wilderness.[28] He will lead us out of here soon! Rejoice Israel, we are going to go home, and the Messiah is coming! Rabbi Perla we will then know, all of us, Who He is . . . I believe it is Jesus Christ . . . you are not sure . . . but we will all know and we are all going to be saved out of Petra."[29] Uri was beside himself with happiness presenting this glorious set of prophecies as well as anyone ever could.

He went on to tell them that according to his best calculations the Messiah would come in another eight or nine months! [30]

This meeting broke up with hundreds of questions pouring at Uri as he stood there defending and listening and understanding their perplexities. But he sent many a family to the caves that night rejoicing, trying to believe he was right. They really tried to believe. He had been so convincing . . . He knew the prophecies and they were so amazing!

Even those who didn't believe had to love Uri for his fervor and unbending faith in what he knew to be truth. No one could dissuade him. Not many wanted to. His message was one of deliverance, and that's what they wanted to hear.

Meanwhile in Jerusalem things were hot and startling events were popping daily. Stanos was growing wild with power. He had nations sending more food to take up the slack of what the United States and Canada had terminated! [31]

The oil blockade had produced the greatest depression ever known in the North American countries as well as in parts of South America. [32]

Europe was being forced to take the insignia and though it was slow, millions were doing so. The job of marking all was a big one and one that many rejected to the last available moment. Deadlines had been delayed and postponed and new deadlines set up.

Stanos' greatest ally for several years now had been the more formal and organized churches of Europe and England. [33] He had exalted a defrocked priest and cardinal to the position of his right-hand man in Europe. [34] While Stanos controlled elements in the Middle East and Africa. Father Antonio Gusseppie controlled political religious events in Europe.

Earlier he had been defrocked by the Roman Catholic church for apostasy. His apostasy was that he taught his parish and fellow priests that Stanos should be the new Pope of the Holy Roman Empire. He advocated the overthrow of the present Pope in the Vatican. Powerful forces within the church saw the wisdom of what Father Gusseppie said but could not overthrow the incumbent Pope and they too were excommunicated along with Gusseppie. They in turn followed Gusseppie to Jerusalem to form the New Holy Roman Empire, with Father Gusseppie heading it as the Universal Patriarch of the church. [35] Protestants,

Catholics, Jews, Moslems and many other faiths merged into the One Holy Church under the New Universal Patriarch who called on all men everywhere to lay down their intolerance and traditions and follow the new Messiah, Stanos Papilos, to glorious world victory. [36]

Father Gusseppie taught that all prophecies in the Bible pointing to the coming world of peace and prosperity would be fulfilled in the New Holy Roman Empire church and that predictions for a universal Messiah were fulfilled in Stanos Papilos.[37] It was he who had the image of Papilos made and set up in the Holy Temple in Jerusalem.

At times it appeared that Father Gusseppie had the power to perform miracles.[38] On television screens across the nations he performed his new mass calling down "Holy Fire," and stated publicly that if he desired even the image of Stanos would be made to speak the voice of God.[39] There was another supreme God in Heaven. He had sent Stanos Papilos to the earth to bring control out of chaos and beauty for all from the carnage of the human race. Though men did not receive him immediately and openly, neither had they received the First Messiah, Christ, with open arms. They crucified Him. Stanos came to complete the work that was stifled on the cross of calvary two thousand years ago. Christ's work was incomplete, his life being snuffed out all too quickly; Stanos would live forever!

Father Gusseppie appealed to Moslems, Christians and Jews by embracing all of their Great Prophets . . . Moses, Muhammad, Christ. All would live happily under the new mystical, ecumenical theological roof of the New Holy Roman Empire Church with its Messiah and Prophet, Stanos Papilos aided by none other than God's forerunner for Stanos—the one who came now as the Vicar of God on earth among men in the spirit and power of ancient Elijah as predicted by the Prophet Micah[40]—Father Antonio Gusseppie.

In order to form the New Holy Order of Beings, the reprobates would have to be exterminated. All unbelievers would be put to death upon testimony of their own faith. They could only live in the New World Order by showing the insignia indicating they pledged allegiance to Stanos.

Millions did just that and lived. Millions died as martyrs throughout Europe, the Middle East and parts of Africa. Wherever Stanos' men went, bloodshed followed bloodshed for the sake of a united world.[41] "The reason the world has never been united," Stanos said frequently, "is that too many ideas had been permitted. Now only the one highest ideal of all would be tolerated anywhere—Stanos Papilos, head of the New World Government.

He was now attempting to destroy all the religions that had formerly supported his rise to power in Europe over the Ten Nations—Catholics, Protestants and others.[42] Unless they denounced their own convictions and accepted him as the supreme head of the church on earth as the Archbishop, the Patriarch Gusseppie had stated, they would die. There was no mercy in this man. He was possessed.[43] He was determined to do what had to be done. His would be the one world kingdom lasting forever.

There had even been circulated a religious theory that he had lived many lives. He was now a resurrected personality out of the distant past![44] Stanos even claimed he was Divine!

Tonya Rae had met her father several times at the airport during the past months—which had flown by. James Hunter stayed on with her working in his various capacities inside the offices in management of computer controls for many new nations in addition to the original twenty-five.

Trades were being made from nation to nation with Stanos' blessing. They traded tax free. Some received their oil grants paid by Stanos. In turn they produced what products he needed for world control and Utopia to come soon.

Germany and Britain were ordered to produce war machinery. Tanks, ships, guns rolled off assembly lines to be joined by more and more as he stockpiled an arsenal large enough to blow up the sun, much less the earth.[45]

His concentration on new weapons, new bombs and new nuclear devices was devilish.

"We will fight China soon," was his message to staff members concerning the mounting arsenal he was building in addition to a powerful army of men. They believed his lie to the bitter end.[46]

Those who did not believe it kept quiet and moved inconspicuously.

Many wondered whatever happened to the thousands who had left and what had happened to the many soldiers lost while trying to kill them as they fled. No one knew the answers.

Tonya felt sure most of them died in the barren wilderness and felt terribly sorry for them. ''There were so many babies and mothers.'' She told her father.

Raymond showed her in the Bible one evening the many Scriptures concerning all that was happening. She called in James, and he listened intently, remembering his childhood days when he had sat in church.

There were so many verses dealing with all that was transpiring, Tonya and Jim found it hard not to believe. They accepted the theories that the Prophets of all knew by some Divine Premonition shown to them that these things were going to come to pass. But so far, they had resisted believing on Jesus Christ personally. They both frankly felt too busy for personal convictions now. ''Maybe later . . . when I see how all this is going to pan out.'' Jim said, honestly.

Raymond flew in and out for the last time. He had all the explosives they would apparently need to do a thorough job. He had learned how to handle it all from a British friend who had handled explosives in World War II many years ago. Raymond had learned easily.

Not one time was he stopped at the Israeli airports and searched, for the main guards knew who he was, and wishing to please Tonya they always smilingly ''let Daddy through quickly.''

James had devised a complete floor plan whereby they would blow the computer headquarters to the heavens. He had it laid out in his mind only not trusting anything to anyone.

That night after dinner, he took Raymond and Tonya through the entire plant. At every major explosion sight he signalled carefully, indicating to them this is where the charge should be laid.

Guards would have to be killed or knocked out during the graveyard shift from midnight to six in the morning, when no one was working.

They would plan that later. For now, it was plastic placement and how to run the wires back to his office quickly and get out using a timing device set for minutes after their escape.

For a month they went over every point in Tonya's car lest anyone hear or get suspicious of them meeting too often in anyone's apartment.

The time was set. It was a Holy Weekend proclaimed by the "Messiah" himself as a time of rest, jovialty and happiness for all his supporters.

Stanos had asked Tonya to celebrate with him. She had to accept wondering how she would get out of it or out of spending the whole night with this evil "beast."

"You will go out with him if necessary." James planned. "You will go back to his apartment and simply drug him quietly while he is not looking. Use a drink, which he always has in his hand, and while he gets amorous, you will put him to bed and leave. He will never remember in the morning's excitement anyway."

Jim was right. It had to be done that way. She dreaded the sensuous encounter and wondered if her nerves would hold up under the strain.

The terrifying night arrived. Festivities were running high in the streets of Jerusalem as Stanos had declared it was His High Holy Day, and all were to have a gala weekend, free from work in worship and homage to his New World Order.

Tonya and Stanos left her apartment fairly early and started the evening by attending a short worship moment at the Shrine of the Messiah. They entered the Holy Temple through the main doors, accompanied by Stanos' men. Stanos stared and purred at the gold image of himself emblazoned in brilliant multi-colored floodlights standing high above them and smiling wickedly down upon them all.

Hundreds of Jews were pouring in for moments of quietness in front of the great statue of the smiling Stanos.

They left, followed by five cars of his men. He took her to a new place that had just opened where reservations had been made and they dined together, occasionally speaking of the business she had under her jurisdiction and her family. She asked him a hundred questions to keep him busy—about Europe and England, the insignia and how it was being accepted.

He told her about African acquiescence to it and, laughingly, how the Europeans looked on it as "mark of the devil." Most just shrug and take it knowing it will bring them food and water.

"I will enforce it all over soon. It is the way to get loyalty and end all evil against my empire." He smiled at her touching the velvet softness of her face with his hands and fingers lightly.

They danced until late. He drank heavily as usual. They left near midnight with Tonya's heart pounding as never before in her entire life.

This night would mean a horrible death of slow torture for them all if they were caught. No one had ever tried such a thing against Stanos. He might even know it was them right away. They had to make good their escape.

A large boat had been bought and lay offshore with a crew of four. It was anchored out about two hundred yards from the Joppa coast just south of Tel Aviv. They could have docked it but decided that if it were not noticed that infamous night they might have a better chance of escaping. They would paddle out to it in a dingy already prepared.

Stanos took Tonya into the Holy Temple and into his palatial like private quarters so large and beautifully appointed with the finest of woods, tapestries, gold and silver bric brac from all over the world.

As he served her her favorite champagne and sipped on some himself, he got up to put on some favorite music as she requested. While he was looking for a certain album she wished. Tonya nervously emptied a small vile of knock-out drops into his fizzing champagne.

It fizzed momentarily and then blended with the drink. Her pulse raced. Stanos came back and drank it with one gulp listening intently to the music.

Within minutes of dancing with her on the carpeted floor of his luxurious living room with their shoes kicked off comfortably, he suddenly slumped out of her arms and fell in a heap at her feet, unconscious.

With great physical effort, she dragged him to his bed. Throwing him on it, she took off his clothes and left him laying there as if he had gone to bed normally. She succeeded with great effort and a strained back.

Quietly leaving his apartment through another door, she slipped past one guard easily and bumped into another walking up the steps. She waved quickly as though to say goodnight as she passed. He murmured good night to her thinking nothing unusual.

Speeding as quickly as she could back to the Hotel in a Taxi, she passed many dancing Israelis walking the streets still celebrating at one in the morning.

She changed her clothes into darker tones including slacks and slipper soft shoes that would take her into the various departments of the building unheard.

She immediately went to James Hunter's office only to find him and her father sitting there chatting with several guards. She was shocked for a moment until she realized James had everything under control.

"O.K. everybody back on duty, gang." He said with a wave and shooed them pleasantly out of his office taking their loaded drinks with them.

Within ten minutes, each guard had returned to his own post and was out cold. Tonya checked them. They were not in positions to see one another as they collapsed on the floors. All doors were locked to outsiders. Radar beam alarms had been reset. Raymond, James and Tonya knew what not to touch and where to walk so as not to trip the alarms.

For three hours they worked feverishly on all three floors of computers, the storage rooms for computer data and the electronic brains. All facets of Stanos' vast computer empire were thoroughly wired and the timers were finally set in James' office for ten minutes after they left . . . four-twenty in the morning!

While Raymond and James were setting up the timing devices, Tonya was rechecking all points of contact with the plastic explosives from one end of the floor to the other and up the stairs as well, she suddenly heard an unfamiliar sound.

She whirled around expecting to see Jim or her father. To her complete mental paralyzation she encountered a guard, half-drugged but half-aware that something was definitely wrong.

He walked drunkenly towards her while attempting to speak and drew his revolver pointing it unsteadily at her.

"What the Hell are you doing here, Tonya?" He snarled at her seeing the look of fear on her ashen face.

"Answer me or I'll blow your head off even if you are Stanos' slut!" He stung her into raging sobriety and immediate action.

Controlling her emotions of burning hatred for this man, she smiled cunningly and said, "You better come over here. You guys really missed something big this time. This place is wired. I just discovered it. Look!"

In his drugged mind he did not catch on to what she was pulling for a moment. The guard came over and stopped to look where Tonya was pointing.

She had a knife with her, having been making connections with the wires to the explosives as they had repeatedly explained and demonstrated for her, realizing all three of them would have to be able to do each part of the task.

When the guard stooped, looking in the darkness for the wires, Tonya quickly and cooly plunged the wicked knife into his left side with all her strength hearing it scrape through his ribs and knew it plunged into his heart instantly killing him.

Blood splattered her clothes and ran all over the floor as the guard fell with a thud at her feet his wind expiring in a gush from his lungs.

Tonya stood there looking at the knife still pushed in to the hilt in his side. She turned and vomited, retching her very insides out all over a desk.

She quickly ran to the men . . . and fell limply into James arms.

She told them the story as her Father wiped the blood from her hands and clothes as best he could.

Everything was set now. Nothing else better stop them.

The timers were set, and they left the building without connecting up the radar alarm system again.

They fled in James' helicopter parked at the landing adjacent to their building. It would take them nearly ten minutes to fly over and out of Jerusalem taking a route over dark forests and through the mountains winding around secluded areas so as not to be seen.

They watched their watches as they attempted to make good their escape to Tel Aviv unnoticed.

James slowed the helicopter down just out of Jerusalem atop a high mountain and looked back. They checked their synchronized watches.

It was nine and a half minutes. They counted breathlessly with hearts pounding in their throats as though they would choke them . . . At exactly ten minutes they heard a deafening roar and saw the bright lights of the explosion and flames leaped into the heavens lighting up the sky as though an atom bomb had gone off.

Then came the second explosion set for seconds later on the lower floors and with that the trio turned the craft and raced towards the sea south of Tel Aviv. They didn't hear the noise of blasts going off nor of the fire trucks rushing to the Hotel from all over Jerusalem. They couldn't see the hundreds of Stanos' uniformed men who rushed to the scene. The whole building was on fire and you could see it from most points in Jerusalem. The fires lit up the sky for them to see afar off.

Later, many of them thought that Tonya was either with Stanos at his Temple or dead in the explosions near her apartment.

In the excitement Stanos was not awakened until nearly six in the morning, about two hours after the explosion. No one thought of awakening him in the burst of initial excitement and shock.

In his stupor from last night's hangover, Stanos stood unbelievingly, two blocks away and saw his dreams going up in smoke and uncontrollable flames.

"Whoever did this, Sir, knew what they were aiming for and did a thorough job of knocking out all communications, all computer records and especially the national inventories of the Ten Nations and participating countries," Aubrey explained angrily, standing beside his boss watching the billions of dollars of machinery go up in flames. Stanos was coming to a fast boil.

Large crowds had gathered in the early morning hours. Television crews and radio reporters were on hand broadcasting live, on-the-spot action news to the world.

The news went out that morning that the "Beast of Jerusalem," may have suffered the greatest blow of his career as world leader and dictator of policies. He had lost his computer control of "ECU," food crops and industrial inventories of every nation. Nowhere could this be duplicated except by starting all over again with the cooperation of the nations if indeed they would. He lost all oil inventories, all access to information on political parties, politicians, programs and enemy lists—even the lists of those with the insignia!

He had foolishly failed to duplicate classified material. Only he had the records and only in Jerusalem were the records of nations stored. Now he had nothing but his army and his controlled oil.

He stood there thinking of it at seven o'clock in the morning watching years of labor go up in smoke. He cursed the nations and cursed everyone around him like the demon possessed man he had become.

He had to know who had done this. But it would take at least a week to sort out who might have pulled this off. The guards were all dead, burned in the fire. No one had seen anyone come or go.

No one mentioned the helicopter for nearly a week, when one day, Aubrey came storming into Stanos' personal office and said it had to be them . . . James and Tonya.

Stanos knew Tonya had been with him, but his mind was so hazy over the circumstances of that night. He could not remember when she left or much of what they had done, or not done! He figured he had gotten drunk.

But after several days of looking for James and Tonya and realizing both of them were the only executives missing . . . suspicions started to grow.

Both of their cars and personal belongings inside the cars looked untouched. Neither James nor Tonya took much with them. They had both packed but one suitcase and taken another suitcase of silver coins and gold coins bargained for in the black markets of Tel Aviv and Jerusalem for over a year's time. Their apartments were ruined.

There had always been some jealousy between Aubrey Miers and James Hunter. Aubrey always wanted more power and thought he could do his and James' job easily. Stanos knew of the personal feelings of Aubrey and at first, after the explosion had ruined everything, discounted him as a misdirected jealous fool.

But now that the helicopter was missing, there was a haunting feeling in his mind tortuously aggravated by Aubrey daily, that maybe James and Tonya did conspire together to do it. But it just didn't seem plausible. How could they?

Reorganization was under way slowly in other rented buildings under Aubrey's swift control. But it would be months before communications could be reinstated and the computers would take another year for installation and reprogramming after they were shipped in from points in Europe.

Stanos was blocked overnight in his economic goals of taking over world inventories. He was stymied on every hand by uncooperative world leaders in their own domain. They now had billions of "ECU" for their nations in a flash. Never had one man had so much and lost so much in the history of the world, so said the press worldwide.

Stanos now knew he had been a fool to trust anyone and not to duplicate the most valuable asset any leader ever had . . . total computerized control of every nation's gross national productivity so that they could not lie or cheat him. His men and political representatives were everywhere in Europe and all over Africa and the Middle East. The United States and Canada scorned him again and rejoiced in his sudden calamity.

They had played the game well. They had increased their military power and their nuclear arsenal in the past months, and beefed up their army, navy and air force. They had developed a new bomb capable of wiping out millions of people and valuable crop land. The President had ordered a strong civil defense program in America, and the people of the United States had finally dug in and sacrificed.

They had even engaged in a period of "full employment" in hardening all their industries and records." This was a term originally used by the Soviet Union in protecting all machinery, everywhere in the Soviet Union from bomb attack or intercontinental missles. They "hardened industries" by sandbagging them with simple earth. Three feet of earth around a large or small piece of machinery would protect it from everything except a direct hit by an atomic or hydrogen bomb. The Americans followed the lead of Russia and did it when their very lives and support systems were finally threatened.

When "hardening" was accomplished and oil development not yet producing well, industries started to shutdown for lack of energy and the great depression had hit. That's where America was at that moment, struggling to overcome the setbacks financially, due to energy losses.

But America was talking war with the "Beast of Jerusalem" soon unless something happened to ease the oil embargo. He had no rights to it exclusively, and it was just possible that America would attack first. Europe did not have the sophistication of nuclear power that America now had. And Stanos' armies were spread out keeping the peace on three continents.

The trio of sabotage experts escaped. Their helicopter was spotted after a week in the forest area surrounding a small village south of Joppa, about twenty-five miles south of Tel Aviv.

Aubrey, eyes blazing in fury, inspected the aircraft and was certain now that Tonya and James had conspired against Stanos and were involved in the destruction of the most powerful part of Stanos' world control.

How they managed it alone he could not imagine. Where did they get the explosives? Who helped them? Did no one suspect? Had no one any idea of their planned sabotage? He snarled infuriatingly at everyone. These and other questions circulated among Stanos' faithful employees. No one knew anything.

While millions rejoiced in the United States and Canada about Stanos' great losses, in Europe and the Middle East, millions of his faithful supporters wept as they witnessed, via television, his loss around the world. [47] Even Stanos's men were tragically affected by the terrible losses thinking it might effect them ultimately.

Of the original twenty-five cooperating nations, only eleven continued to cooperate with Stanos and sent in regular inventoried reports of national production of needed products. The rest were revolting against his control.

Anger was rising out of nations everywhere against his dictatorial powers. They saw this as their moment for freedom from his tyranny.

Leaders had secret meetings in the Far East with Peking's leadership. In the West many journeyed to Washington to view the situation with the Americans.

The United States had needed this impetus to action now. It would be the key to rebuilding America out of the dust of the most hideous depression ever.

China wanted it for world domination. There was little parleying between Peking and Washington, but each knew the other wanted Stanos dead, and his world monopoly destroyed with him—each, for differing reasons.

Stanos prepared for war with all stops pulled out! He hated Tonya and James and had an immediate all-out watch for them, figuring they were moving by ship somewhere. The airlines were blocked out of Israel. Had they been bluffing by leaving the helicopter by the ocean in that forest, he would catch them. Whether they elected to go by land or air, he had that covered.

Only by sea could they escape, Aubrey furiously deduced and convinced Stanos of the same. Ships everywhere were alerted that a huge reward was out for the saboteurs, one male and one female and their accomplices. Their descriptions and pictures were sent everywhere.

The descriptions were picked up by radio on board a United States Aircraft carrier in the Atlantic Ocean. This was radioed back to shore, and the Pentagon relayed the message to the President. It hit the press and television from coast to coast.

Steve picked it up on television just ten days after the mighty blasts had been reported in the United States.

He heard the names and descriptions. He was shocked to learn James, Tonya and probably Raymond Morgan had pulled this master stroke. Who else they had with them, no one knew. Charlotte was about to be hospitalized over the news, and Steve finally gave her a sedative to calm her down.

They would quietly and fervently pray, hoping for the best for the desperate trio as they waited for further word.

"Imagine," Steve pondered with inner panic, "They helped fulfill Revelation, Chapter eighteen! My God!"

Tonya, Raymond and James were safe thus far. They had swiftly left the abandoned helicopter and were in the boat going southward, through the Red Sea now, having traversed the Suez Canal on board their sixty foot yacht, with four crewmen hired on board. He had used this ship several times before, when he and friends had taken quickie vacations out of Jerusalem, into the Mediterranean over to Athens.

They had hired the ship and the crew for a large sum of money, all in gold coins. It was an enormous price to pay and the lavish amount bought the loyalty of the crew, who had planned on taking them to England staying close to the coastlines all the way. But when reaching Alexandria, they had to turn around and go back to the Suez Canal. Word was out they were going in the direction they originally desired. They would be caught by Stanos' ships and men for sure. They had all decided any port of safety was better than none.

After a day of great deliberation, while hiding from passing ships, some of whom might be looking for them, they decided on the trip down the Suez Canal and Red Sea, through the Gulf of Aden, into the Indian Ocean, stopping at ports along the way for fuel and food. They could reach Singapore in about a month. Then, if necessary, they would go on through the Flores Sea, into the Indian Ocean again, and head for Australia, and come in at Darwin on Australia's north coast, or at Perth down the Western side.

It might take two to three months, but they had plenty of money, plenty of time and could pick up fuel, repairs, and good food at any one of a hundred friendly ports enroute to safety in a British country that also hated Stanos. Or, they could all try to fly out to the United States and freedom.

No one would dream they would go this way. It was too long and arduous a task. But they did. Seas were rough at times, but the food was good, and it was like being on a luxury cruise, having most of the food fixed for the happy trio by the crew. They only wished they could communicate with their families, but could not for several more days.

It seemed their crew was indefatigable. They took turns at the wheel and between the four of them kept the cooking going, powerful diesel engines purring like twin kittens and the ship clean as she sliced water foreign to her tough sleek hull.

One of the danger points for them would be the mouth of the Red Sea, called the Gulf of Aden. On one side, would be the seaport of Aden, in Yemen, a former British Protectorate Country and filled with Arabs. On the other side would be the Djibouti, in the country of Ethiopia, where it joined hostile Somalia. There were two great naval bases there, and they had to maneuver between them, missing Stanos' great ships.

It was a fairly wide body of water and with luck they could escape detection as there were many ships coming and going in either direction.

Once they were out of the Arabian areas, but down into the Arabian Sea on the west coast of India, headed for Karachi in Pakistan, and then to Bombay, India, they could breath easy from Stanos' fleet.

They had heard broadcasts, alerting anyone finding them to turn them over to Stanos' men anywhere in the world. Rewards were posted for James Hunter and Tonya Morgan of a half million "ECU" each, dead or alive, with a special unnamed bonus, if they were alive.

Tonya had ignored James' romantic overtures now for several weeks, having been all consumed by the treacherous plans and overwhelmed by the immensity of it all. She was not sure of her emotions for him at this moment.

At home in their Jerusalem, Stanos was preparing for all-out confrontation with China. But he was also stinging daily by the strange preaching of two evangelists, parading up and down the length of Israel, wildly proclaiming that the Messiah was coming soon and that to denounce

Stanos, and his regime and his mark, and to worship the true and living God in Heaven, and His Son Jesus Christ, was the only answer. [48] Everytime Stanos tried stopping them, his men were somehow killed. It appeared mobs had attacked his soldiers, though strange reports came to him about "supernatural death" falling upon his men.

He hated those preachers . . . They were right under his nose!

---

1. Daniel 7:7-8, 19-20.
2. Daniel 12:11.
3. Revelation 16:15.
4. 2 Thessalonians 2:2-5.
5. 2 Thessalonians 2:1-8.
6. Revelation 13:11-15.
7. Revelation 13:15.
8. Matthew 24:15-22.
9. Revelation 12:13-17.
10. Luke 21:21-23.
11. 2 Thessalonians 2:4.
12. Revelation 12:15-16.
13. Revelation 12:14.
14. 1 John 2:18.
15. Daniel 7:7-24.
16. Daniel 9:27.
17. Daniel 9:27.
18. Daniel 12:11.
19. Daniel 11:31.
20. Matthew 24:15.
21. 2 Thessalonians 2:4.
22. Revelation 13:11-15.
23. Daniel 11:41-45.
24. Revelation 13:16-17.
25. Revelation 13:18.
26. Daniel 12:7.
27. Daniel 12:11.
28. Isaiah 26:20, 42:11-12.
29. Zechariah 12:9-14.
30. Daniel 12:10-12.
31. Daniel 11:39.
32. Matthew 24:20-22.
33. Revelation 17:1-5.
34. Revelation 13:11-12.
35. Revelation 13:14.
36. Revelation 13:12.
37. 2 Thessalonians 2:3-5.
38. Revelation 13:14.
39. Revelation 13:15.
40. Micah 4-5.
41. Daniel 11:33.
42. Revelation 17:16-18.
43. Revelation 13:2.
44. Revelation 13:3-4, 17:8.
45. Daniel 11:37-38.
46. 2 Thessalonians 2:9-12.
47. Revelation 18:10-19.
48. Revelation 11:3-13, Zechariah 4:11-14.

Chapter

9

The Battle
Of
Armageddon

The Battle of Armageddon

A spirit of fierceness had gripped the nations of the world. [1] One country after another fired verbal volleys at Stanos' regime. The Western Nations had met to find a way to rid the earth of this scourge. Through the United Nations, Chinese representatives met with the American Ambassador along with the Japanese and Australian Ambassadors.

They had a private conference on how to rid the world of Stanos Papilos, now that he was hurt badly by the destruction of his computer headquarters in Jerusalem.

The Chinese thought the Americans had done it and vice versa. It made for moments of humor for the group as they met, each blaming the other for one of their greatest victories ever over Stanos. All Ambassadors agreed that now was the time to attack Stanos. He was at his weakest moment politically and militarily.

It was agreed they should ''strike first'' at Stanos, or else they would suffer greater damage by allowing him the opportunity to do so. Right now they had the numerical military advantage over him.

China's arsenal of weapons was ready now. Her armies fully trained, and her highways to the Middle East nearly done. They had built a super passageway from the roads in Western China, out into Tibet and across the Himalayan Mountains, touching the top peak of India and into Pakistan, nearly to the borders of Afghanistan, where she stopped. It was but a short hop through Afghanistan into Persia and over the Euphrates River into Stanos' country of Israel, after taking Iraq and Iran if they gave any opposition.

By joining forces with the United States, common enemies buried the hatchet for the time being, maybe forever. They would attempt to conquer the world's most wicked, evil man. If they did not try, he would eventually conquer them. It was a life or death situation!

China started the massive march westward through her own large territories and into ancient Tibet. They seemingly crawled over the mountain highway, built by the lives of several million coolies over a period of fifteen years. The Chinese moved heavy armor, trucks, tanks on heavier army equipment, munitions, mobile missile launchers, men and engineers to help them get them over the Euphrates River, in case it flooded. They were planning on next summer when the river was virtually high and dry, thanks to the Soviets. The Russians, back in the early 1970's, had built a large dam on the Euphrates River, north of Damascus about five hundred miles. It was called the Tabqa Dam and it made Iran and Iraq very, very angry. It tended to dry up the Euphrates River to a trickle in the summertime[2] cutting agricultural production in both countries. Ways had been considered in which to bomb the dam. But now, the subject was dropped, for Stanos controlled its flow. That meant they could either get over easily, or Stanos could open the floodgates in time to catch them, making fording it impossible. They were counting on him being preoccupied. They had planned a large diversionary effort in Africa. Fortunately for the Western Alliance, three African countries were rebelling against Stanos and would join the force against him to the fullest.

Through these countries arms could be shipped and men arranged and made ready for the massive diversionary attack from the southern flank. There was to be a threefold thrust. First from the south, diverting Stanos' men and armies into Africa and the desert, where the Africans had excellent experience and equipment.

The second thrust would be the navies entering the Mediterranean Sea, directly confronting Stanos Papilos' navy, pushing towards Israel.

While these two moves would create a diversion, the main body of the Oriental Alliance Forces could quickly move in over the Euphrates and push across barren land into Israel, through Amman, Jordan and Damascus, Syria.

Stanos was alerted to the action out of the Far East and sent army intelligence to watch maneuvers.[3] They reported every move to him daily.

Stanos was not aware of American ships moving in crated tanks and trucks to African ports. They were accepting the crates up and down the coast in unmarked naval vessels or vessels with incorrect markings. Some ships were marked with Stanos' own insignia, and if any of his ships passed by, they communicated in friendly fashion on the open seas or close to ports. No one suspected that this was a massive arms buildup.

Troops were moved up the Chinese built Tanzanian railroad right through the Central part of the continent, undetected, into Kenya and then to Somalia, from where the attack would begin. From there they would go up the Red Sea, into Israel from the Gulf of Aquaba and Eilat, and through the Suez Canal into the Sinai Peninsula where many wars had been fought before, between the Israelis and Egyptians, prior to Stanos' time.

While Stanos was hurriedly rebuilding the computer project, somewhat concentrating on new programs with which to further control the output of nations and use it for all his own good, the world was on the move. Never in world history had so much military hardware been amassed.

Military maneuvers were underway for Stanos as well. He was fortifying his establishments in Europe, in case the threatened attack from America caught him off guard there. He felt that if the Americans attacked him, they would do so in Europe first, thinking he would be weakest there, and stronger in the Middle East areas. He intended to prove them wrong.

S.A.F. was designated as the code for the operation from the Southern Attack Force, representing all the Allied armies of the African theatre.

C.A.F. was the code for the Central Attack Force, representing all the nations of the Americas, attacking on the western flank, leaving O.A.F. to be the code letters for the Oriental Attack Force, attacking on the northern and eastern flanks of Stanos' mighty empire.

The timing had to be perfect. Stanos would know of the approaching Oriental hoards. They could not be concealed to aerial surveillance. He would be somewhat preoccupied with them, watching, observing, planning and worrying. They would stop temporarily. C.A.F. would then move across the Atlantic Ocean swiftly, while S.A.F. would attack in full force from the south. With good fortune, Stanos would be drawn away from Europe and from the Far Eastern enemies, and would plunge into the African theatre of war. That would contain him for several days or weeks, maybe even longer. During that time, the Orientals would push westward across the Euphrates River and swiftly come the remaining distance into Jordan and then Israel.

Simultaneous with the Oriental attack, the Americans and allies would come into Haifa and perhaps Tel Aviv, drawing Stanos' forces up and away from the beleagured Africans long enough to give them time to reorganize if necessary, to hit him further from below.

On paper it looked good. All the preparations were underway, brilliantly executed to date.

Without attacking Europe with ground forces, the Americans and their allies all agreed, that for the first time nuclear powered submarines would blast virtually every major occupied city in Europe with nuclear weapons.

It was a terrible decision to have to make. But it seemed to be the only decision they could make. All of Stanos Papilos' followers who had taken his insignia were another breed of human beings. They had no mercy, no feelings and mercilessly killed and butchered anyone found in Europe without the "Mark of the Beast of Jerusalem." To rid the earth of Stanos meant they had to rid the earth of his followers. When one took the mark, they hypothetically followed Stanos' every word and every suggestion to the superlative degree. They seemed inflamed with the same passions that directed this would-be-god-among men! They would all have to be killed.

Everything was made ready. Americans were suddenly alerted to the possibility of using their bomb shelters, evacuation routes, and underground hideaways in case of retaliation by Stanos, which was virtually assured.

S.A.F. attacked on schedule early one morning, just before sunrise. All of Stanos' ports of operation were destroyed at the mouth of the Red Sea, where the Indian Ocean joined. His mighty ships there were sunk, and his armies stationed there were destroyed in less than a week.

Addis Ababa fell quickly to the superior forces of the armed black Africans and Americans. Khartoum fell to the ground forces, as did Cairo, along with Jidda, and Mecca, in Saudi Arabia, which were not heavily fortified.

The Orientals had stopped as planned, and were waiting patiently. The Americans were now moving across the Atlantic, steaming towards the Mediterranean and soon their strategically placed nuclear powered submarines would launch their nuclear missiles at European capitals, attempting to destroy all power bases there of Stanos' operation.

Suddenly, as planned, Stanos moved his armies southward and turned his Mediterranean ships and large heavily armored navy into the ports in North Africa. [4]

By the time African and American forces on the ground and in the air attacked Cairo, Tripoli, Begasi and Tunis, heavy fighting broke out and stiff resistance was encountered, driving the Allied attackers back into the northern deserts of Africa.

Extremely heavy fighting was taking place in the Sinai area, with no advances being made by the Allied forces there. Stanos was throwing the best he had in that direction.

Then, while he was distracted in this area of conflict, driving back the allied forces with fury and destruction, a three point move was enacted against him.

Simultaneously, American forces entered the Mediterranean Sea in the largest American task force ever to take to the waters. They steamed for Haifa.

While the Americans headed for Israel's western flank, the Orientals made their move across the Euphrates River en masse, with thousands of tanks, tons of military equipment and hundreds of thousands of fully armed men racing for the hills of Jerusalem a few hundred miles distant. They came like a cloud covering the land. They had the fuel, the drive and ambition, and had been taught to hate this man with a burning passion.

They would take Jerusalem, killing all, and immediately turn on the Americans, their allies, and complete their takeover of the world. They had only joined the Americans and their allies to this good moment, in order to secure their help in the destruction of their mutual enemy. All plans were laid. With the Americans nuclear bombing of Europe, and the natural reaction of Stanos to bomb the Americans, they would take the Middle East oil fields and turn their vehemence and wrath on the suspecting Western Nations and destroy them with their own nuclear weapons on hand for just that move. It would make for the greatest trickery, and the greatest destruction in the history of the world. [5]

Australia and New Zealand would be attacked by Japanese task forces, already designated for that takeover, and the world would belong to the yellow races, at long last. Their patience and endurance would be well rewarded. They would control Moscow, Washington, Ottawa and all the major capitals of the European sector that remained after the nuclear attack. They had the manpower to do it. Communism would finally conquer the entire globe in one sweeping move and end all opposition forever.

Had not their great former founder, Mao, said time and time again, "Patience will give us the world. We have the numbers, and the West will give us their science for the right price. We will conquer all, if we but have the endurance to push, work and wait." Now that day was about to dawn!

Suddenly, Europe exploded like no land mass had ever exploded since the creation of the world when God moved the mountains, and churned up the oceans.

Beginning with Brussels, Belgium, former home of the "Beast," then Paris, and specialized locations in the South of France where great military operations were based formerly in NATO, now under Stanos. Luxembourg, a large headquarters for much of Stanos' operation, and Rotterdam, Amsterdam and westward to Hamburg, Hanover, Berlin, Bonn, Frankfurt, Munich, Prague, Vienna, Holland, Germany, Czechoslovakia, Austria—all were bombed including Milan, Genoa, and Rome. All key ports where Stanos' followers lived; his military based powers were destroyed.

Massive industrial centers, food storage buildings, nuclear missile silos, diamond industry headquarters for industrial and commercial diamonds, including gold storage vaults in Switzerland, and "ECU" headquarters in Geneva, were also completely destroyed and flattened to the ground. [6]

In one hour nearly two hundred and fifty million people were wiped off the face of the earth in Europe. Two-thirds of the people of Europe were gone—they had vanished from the face of the earth without hardly a trace. The nuclear power was of such destructive force that bones were burned instantly without a trace of dust where they had been standing. [7] It was the greatest destruction and the worst human carnage ever inflicted on any generation of humans.

Stanos ordered immediate retaliation from what was left of his missile silos in Europe and from his nuclear powered submarines in the Atlantic Ocean and the North Sea.

They had a range of over six thousand miles. Many were preaimed at major centers of political, industrial and military power throughout the whole continent of the United States and Canada.

North Americans were immediately told to vacate all premises, and go underground until further notice. Food was there, water was ample, and over two hundred million people went into shelters, envisioned before, by Civil Defense Authorities. They waited as they heard the missles destroy their cities above in horrid retaliation.

At least half of Stanos' missiles were knocked out of the air by the U.S. Antiballistic system. The Atlantic Ocean was the scene of many a dropping, exploding missile device. Many ships were caught in the crossfire.

Americans survived the first attack fairly well. Religious leaders said it was the mercy of God, for America had preached more Gospel than any other nation in history and had been a friend to the Jew for a long time. God was honoring His Word as He cursed those who cursed Israel and blessed those who blessed. 8 America was being blessed at this moment for following His Word.

Underground radio communications were all Americans had after the attack. Virtually every city was hit, but not nearly as much as they thought they would be. Only about twenty-five percent of the enemies' missiles hit anything like their intended targets.

Several shelters were hit directly by large destructive missiles, and those in them died. The death count was not out yet. All had to stay below for at least two weeks for the fallout to blow out over the oceans. But the latest reports indicated that less than ten million were dead in the United States. That was considered a miracle!

South Lake Tahoe, as with many other rural areas, was not in the area of destruction at all. The missiles overshot them, but the Scotts heard it all on radio, and took cover within, in case fallout from nuclear bombs would blow their way. Until now they were safe, and rejoiced with Americans at all their good measures of defense and safety. They too, attributed it all to God and gave praise to Him.

The Southern Attack Force was being thoroughly and murderously wiped out by Stanos' superior forces and quick thinking. He was beaten in Europe and so he now concentrated his fire power on Africa, and introduced his nuclear missiles into the operation, wiping out thousands of Americans and Africans in this surprise attack.

Stanos knew this was to be a bitter battle to the finish. He also knew the Americans and their allies were steaming eastward to Israel and had already entered the Mediterranean Sea, armed to the teeth.

His reconnaissance over the Oriental Attack Force, told him they were approaching the Euphrates River en masse, and he had speedily opened the floodgates of the Tabqa Dam to try to stop them. But he misfigured the distance the rushing waves of water would have to travel before encountering the enemy in the great river bed. It was too far to stop the early task force. Hundreds of thousands of men, and thousands of tons of equipment, were easily moved right across the Euphrates River by the Chinese engineers, who excelled at moving equipment over rough and unyielding terrain. Within two weeks they had nearly every piece of equipment over the river bed, and then, the water hit with terrific force. But it did little damage as the Chinese watched it approach from miles away in safety, while rushing last minute pieces of vital equipment over for their Battle of Armageddon with Stanos and the Americans.

The Oriental Attack Force had marched through Iran, encountering nothing from its angry leaders but a small show of military force, which they suppressed easily. They were like a creeping hoard of locusts, crushing, eating and completely devouring everything in their unstoppable wake of terror and power.

Iraq did nothing to stop them, as leaders in Bagdad knew it would be futile to try to stamp out this army of elephants. They gave the Orientals free sway to enter and pass through their land, supplying them with water and food while draining all food reserves in every storehouse the country had. It had taken the Chinese nearly five months to go this far from Peking and Canton centers of military development, and they would not be stopped by small bands of Arab fighters or Arab nations, even if the same tried to protect themselves and their stores of food and water. Everything edible was confiscated.

Passing through the rest of Iraq and entering into Syria was no small task for the terrain was rough. The mountainous country was forbidding, even to these mighty conquerors of the Far East. But no obstacle could possibly come their way that had not been planned out first. Every conceivable foe had been accounted for. Every physical need of well trained and battle hardened men was thought of. This was the Orient's one chance, and they had to make it the most undefeatable effort ever launched against joint enemies and primarily against the white race. This was the dawning of the age of the Oriental supremacy. Everything was proceeding to perfection.

The Southern Attack Force was knocked out. Stanos had elected to use all his powers there. After seeing what the United States had done in Europe to his leaders, supplies and followers, he maliciously used his nuclear arsenal to stop the S.A.F. in its tracks. They could neither retreat nor advance. He had them pinned down. The American General was killed when the first mobile missile unit opened fire.

It left the command in total disarray, the men not knowing where to turn and what to do. Many fought brilliantly and indefatigably against overwhelming odds. But they lost the Southern battle completely. The news came as swiftly as it happened. Stanos' forces had beaten back the African coalition of nations, and there would be no more attempt to attack Stanos in Israel from the south.

Now, the approaching ominous looking Oriental hoards were into Damascus on the north and Amman to the east of Jerusalem, less than one hundred miles away.

That was where Stanos' main counterattack began. He unleased intercontinental missiles from mobile launching sites from all over Israel's eastern quarter, from the Sea of Galilee south to Beersheba.

The Chinese were ready for him with small mobile antiballistic missile systems of their own development, fine tuned by the best of military scientists. They succeeded in knocking a great many of his missiles out of control and out of direction, or out of the air, within minutes after he launched them.

However, many of his missiles hit directly and effected great losses to the Chinese and Japanese armies. Mayhem was everywhere momentarily.

Almost all of the Orientals had been equipped with nuclear fallout protection suits of a silvery substance, having been shown how to make them by American firms and military strategists years ago. They made them like Chinese make flowers for Christmas export to the West. Every soldier had a suit and many of them had time enough to put them on.

In any given area, fallout would usually blow over with tradewinds, in less than a week, two weeks at the most.

The Chinese responded with several missiles of their own, controlling their projections carefully so as not to hit any areas of oil production. Israel had recently discovered large deposits of oil, just ten miles north of Jerusalem, near Ramallah. The Chinese only wanted to kill off the enemy, not destroy his oil or natural resources, especially the mineral powers lying within the waters of the Dead Sea.

They moved troops into the Golan Heights area and pushed past the great Mount Hermon, taking control of it with fierce fighting in that northern Galilee area.

Heavy artillery fire was now being exchanged from both sides. While the Chinese slowly but steadily were pushing into the Holy Land proper, starting in the north and later would push southward to Jerusalem, the Americans were on the western flank of Israel. *This was the dreaded Armageddon!*

It was far from over and already two hundred and fifty million had been annihilated in Europe, added to the several million in African forces combined with the Americans, and now another million or two of the hoards of Chinese and Japanese, to say nothing of the losses in Stanos' manpower. It would be safe to say that by the time the armies had reached the borders of Israel, nearly three hundred million people had lost their lives, mostly civilian followers of Stanos Papilos in Europe.

With the close proximity of the fighting forces, only limited nuclear power could be involved for fear of wiping out one's own forces.

The U.S. sixth fleet was bottled down in a naval battle equal to anything in history ever fought on the waters. Missiles were launched from submarines, not always hitting their moving marks and targets. The U.S. had brought in every aircraft carrier it had, along with destroyers and cruisers with the largest guns ever. Every size ship imaginable was afloat, fighting for the survival of the western powers. They knew the consequences and fought accordingly.

Stanos was moving the armies he had left, after the European wholesale slaughter of his forces there, into the central Israel area between Galilee and Jerusalem on the north. He was moving more of his men up from the southern flank now to aid in the defense of Jerusalem itself on the north.

He had decided that if worse came to worse, he would unleash his final volley of nuclear devastation and wipe Israel's northern half right off the map along with the armies gathering there. He would have to sacrifice many of his own men, but this was going to be his last desperate move for victory over an enemy that was approaching him with such ferociousness as to be indescribable. His defenses were known to no one. He could destroy nearly everyone in the country with the push of three buttons in his private offices in the Holy Temple.

The first thing Stanos had done when he moved to Israel over three years ago now, was to establish a Final Missile Operation Center.

It was only for final hour battling, to be used only by him if all else failed. It would win. Not much would be left, but it would put him on top.

With the south under control with Stanos' troops, he made his move to the north of Jerusalem, shocked that his enemies had gotten this far.

All armies were gathering in the northern part of Israel now, in the great Valley of Esdraelon, the Breadbasket of Israel, commonly called by some religious leaders the Valley of Armageddon. It was the place where the predicted blood and bodies would rise as high as a horses bridle, for two hundred miles of . . . "four feet of blood and death!" 9

Only because of the tremendous numbers of millions of their men, fighting like mad men, had the Orientals arrived in the land of the Bible. Had they had less armed men they would never have succeeded. But now they controlled Galilee and Tiberias of old as they advanced west into the Valley of Megiddo for the final thrust at Stanos' mighty resisting powers. They would soon take Jerusalem. For the first time in world history, an Oriental would claim the Holy Temple, while laughing at Jews and Christians alike.

Stanos had most of his executive staff with him in the Temple communications room. He had a complete picture of Europe's losses with the U.S. seventh fleet taking over everywhere in western and northern Europe.

He saw the southern flank of Israel was his and no one was approaching since he devastated the southern armies of blacks and whites.

He saw the enemy approaching the Jordan River en masse, and knew it would only be a matter of hours before they would come over in spite of the best fighting his fortified positions on the tops of the Judean mountains could do. They had the advantage of height, but the Orientals had the advantage of a million more men to throw into the battle, even though a million were dead in front of them. Strange how they numbered in the millions 10 . . . the greatest army ever amassed in history. "It would be the greatest disaster, too" . . . he thought, as he planned on— "three red buttons" for his final victory and defense. It would mean human carnage everywhere. But he knew he could beat them here. By defeating them on the Mediterranean and keeping their forces from entering Haifa, or Tel Aviv while destroying the Orientals in their tracks, he could regain the world in time. He never thought for one fleeting second he would lose this battle of battles . . . Call it anything they might . . . This Battle of Armageddon was his victory over the last opposing forces of the world, and he would recover! The thought of defeat never entered his evil head.

Aubrey looked at his leader and confirmed, "Within two days we can know what will happen in the Galilee area. Our fight is here in Israel. This is where victory will be won, and the final defeat come. Once you conquer the Orientals, the Americans will hightail it home and may even leave Europe for us. Or we'll eventually chase them out. Our people are not all dead there." He cursed the Americans and their atomic bombs.

"You are right, Aubrey," Stanos devilishly conceded. "We will beat them. By all the powers of Hell we will conquer them now." He was bristling with violent emotions, cursing in a strange language that not even Aubrey had heard before.

It was as though everything ever said about this fiend from Hell was true and was readily ascertained by anyone coming into his terrible presence.

"They will not win," he snarled to himself. "They will never conquer me!" He elicted a shudder, even from Aubrey, with his looks and strange remarks.

"So far it is a stand-off battle. No one is winning yet in the Megiddo area." Aubrey stated, looking at the military intelligence reports just in.

But a report from the Jordan Valley area indicated the enemy was blowing the tops off the Judean mountains with mini-missiles from down in the Jordan Valley itself, destroying Stanos' emplacements and men in those ancient hills—from the Dead Sea north to Samaria. The Chinese were pushing all along the Jordan River into the State of Israel.

"We are not stopping them at all along our eastern flank. They're pouring in like water, and we cannot stand much longer without missile action in the Jordan Valley," an aide shouted above the excitement to Stanos.

Without further thought, Stanos walked over to his private board of technical dials, telephones and screens, and with a devilish jeering smirk on his curled lips pushed a button colored red!

Within seconds, massive underground silos opened on the eastern side of the Mount of Olives, overlooking the Jordan Valley thirty-five miles or more away.

Within another ten seconds, they had fired themselves automatically, and within thirty more seconds, had blasted the Jordan Valley and advancing Oriental battalions and weapons to smithereens. The blasts shook all Israel.

Eighteen short-range missiles snuffed out the lives of several million more men and their mechanized war machinery. The billows of smoke like giant mushrooms into the heavens were seen by virtually every frightened soldier to the north in the Galilee area and Valley of Megiddo.

It came as a shock. It also indicated to the Chinese and Japanese Generals that what happened there might happen in their areas. Immediately, mobile missile units were brought into positions to fire upon command.

The instant butchery and mass slaughter of human life was unbelievable. The dead and dying lay on the hills as far as the eye could see. Everything was burning. Every truck, tank, piece of artillery, jeeps, amphibious vehicles, and even the roving mobile missiles units operated by the Orientals, had been hit and had exploded, killing and destroying everything near them for many miles. Now, the only Oriental powers left on the eastern flank were those to the east of Amman, Jordan, who had been waiting to be called up when they were needed.

The nuclear missile fire now covered an area of two hundred square miles in Jordan primarily, but with tips of Israel jutting into Jordanian affected areas as well.

In all, when the official count was heard on radio being transmitted to the Generals, there were over seven million dead, and the total loss of at least ten percent or more of all the machinery the Orientals had brought with them.

By now, uncountable millions of all troops and nationalities, lay strewn dead or dying in Jordan and Israel.

Stanos had "two red buttons" left. One pointed his furious multiple entree missiles out to predetermined areas in the Mediterranean Sea. The other aimed and released missiles covering the northern half of the tiny State of Israel, and would devastate the inhabitants, intruders and productivity of the land from the Mediterranean Sea on the west, to the city of Damascus on the east, and would leave nothing, . . . no living thing . . . alive!

If the winds reversed and blew back towards Jerusalem, most of the inhabitants of that area would die, unless protected underground for at least two weeks.

Stanos knew he had plenty of men to aid him in rebuilding Israel, and hopefully his world government, even if his armies in the north had to be sacrificed.

All the world would want minerals and oil. He could rebuild by charging astronomical prices and wait for each area to do their share of reconstruction. In the meantime, he had to win this war now!

Stanos unhesitatingly pushed the second "red button." Within forty seconds the eastern half of the Mediterranean Sea was showered from the air with multiple entree nuclear warhead missiles, capable of inflicting total damage and death to everything nearby as they exploded in the air, and then, to rain death and destruction like hailstones of atomic death in thick deadly profusion on everything and everyone below.

The cries of agony and the vision of ships exploding like toys was terrifying as meteor-like missiles struck and tore them apart like paper. The hideous pain inflicted on Stanos' own men, the Americans, the South Americans and Central Americans on board fighting ships, was totally petrifying.

Within minutes the sea was a color of blood. Ships were sinking. Very few men attempted to jump overboard to safety or take a lifeboat. Most all lifeboats had burned upon the impact of the burning hailstones.

Was this an act of God or man? Was this death produced by man's evil genius, or was God so sick of them all fighting and killing that He wanted them all done away with and off the face of the earth? It was both. [11]

Christians throughout the world knew that God was alive. [12] The enemies were destroying themselves by throwing at one another every powerful weapon ever devised by man in the evil, self-destructing ingenious laboratories of science. Motivated by the demoniac forces of Hell, [13] mankind had devised the means by which to destroy the last vestige of life on earth. Within another week, mankind would obliterate most of the populations of the earth, with the rest of the atomic energy harnessed in the death dealing explosives, laying in wait for the final buttons to be pushed. [14] One of them was in Stanos' office . . . The remainder would completely destroy America with the remaining missile-carrying submarines laying quietly offshore in the Atlantic and Pacific Oceans, awaiting the final command they knew would surely come now.

Seventeen more nuclear powered submarines were waiting for the final salvo of multiple entree missiles to be shot, and the end would come for North America. There would be nothing left but ashes.

Stanos was nearing the moment when the alert would be given and the final message sent to fire. That would come when he pushed the "red button" still remaining at his board.

Those fatal buttons would give him back his world—ravaged, bloody, desolate, devastated and filled with death and the dying. But, it would clearly be his world then. He would repair it.

Who then could make war with him? Who is like unto the beast? [15] Was he not the Son of Satan; the resurrected spirit of every dictator who ever lived and died [16] Would he not, in the spirit of Nimrod, Antiochus, Epiphanies, Alexander the Great, Napoleon and all the Emperors of once mighty Rome, finally conquer this infernal world, making it his permanent domain and would never see death again?

Was not his father, the Prince of this World, the Evil One, [17] that knew all, saw all and conquered and controlled all in this sphere? Let another God stay in his heaven . . . Let angels attend Him . . . He is far away in other worlds, on other planets . . . But this world, . . . this planet belonged to Stanos Papilos and his Father of Evil. . . . The controller and usurper from God. For had he not stolen this planet from the Deity that produced it? Right out from under Him? Who was God anyway? . . . His forces soon would be dead, . . . and this bleeding world would belong to Hell and its inhabitants forever.

"Rejoice, oh Kingdom of Darkness, you have brought to nothing the kingdoms of this world. You have conquered the Christians, [18] and the saints of all ages will fall at your devilish feet in humility and pay homage to the one who is finally proven the Greatest of all deities in history and in the earth."

One more message to the submarines simultaneous with the one diabolical button to be pushed, and it would all be over! It would be all his!

Stanos walked over to the red phone and picked it up, dialing a coded number to reach the commander of the waiting submarine fleet.

He smiled ever so villianously at Aubrey and said, "This is going to be the moment to relish. It is our moment of final glorious triumph over everything, and everyone." His capricious smile was that of a convinced fiend from hell.

The Scotts were still safe in Lake Tahoe seclusion, listening to the earthshaking epochal events about Europe and their London. They followed the events happening in Israel and in the Mediterranean Sea with their Bibles open in shocked horror!

The trio of Australian bound escapees with their crew, followed every broadcast of the news, realizing all they ever had in Europe or Israel was totally destroyed. They could not believe the immensity of the war. It was beyond their comprehension in its magnitude.

Life for Tonya, James and Raymond was anything but boring on the high seas, skirting ships in the distance that worried them for fear of Stanos.

Tonya's nerves were still taut and her relationship to James pleasant, but romantically cool. It was not because of her father's presence, nor could she fathom why she was "drained of all love" for the moment. But she attributed it to her overwhelming experiences with the plan, the killing of the guard, the dangerous escape and the daily "diet of death" as each ship passed them. She was so full of womanly fear, not even her father comforted her much.

Her appetite was gone . . . She could only force herself to eat occasionally, and then usually alone in her cabin with the radio playing music via the eight track. She was morose and sad and acted so threatened as though at times like she might be on the verge of a nervous breakdown.

James and Raymond were constantly discussing it. James had told Raymond of his deep love for Tonya, but that he had never had a chance to tell her how he really felt, and sincerely wondered now if he ever would. He was worried himself about getting caught, but far more so about Tonya and her health.

---

1. Revelation 16:13-14.
2. Revelation 16:12.
3. Daniel 11:44.
4. Daniel 11:41-42.
5. Isaiah 24.
6. Revelation 18:19.
7. Joel 2:1-7.
8. Genesis 12:1-3.
9. Revelation 14:14-20.
10. Revelation 9:14-16.
11. Revelation 14:14-19.
12. Daniel 2:28, Ezekiel 38:23.
13. Revelation 16:13-14.
14. Matthew 24:21-22, Luke 21:34-36.
15. Revelation 13:3-4.
16. Revelation 17:8.
17. John 12:31.
18. Revelation 13:7-8.

Chapter

10

They Saw The Second Coming Of Christ

They Saw The Second Coming of Christ

Prophets predicted it;[1] angels foretold it;[2] disciples preached it;[3] scientists discredited it; atheists scoffed at it; agnostics ridiculed it; born-again Christians believed in it; Jesus clearly taught it.[4] Now, the world, made up of all believers, and unbelievers, scoffers and ridiculers, would finally see the greatest of all earthly epochal glories.

While Stanos Papilos, the predicted antichrist, dialed a number to produce the death of the United States of America and Canada, which were the last bastions of Christian influence now, the earth suddenly shook violently under his trembling feet.

Stanos dropped the phone, leaving it hanging, undialed. He staggered to a doorway as others screamed in fear and fell to the floor of the Temple. He managed to run, swaying, stumbling, falling, standing awkwardly up again, to the doorway of the central hall leading into the Temple proper. He was now out in the Outer Court and impulsively pirouetted at a strange sound behind him, and saw his Temple home disintegrate before his very eyes, crumbling in horrible devastation and destruction at his feet. While hopelessly watching, all his plans for his enemies' defeat collapse like a house of cards.

He knew an earthquake had taken the Temple. Feeling another tremor, he screamed in terror while running with some of his men to the Gate on the Eastern Wall, just a hundred yards further to the east.

This was the only Gate not in use, as it had been sealed for centuries by the Turks, and was a fulfillment of prophecy, though Stanos didn't know it.[5] Outside it, on the eastern slopes of the Mount called Moriah, was a well-used Moslem graveyard. As Stanos' eyes ran down the valley, he could not believe what was happening to the famous Garden of Gethsemane. As he looked in utter horror, the Garden at the northern point of the Kedron Valley split in two. The foot of the Mount of Olives suddenly divided; part went southward and part northward, and the widening split in the earth opened even further as the division in the earth's surface undulatingly careened wildly right up to the top of the Mount of Olives, from the bottom of the Valley floor.

Stanos stood, half leaning against the Eastern Gate in shock, feeling the movement of the earth beneath him, 6 watching the ever widening crevasse in the Mount. Then he heard the sounds of a mighty roar coming from the heavens.

He looked up to see the sky lit up brightly, with every conceivable color in the rainbow, 7 blending into harmonious hues of marvelous tones. The heavens seemed to be opening up with such brilliance and inexpressibly shocking, piercing, brightness that it threw Stanos and his men on the hill back against the gate with great force. They were screaming and holding their heads between their hands and then down to their legs, because of an excruciating pain swiftly stabbing at their ears. They felt like their brains would literally explode with the tortuous, grueling, internal pressure.

They heard the sounds of a thousand hurricanes whirling with cyclonic-like force above them. They could feel the winds blowing them with terrific pressure and heard in the distance the sounds of a million singing voices, 8 in perfect harmony. But they dared not look up. Stanos could feel the crushing, intense heat upon his head and body, emanating from the source above, that nearly blinded him completely, when he had first glimpsed it.

He could hear humans moaning near him and felt the squashing weight of death all around. But he was powerless to move a muscle in his body, or get away from the Eastern Gate. By now, he was pushed so hard against it by the winds he could barely get his breath. His breast heaved in horrible agony, trying to gulp in the toxic-like hot air. He could not fall to his knees, nor to the ground. He was firmly planted, vertically, and had no power over his muscles, or any limbs, nor could he even move his neck. His body had suddenly gone rigid. He was completely paralyzed!

He could only move his eyes, slightly. Now, with the brightness toned down some, he saw marvelous colors fill the sky like a changing series of ten thousand western sunsets on a warm summer night. It was a kaleidoscope of colors. Singing could be heard in the background, coming from somewhere. But something ominous and uncanny kept silencing the singing with a deafening roar. The earth shook again. Tombstones turned over in the Moslem graveyard, where he was. Olive trees shifted position, as though they would fall over. Stanos' men were in the same physically agonizing position, unable to move. Nor could any of them get enough breath to utter distinguishable words. They screamed in their pain when breath was gaspingly available. Their tortured bodies were stone rigid against the Eastern Wall of the City of Jerusalem. But the Wall did not fall with the quakes, nor did the Gate open or move. Not a block fell out of place from it.

The extreme brightness of the heavens was not like the mushroom brightness of the hydrogen-atomic explosions of the missiles, or the bombs of the armies. It was a magnificent brightness; so unearthly, so indescribably beautiful, so immeasurably boundless that no man could characterize it. The whole earth stood frozen at the infinite grandeur of it all.

The Oriental commanders with their armies gathered on the hills and in the valleys of Megiddo were transfixed, as though something invisible, yet nonetheless real, had impaled them to the very ground they stood on. Not a soldier moved. Every man fighting for or against Stanos Papilos was glued to the ground. His body rigid in excruciating pain from the pressures he was sensing from an invisible enemy. Each soldier's head was ready to split open with the brightness from the heavens and the unseen pressure jamming their temples.

No one knew what was happening, though they realized in a second it was not a man-made power causing this phenomena. It was both deathly frightening and yet was a glorious portrayal of Divinity unfolding before their very eyes, involving the whole heavens. They heard the sounds of singing, and the sounds of trumpets in the distance, but could see none of the actual participants, as they continued at times to hold their heads in agony.

Men, falling from the ships into the Mediterranean Sea, beheld the same glory while they plunged to their death. Some drowned with eyes paralyzingly transfixed on the heavens as they opened up before them.

This was no extraterrestrial planet visiting the earth. This was not a Hollywood star war. This wasn't even Jupiter lining up with Mars, or Venus, to exercise a magnetic tug on the earth's surface, creating great earthquakes and cyclonic lights, as had happened on the earth back in the year 1982. Hundreds of thousands of earth's inhabitants died then, even though they had a warning it was coming.

This was no calling down of so-called supernatural fire from the atmosphere as Stanos' companion in evil had accomplished on several occasions, using Satanic powers. No, this was not an act of Stanos Papilos, or any man, or any nation, or any gathering of world powers.

This was not of man. It was of man's God!

This was not of earth, earthy. It came directly from Heaven.

This was not natural in its origin. It was marvelously supernatural in every glorious aspect.

This was not a fleeting flash of summer lightning. It was a permanent blaze of celestial glory in the heavens. It could not be turned off, nor could it be changed by man, or altered by might, or power on earth.[9]

The world stood reverently still. Every bird was silenced in the jungles and forests and in the glades from America to China, from Russia to the Antarctic Ocean, beneath Tasmania and the Tasmon Sea.

Boats bobbed in the ocean waves, but humans on board were transfixed, staring at the heavens, immovable. Planes suddenly, inexplicably stopped in midair, as though suspended by an unseen hand or power. Passengers were glued to their seats looking at weird skies changing, bursting with a thousand sunrises above the clouds. They felt the same pressures that their compatriots on earth felt. They were impaled. They too were totally immovable and were in agony.

Motors stopped as if instantly wound down, or shut off with a key. Cars stopped, trains refused to budge. An unseen power had stopped all movement on earth, only the leaves in the trees shuffled lightly paying homage to the One who was producing this strangest of all inner action on the earth's surface.

Nature seemed to gladly obey Heaven's commands. The fowls of the air stopped flying; even the creatures under the surface of the waters stopped swimming and gazed with sudden paralyzation of their senses to the tops of the waves and beyond to the Heavens.

In those few short minutes throughout planet earth, the world stopped moving. The earthquake terminated its massive shaking; then, graves opened up all over the whole earth. In a flash, humans instantly disappeared, right out from the sight of those looking at them, leaving their clothes behind.

It was as if you blinked your eye and the person next to you was now missing. One moment you stood by a graveyard with the graves closed as always. You blinked and certain graves opened up. Tombstones rolled over and crashed on unopened tombs.

Then, the shocked world heard the rejoicing of voices in the distance . . . happy, joyful singing! It was the immeasurable din of a million times a million voices singing, laughing, rejoicing in the heavens. Not all words were distinguishable. But the sounds were coming closer.

The Heavens took on the form and dimensions of a thousand noonday suns, all pointing to their center. It was as if a myriad of suns were turned sideways. They were beautifully crimson on their outside and so brilliantly illuminated with a million fires on their inside, reflecting into a giant emerald, diamond-shaped center with nothing in its effulgent center to catch the glory of the suns, nor to reflect it back. But there they were, all turned in, lighting up the Heavens with the glory heretofore unexcelled to mortal eye. An inexpressable Divine Revelation took earth's breath away from them as they beheld it all.

Then, in the midst of millions upon millions lifting their voices singing louder and louder . . . "HALLELUJAH . . . HALLELUJAH . . . HALLELUJAH!"[10]—There suddenly appeared the giant, unmistakable, beautiful form of the JESUS CHRIST OF THE BIBLE.

At first, He was totally, indescribably lovely. And within seconds of time one could then behold His fine features coming into perspective.

He stood smiling so softly, with arms outstretched to those near Him—those whose voices were raised in exultant praise as He appeared majestically.

The color of His skin was almost golden. His majestic robe was as white as the eye could behold, without having to look away. At the bottom of the whitest robe ever seen was the blood red fringe, falling down to His feet, covering them with the red border of the marvelous garment. The red fringe was also on the bottom part of the sleeves, and most evident as He lifted His arms in a welcome gesture to those He was looking at, whose voices earth heard so clearly. No one had ever looked so regal, so Divine, so gloriously beautiful, in countenance and body.

His long hair was jet black and glistening with the sun's reflections. It was bushy, beautiful, masculine.

His eyes were the strangest of all. One second they would be like the eyes of doves—soft, loving, tender, appealing; then suddenly changing as He moved His gaze from around Him to below Him to the world. Then, swiftly, His eyes turned to blazing balls of fire, set deep in His head. It was shocking!

His hands were long and graceful, beautifully formed and out-stretched, in loving gestures to His invisible guests.

Then, He turned his hands towards the earth, bringing his arms slowly downward and turned the palms of His hands upward. All earth beheld the unmistakable marks of suffering in the very palms of His hands . . . They were golden hands with flaming red drops of blood emblazoned on the palms distinctly, for all to see.

There could be no mistaking Him for anyone else. He was the Christ of Prophecy. He was the Jews' Messiah, and the Christians' Lord, who had stepped into the diamond-shaped ring, with a brilliant emerald back-ground contrasting the golden texture of his skin and the shocking whiteness of his robe, trimmed in firey red.

He was the Promised Judge of the Earth, and Savior of the Saints, who finally made His appearance just in the nick of time to save civilization from the last stroke of Satan.

This was His prophecied Revelation. 11

The suns turned even brighter as they focused their reasons for being on Him. This was the most brilliant of illuminations. The brightness of His appearing, 12 stung and blinded the eyes of millions on earth. Only by them being impaled by some unseen force greater than anything earthly had they all held up from falling prostrate on the ground, blinded forever, and deafened by the roar of the jubilant singing above.

But God in Heaven wanted and had planned for the whole world to see the Revelation of Jesus Christ at long last.

They could not blink, they could not speak, they could not move. They could only behold with bursting emotions of soul and hearts stricken with the majestic glory in the Heavens and know that it was the dazzling Person of the Lord Jesus Christ, appearing to earth the Second Time.13

Then, outside of the ring of bathing, blazing suns, shining on His Face of love and unexcelled beauty, you could see the blurred vision of white and gold clouds, filled with human beings, singing and standing, all in pure white robes . . . all with hands raised, millions upon millions of them. Singing, and moving in perfect rhythm; swaying before Him in adoration, paying their deepest of homage to the King of Kings and Lord of Lords!

The vision cleared and you could see them clearly now. Swaying by the millions upon millions, all around Him . . . above Him . . beneath Him . . . on both sides of the Christ! All looking at Him with outstretched arms and hands, gazing at the Messiah, singing. It was a clear vision now, to all on earth.

The whole vision was so immeasurably glorious. It was so incredibly, unbelievably immense, that as the planet seemed to turn, the vision circled the earth so every eye could see Him and behold the glory that was His.14

Seconds after Tonya and her group had seen the lights flash and felt the ocean waves heave terribly, nearly knocking them overboard and while they heard the music from the skies and were paralyzed in their bodies, Raymond Morgan vanished from their sight while Tonya was looking at him! He vanished without a trace and to Tonya's consternation, while her eyes were on his vanishing body, his clothes fell crumpled to the floor of the boat, barely covering his shoes, which poked out, from beneath the dropped togs of a seafaring man. Tonya wept for her father feeling she might know what was happening to him. "My God," she thought, "Could all of this have been true?" She wanted Jim's arms so much, but couldn't move.

In South Lake Tahoe there was a completely empty cabin, with only the kettle still steaming away. Five cups were set out with the sugar and tea nearby. But the cabin was empty, except for the static coming over the radio. All persons within had vanished, leaving their clothes where they had sat.

Within the exultantly thrilled group of Jewish followers, down in Petra, there had come the ecstatic thrill of realizing what was happening in the Heavens. This was the prophecy of Zechariah at long last! All Jews were impaled to the ground, but unlike their Gentile counterparts left on earth, the Jews were painlessly paralyzed. This was true of Jews everywhere in the world. They felt no pain. It was as though God felt they had had enough pain in life.

Petra Jews realized their Messiah was coming. He was coming just as the prophet stated. [15] They too could use their eyes, but their lips were silent as they beheld the glory of the ages appearing as He said He would.

He came enshrouded with a million diamonds of brilliant suns, acquiescing to the Messiah's position of the eternal light. [16]

To their immediate consternation, every Christian Jew had vanished in the twinkling of an eye. [17]

They had been there together a second before. But in less time than you would take to snatch a breath, they virtually dissolved in front of the remaining transfixed eyes, and faded out of sight. Their clothes dropped to the ground where they had been seconds before. It was baffling. The Jews were dumbfounded at their mysterious vanishing into thin air. But in a moment, all thought of the vanishing Christian Jews was gone! They now beheld the wondrous glory of the vision in the Heavens. It surrounded their mountain fortress of Petra, with the greatest of brilliance, illuminating every crevasse, penetrating the darkness of the deepest caves with marvelous light.

Now, the mysteries were solved. Now Dr. Raymond Morgan understood how "all could see Him come in His glory," even if they were on the other side of the earth as his wife had been. They didn't need television—man's creation. They only needed the gift of eyesight from God. There it was, filling the Heavens above and below the equator . . . from the east side to the west . . . not a nation missed it . . . not a black girl in Africa . . . not a Chinese boy in Canton . . . not an Eskimo in Alaska. They saw and they knew instinctively . . . The papers would never print it . . . Announcers need never describe it. They were seeing it. "The Heavens were declaring the glory of God!"[18]

Every believer was now in the Heavens; either resurrected from the dead[19] or "raptured" out from among the living still on earth.[20] They had been caught up to Heaven as sure and certain as the prophets had said . . .

Tonya Rae Morgan knew it for she had heard these teachings, time and time again. But she missed the glory being revealed to them and her parents as she viewed it all from the deck of her boat floating in the ocean.

Her mind flashed to the favorite scripture her father had often quoted to her. With agony of soul she quoted it to herself, impaled to the deck of the ship, rigid, motionless, with time to behold and to think . . . . "Daddy would say:

"For if we believe that Jesus died and rose again, even so them also which sleep in Christ will God bring with Him.

For this we say unto you by the word of the Lord, that we which are alive and remain unto the coming of the Lord shall not prevent them which are asleep.

For the Lord Himself shall descend from Heaven with a shout, with the voice of the archangel, and with the trump of God; and the dead in Christ shall rise first; Then we which are alive and remain shall be caught up together with them in the clouds, to meet the Lord in the air; and so shall we ever be with the Lord."[21] She thought of those words again and again . . .

Tonya Rae knew where her mother and father were. The thought gave her much comfort for the moment, but then plunged deep conviction into her soul. All she could think to say to herself while viewing the majestic sights of the Heavens, was, . . . "Why am I not there with them? Oh God, why am I such a fool! I am such a fool." Tears coarsed down her cheeks.

"I had every chance . . . I had a father who believed and begged me to join his faith too! My mother . . . even as carefree as she had been in life . . . she accepted and loved her Lord. Why was I so blind?"

She wept inwardly as never before, so deeply in sorrow, she had to look away from the spectacle of the Heavens. Her own words burned in her as fire: "Am I too late? Is all lost? I have lost what they have, . . . that glory, that marvelous mystery, unfolding to them . . . . Oh God, please help me. Don't damn me Lord . . . . I had no faith, but I never really disbelieved. I just," she hesitated in deep sorrow knowing the truth, "didn't activate what I knew was right within me. I knew they were right. The Bible was always respected as truth with me. I just never applied it . . . . My God, what will happen to all of us now?" Her soul wept as did millions of others throughout the earth.

At the end of one complete circulation of the twenty-five thousand miles of the earth's surface which took a much shorter time to revolve than the normal twenty-four hours, there was tremendous movement in the Kingdom of the Heavens, observable by the earth's paralyzed persons.

Earth's inhabitants did not know that during that time immeasurable glories had been beheld and thrilling events to proceed on earth had been announced to the ones redeemed above them in the Heavenlies with their Messiah. Earth had no idea that awards and rewards were now being distributed as the Saints of all ages stood before the Lamb of God, Jesus Christ. [22]

This was the Throne of God established in the Heavenlies for this time of eternal bliss, and constituted the "Judgment of all Believers." This was the Judgment Seat of the Christ. It was clearly prophecied by Paul and others. [23] This was the beginning of "Pay Day" for the ones who served the Lord with gladness through martyrdom, suffering, labors abundant and from every walk of life. They had now come, resurrected, raptured, redeemed, giving Him the Glory, all due to His Sacrifice on Calvary, and now, His glorious descent from Heaven to Earth. to end earth's misery and stop the last mortal crime of extermination [24] . . . genocide by Stanos Papilos, the Antichrist of Hell.

He was stopped. Everything stopped. All beheld, all gazed unflinchingly as the God of all Grace and Love cemented forever the union of the Bride and the Lamb. The redeemed followers of Christ were the Bride as mentioned in the Prophecies. [25] She was presented to the Heavenly Groom, Jesus Christ, who had paid the dowry of His Blood for her purchase. She was betrothed to Him and was now being married to Him in a celebration designed only for the immaterial, incorruptible immortal eyes of the redeemed, and Heaven's angels.

The earth and Stanos with Satan had had their time of wretched noise, death and revelry. Now it was the hour for the persecuted and murdered ones to rejoice. Let martyrs sing as their bodies came to life, and were transformed into immortality, never to see death again. [26] Let the lame leap and walk in their new bodies, never to know crippling or pain ever. Let the dumb speak and sing, . . . the deaf hear and rejoice. They had traded their illnesses, their plagues, their infirmities and their terrestrial bodies, for a celestial one, never to know earth's impediments ever again.

Let the aged leap for joy in their new bodies of eternal youthfulness! Let babes sing with mature voices of fully developed bodies, since being resurrected as infants, but raised in maturity!

Let the jailed and tortured shout, as they have just exchanged gnarled bodies for beautiful temples to live in forever.

Let the earth be quiet, as earthly wrongs are righted in Heaven's peaceful atmosphere. This is where all hurts are healed, all wounds vanish, all broken hearts are put back together again; this is where every trial on earth is rewarded by Him who endured the worst of trials. This is where Heaven touches the tempted with love, peace, and superlative happiness for overcoming and living by faith.

This was the First Resurrection completed! "Blessed and Holy are all those in the first resurrection. [27] These were the only ones to reach the greatest of Heaven's rewards, the High Calling of God in Christ Jesus, to be His Bride forever.

Time had stopped for hours. The world firmly knew Who it was by now that had conquered all on earth, and in Heaven, and Who had stopped the last touch of inhuman torture and death. Christ had promised before He left that this would happen.[28] He stopped it before complete genocide of the races had been finished by Satan through His Man of Sin, the earthly Antichrist.

Stanos was immediately taken, and with him the False Prophet. They were visibly flashed out of existence [29] as his guards and aides saw them writhing in excruciating pain, carried out into the air, into the universe, as though unseen hands carried them far away from their very eyes on the hillside of Mount Moriah. The very hill where Christ had died a little to the north, Stanos Papilos was finally destroyed forever, never to be seen again.

His armies were wiped out in a flash of lightning from one end of the lands of occupation to the other. Brilliant flashes of lightning rocked the earth in the destruction of every soldier in Stanos' military entourage. [30] Every civilian with the "Mark of the Beast" was instantaneously killed. [31]

Within hours, every human that had followed Stanos in any way, and every human that had taken the mark, were dead. Their bodies lay from the North Sea to the Antarctic Circle.

Shortly thereafter, the feet of Jesus Christ touched the Mount of Olives, [32] which split in two, part to the north, and part to the south of Jerusalem, leaving for a moment, a large cleft in the mountain. It formed a valley. 33 The valley was great and changed the face of the eastern section of Jerusalem like no earthquake had ever done.

Suddenly, on the same day that Christ's feet touched the Mount of Olives, a river sprang up like an artesian Niagara Falls in the middle of the ancient city of Jerusalem. The river went to the east and to the west.34 It drifted swiftly towards the Mediterranean Sea, and backwards from the heights of Jerusalem nearly four thousand feet above sea level, down to the Dead Sea. The river was of pure fresh water.

In the hours to follow, every creature that had been clothed with an immortal body came down to earth, from the skies above.

They received no retaliation, nor was there any effort to resist them as they organized the remaining beings into a living human family.

The world would bury its dead, remove its corruption and devastation and build again. They were told by these lovely creatures from "outer space" that they would be governed by the Lord God Almighty, through His Son Jesus Christ.

Eventually, the nations were brought before Christ in Jerusalem. 35 As they came, each individual was judged as to how they treated the Jews of Christ's earthly family.

Had they opposed the Jews personally, they perished instantly. Had they befriended the Jews on earth, during their centuries of plight and hours of agony, they were placed into a separate category and lived. 36

None who had ever taken the "Mark of the Beast" were ever seen again. No one who had opposed the Jews in any way, were ever seen again. The only ones surviving were the people from every nation who had never taken the "Mark" and who had never hurt the Jewish race.

They were not accorded places of honor, but they lived and were to rebuild the world. They were told that Christ would rule the world forever in love, justice and perfect equity for all. These living earthlings were to be evangelized by the new "Stars from Heaven."

Tonya Rae and those with her lived. Even James Hunter lived. His heart was judged as a friend to the Jew, for his final actions on their behalf.

Earlier when the physical pressure on human bodies was released, Tonya had literally fallen into James' arms.

She sobbed for an hour, clinging to him as though clinging meant life or death to her.

The absolute enormity of all that had transpired was so completely exhausting to her, she could only lay across the deck, with her arms wrapped ever so tightly around his waist, and her head buried in his chest. She cried convulsively, then softly and more quietly, as he stroked her brow and ran his fingers through her lovely but disheveled hair.

His touch was healing to her. Her thoughts were of the spectacle of space and that brought a psychological healing and tranquility such as she had never had before. She knew the truth now . . . she knew it thoroughly.

"I've been such a fool all my life, Jim." She lamented weakly, while looking at his eyes, laying still. "My Dad was so right and so wise . . . We could be with him now . . . We could be up there!" She pointed to Heaven.

"We were stupid, we will survive however, because we have one another and we now know the truth. How can we help but believe in Jesus Christ?"

"I love you so much Tonya darling . . . . I have loved you so long . . . so deeply!" He just gazed at her, with no gesture to kiss her, and barely hoping for any response from Tonya at all. He just wanted her to know . . . "

There was quietness in her eyes and spirit now. She was relaxed. Her eyes never left his.

Then, in a quick upsweep, she swung herself upward towards his face, and threw her arms around his neck. With the crew looking, she kissed him as she never had kissed a man.

This was real. It would be forever real. Her spirit touched his inner being and told him about a love for him no other woman had ever had, nor would have. She was his now. She was his forever.

Tonya saw her parents again in their immortal bodies, and immediately became a believer in all her father and mother had taught her in their former lives. They appeared to her on her boat.

The Messiah had a new magnificent Temple that came into existence that first day His feet touched the Mount of Olives. It took in the whole city of Jerusalem and was so large, the new building program of the city of Jerusalem had to be extended far into the outer regions of what had been hills and valleys around the original city.

The New Temple described by the Prophet Ezekiel [37] flashed into existence. It was to this Temple that all would come in holy reverence and love. Here is where they could fall at His feet, Who ended the terror of all terrors and the tyranny of Satan. [38] Millions were coming and believing. Others would follow. The new human race would know no war, [39] no bloodshed, little death, [40] hardly any disease, [41] and no ill will from one man to his neighbor. [42]

A spirit of special love prevailed everywhere. There was hard work, but no evil. There was rebuilding, but no dishonesty anywhere on earth. [43] They were not all Christians, but they were rapidly turning to the Christ who was bringing a new kind of salvation to the earth, and there was perfect justice, perfect law and there would soon be perfect order. [44]

The earth had entered into her day of rest . . . . All nature seemed to sing. Birds flocked everywhere with new notes of happiness in their praising of God. Even the beasts of the jungle and forest lost their carniverous spirit and lions and tigers and other beasts usually eating flesh, were eating hay and straw. [45]

Children played with snakes and reptiles and let formerly poisonous insects walk across the palm of their hands. [46]

The world was knowing peace [47] —genuine, lovely peace. There was singing in the streets. [48] Greed seemed to be missing in the human spirit. A spirit of kindness and helpfulness prevailed everywhere in the rebuilding of the earth.

The Second Coming of Jesus Christ proved to be a point of joy and sadness for the Jewish race. They had been protected more than once by Him. But they had rejected him, [49] and consequently were in mourning for days. [50] But they now knew that two thousand years ago, they had only accepted the prophecies they wanted for that moment. They had wanted an instant King to deliver them. He had to come as a Suffering Servant first, [51] then He would come again as King. [52] It was so easy to see now . . . Why had they not seen it then?

The Scotts in South Lake Tahoe, like millions of other faithful believers, had escaped the real ravages of Europe, by moving to America. They saw the Second Coming . . . But even better, they were a part of the Second Coming. They left at the first instant of hearing the trumpet sound and voice of God bidding them into the New World. [53]

Raymond had escaped the powerful hand of Stanos, and he too, saw the Second Coming from his stilled boat in the Arabian Sea. He heard the blast of trumpet by Gabriel, and left this world in a flash to behold the

Glory of the Only Begotten of the Father, Jesus Christ, in the clouds of the sky.

Dr. Robinson, the Scott's pastor in London, saw the Second Coming from a deep dark prison in England, for having preached the Gospel of Jesus Christ after Stanos had ordered all churches closed and ministers marked.

He was released from his prison . . . in spirit and in body. They say they found his clothes and worn out shoes, worn terrible on the toes, as he had prayed so much, on his knees. But his body was missing!

The Rosenbergs all saw the Second Coming, with millions of remaining faithful Old Testament style Jews, who had fled from the evil "Mark" and hid in the hills or went to Petra. Now, the Rosenbergs were complete believers in the Lord Jesus Christ. They missed participating in the eternal joys of the first believers, as they had witnessed. But they now believed, and lived in Israel, near Jerusalem, watching the millions of pilgrims come and go, visiting the earth's Prince, the King of Kings.

Americans saw the Second Coming. Those that knew Christ personally, as Lord and Savior, rose to meet Him in the air. The rest, and all the remaining nations, were under the strict rule of Christ and his governing emissaries.

The nations of the world saw the Second Coming. From China to Buenos Aires they fell on their knees to worship Him, Who came to bring them peace forever.

Satan himself had seen the Second Coming, and was now bound in Hell by the power of the Living Christ Who had taken the Throne of David in Jerusalem. 54

The earth would rest now from her toils, cares, wars and bloodshed. If anyone died, . . . we understand, they will be considered the exception to the rule here on mother earth.

Longevity is setting in. They say Tonya and James Hunter will live forever in their new faith. They believe it. Others who are not even believers in Christ as yet, are living long happy lives.

The flowers are brilliant colors now. Peace is everywhere. A new bright and love-filled world is bursting forth like a baby bird out of its shell.

Even all of nature saw and beheld the Second Coming. And all of nature is at peace with itself. Natural disturbances are gone. The seasons are perfected. There is no area too cold, nor too hot. All natural laws are undisturbed.

Will you see the Second Coming? Yes, you will, undoubtedly. For even the inhabitants of hell saw the Second Coming. God allowed it as part of their inextinguishable agony, realizing what they had irretrievably lost forever.

You too will see the Second Coming when earth is the recipient of her maker.

But, will you rise to meet Him in unutterable splendor and superlative happiness, as a believer in Him now? Or, will you see the Second Coming, only to be damned for having taken the "mark of the beast" and having followed the Antichrist?

---

1. Zechariah 12, 14.
2. Acts 1:11.
3. Matthew 25:31, Luke 17:24-37.
4. John 14:1-3.
5. Ezekiel 44:1-3.
6. Revelation 16:18.
7. Luke 21:25-27.
8. Zechariah 14:5, Revelation 19:6-7.
9. Revelation 19:11, Zechariah 4:6.
10. Revelation 19:1.
11. 1 Peter 5, 4.
12. 2 Thessalonians 2:8.
13. Hebrews 9:28.
14. Revelation 1:7.
15. Zechariah 12 and 14.
16. Revelation 21:23.
17. 1 Thessalonians 4:16-18.
18. Psalm 19:1.
19. 1 Corinthians 15:23.
20. 1 Corinthians 15:51-54.
21. 1 Thessalonians 4:13-18.
22. 2 Corinthians 5:10, 1 Peter 5:4, 2 Timothy 4:6-8, James 1:12, Revelation 3:11.
23. 2 Corinthians 5:10, 1 Corinthians 4:5, 2 Timothy, 4:1, Jude 14 and 15, John 14:3, Philippians 3:20-21, Colossians 3:4, 1 John 3:1-2.
24. Matthew 24:21-22.

25. 2 Corinthians 11:2, Psalm 45:9-17, Song of Solomon 6:8-9.
26. 1 Corinthians 2:9-10.
27. Revelation 20:1-6.
28. Matthew 24, Luke 21.
29. Revelation 19:20.
30. Revelation 19:18-21.
31. Revelation 14:9.
32. Zechariah 14:4.
33. Zechariah 14:4.
34. Zechariah 14:8.
35. Matthew 25:31-33.
36. Matthew 25:31-46.
37. Ezekiel 40, 48.
38. Revelation 20:1-3.
39. Isaiah 2:1-4.
40. Isaiah 65:20.
41. Isaiah 32:1-4.
42. Isaiah 65:22.
43. Isaiah 65:21-24.
44. Isaiah 9:6-7.
45. Isaiah 11:6-7.
46. Isaiah 11:8-9.
47. Revelation 20:1-5, Isaiah 65:25.
48. Zechariah 8:5-8.
49. John 1:11, Romans 11:19-27.
50. Zechariah 12:9-14.
51. Isaiah 53, Daniel 9:25-26.
52. 1 Timothy 6:11-15.
53. 1 Thessalonians 4:16-17.
54. Revelation 20.

Notes